Advance praise for
IF YOU'RE SEEING THIS, IT'S MEANT FOR YOU

"[An] incisive social satire . . . a funny, dark look at the new creator economy in a way only Leigh Stein can."
—*Town & Country*
("The Must-Read Books of the Summer")

"With this gothic tale of influencers caught in a Los Angeles mansion, Leigh Stein writes the horror story of our modern reality: dancing for dollars, fighting for sponsors, building your platform while losing your housing and your loved ones and your mind. She captures all the terror and glamour of what it is to exist, both online and off, today. Stein's work provokes you like the most unsettling clip you've ever seen on a screen—and you won't be able to look away."
—Julia Phillips, author of *Bear*

"Leigh Stein is an absolute master at noticing and excavating meaning from corners of the internet that most people scroll past. In *If You're Seeing This, It's Meant for You*, she blends gothic mystery with sharp cultural critique to reveal the strange, aching humanity behind the creator economy. This is a smart, funny, and incisive novel about fading relevance, digital reinvention, and the people addicted to making content even as it consumes them."
—Andrew Boryga, author of *Victim*

BY LEIGH STEIN

IF YOU'RE SEEING THIS, IT'S MEANT FOR YOU

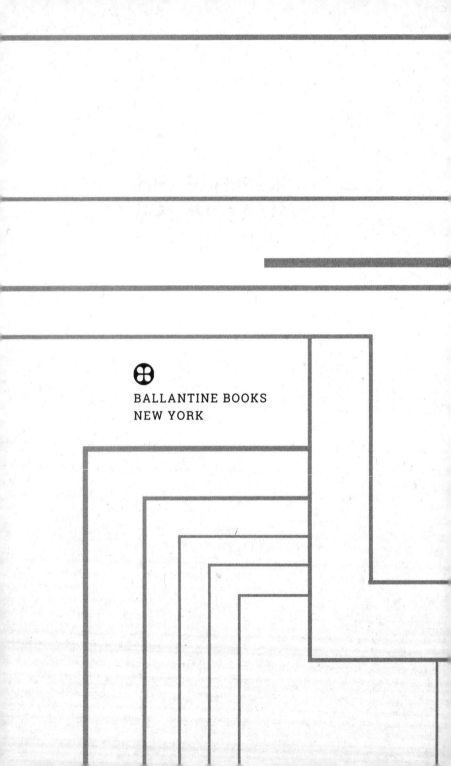

BALLANTINE BOOKS
NEW YORK

IF YOU'RE SEEING THIS, IT'S MEANT FOR YOU

A NOVEL

LEIGH STEIN

Ballantine Books
An imprint of Random House
A division of Penguin Random House LLC
1745 Broadway, New York, NY 10019
randomhousebooks.com
randomhousebookclub.com
penguinrandomhouse.com

A Ballantine Books Trade Paperback Original

ISBN 978-0-593-98364-5
Ebook ISBN 978-0-593-98365-2

Printed in the United States of America on acid-free paper

1st Printing

BOOK TEAM: Production editor: Cara DuBois • Managing editor: Pam Alders •
Production manager: Ali Wagner • Copy editor: Jennifer Sale •
Proofreaders: Julie Ehlers, Brandon Hopkins, Megha Jain

Book design by Elizabeth A. D. Eno

The authorized representative in the EU for product safety and compliance
is Penguin Random House Ireland, Morrison Chambers, 32 Nassau Street,
Dublin D02 YH68, Ireland. https://eu-contact.penguin.ie

For Callie and Theodora
and in memory of Ami

So many people are beginning to treat "youth" as the ultimate judge. . . . They want to be on the side of youth; they're afraid of youth.

—Pauline Kael

If someone tells me one more time
"Enjoy your youth," I'm gonna cry

—Olivia Rodrigo

IF YOU'RE SEEING THIS, IT'S MEANT FOR YOU

How do I (44M) tell my girlfriend (39F) that I changed my mind about her moving into my house?

My gf and I have been dating for 8 years, but I identify as a bachelor.

Diane (I'll call her Diane) rents a one-bedroom, where she keeps a metric fuckton of plants and a rabbit that looks like a lion. I own my own place in Los Feliz (I was an early hire at a startup that was acquired at an insane overvaluation and before anyone jumps down my throat, I know the American Dream isn't possible for everyone; it wasn't possible for Diane).

We used to have this good thing going, where we would spend most of the week at our own places, and the weekend together at my place watching our shows, but during the end of the world we started spending a LOT more time together. Diane only went home to water her plants.

The number one thing you need to understand about rabbits is that they're not cats. They can't really be left alone for more than 24 hours, so I let Diane keep a rabbit cage (she calls it a "habitat") at my house. Owen Wilson (that's what she calls the rabbit) needs fresh herbs fed TO him. It's a lot.

So our new baseline became 24/7. I could go in my music room and put on my noise-canceling headphones, but I could still hear her yelling at her elderly father on FaceTime to put in his hearing aids. When she got laid off, I felt as an empath how demoralized she was when she stopped wearing actual pants. At this point, I think she's supporting herself with credit cards (before anyone accuses ME of being the asshole, I offered to make her a budgeting spreadsheet). I asked myself, how should we sync up on this?

One night, after we split a bottle of a nice Cab from Napa I was saving for a special occasion before special occasions got canceled, I said I had something to ask her. I'm sure she thought I was going to ask her to marry me.

"Would you want to move in?" I said.

Fast forward six weeks. Diane didn't renew her lease. She read that self-help book that says to throw away anything that doesn't give good vibes, but while she was packing, I did a holotropic breathwork session and realized that after all this time together, the thing I want is LESS time together, not more. My therapist helped me articulate my needs: I don't want to share space. I want my space BACK.

Diane is hot. She's smart and she can take a joke without running to the police. She has this sexy, low-pitched laugh that I love. But I'm sitting here right now with Owen Wilson while Diane follows the guys in the moving truck to my place and my resting heart rate is in the cardio zone. I feel like I'm staring down forever.

TL;DR How do I tell Diane I love her, but this is a huge mistake? I want to go back to what we had before.

YOU STUPID MOTHERFUCKER was all I could think when I got to the end. *You didn't think to give Owen Wilson a pseudonym?*

I was stalled in traffic on the 101, behind the Lopez Bros. moving van. It was Mollie who had sent me the link, followed by a parade of red alarm emojis. If she had already seen it, who else had seen it? I wasn't going to cry. I never cried. I thought about taking my revenge in the form of a hysterical blurt of happiness: *on my way see you soon can't wait for our new lives together to begin!!!!* I thought about texting him a screenshot of his own Reddit post, no comment. Or maybe a photo of him cuddling O.W., if I could find one on my phone without killing myself in a wreck.

I remembered every detail of the night he'd asked me to move in. In a blind taste test, I would not have been able to tell the difference between that cabernet and a bottle of Yellow Tail Shiraz, but for Luke it was all about the ceremony of selecting the bottle, followed by the ritual of slowly uncorking it, decanting the wine, pouring and swirling and sniffing and reciting the flavor profile: black cherry, vanilla, plum. As a sommelier, Luke was certified. This was the kind of thing Luke did. He was also certified as a power yoga instructor at the two-hundred-hour level.

What he'd actually said to me that night was "I was worried at first that if we spent so much time together, you would get sick of me."

"I could never get sick of you," I said. Luke had all these talents. He did oil paintings of our friends' pets. On YouTube, he taught himself how to refinish hardwood floors. Once he even knit me a hat. It was like he was accumulating skills that would make his summer camp counselor application stand out. But Luke was forty-four years old. He wore a full beard and a baseball cap to hide his balding.

"I'm not sick of you either," he said, clinking his expensive, delicate glass against mine.

I never would have asked to move in. If I had been the kind of woman who wanted a husband and kids, I would not have devoted my thirties to Luke, who was incapable of committing to anything beyond a thirty-day challenge. I told anyone who asked that I had chosen having a career over having kids, because choices were empowering. The truth was that, in my twenties, my gynecologist had diagnosed me with a condition that would make conception difficult, if not impossible. Working all the time allowed me to inoculate myself against wanting what I couldn't have.

And then I got laid off for the third time in five years. I'd started my career covering celebrities—their vices, their breakups, their crashes, their comebacks—but once they started using social media, there was less of a need for editorial. Print magazines starved to death. I survived the media industry's pivot to digital and the pivot to video and the pivot to podcasting, but it was the collapse of live events, after we'd all pivoted to live events, that crushed me. On paper, I was "deeply passionate about community building" and "comfortable in a fast-paced environment," but my years of experience had become a liability. It signaled to potential employers that I was old and expensive. On my résumé, I deleted my first two jobs out of college and changed the date of my graduation so I appeared to be thirty-four. It still wasn't enough.

"Why would they hire me when they could get a twenty-two-year-old who, this is a direct quote, 'lives and breathes social' and has on-camera experience, and evening and weekend availability to, I quote, 'mine' user-generated content from their online community?" I asked Luke as I read a job listing off my phone.

"Dayna, if you need . . ." Luke looked so uncomfortable. I

thought he was about to offer me money. This was unforeseen, but not unwelcome. Would it be a loan? Or a gift? Because he'd gotten lucky in tech, he now had a lucrative consulting career, advising founders on cultivating "a culture of lucky." The income inequality in our relationship typically went politely unacknowledged, but I'd let slip that I'd opened a new credit card so I could transfer the balances from my other credit cards. I felt like the dealer in Monopoly, exchanging one pile of unreal money for another.

"If I need what?"

"Let me start over. Do you want to move in?"

"Why? Because I'm broke?"

"Not because you're broke. Because I miss you when you're not here."

The wine was finished. I'd hardly tasted what I'd drunk. Luke picked up his phone and started playing a Wilco song through the Bluetooth speakers. As we slow-danced to the melancholy violin, my left cheek pressed to his chest, I almost broke down. Luke knew all my favorite songs. I slept so much better at his place than at mine. I thought my life was about to get easier. I thought I'd finally earned a promotion.

Now a beige Corolla ahead on my left had its right turn signal on. I wasn't even going five miles an hour. She had room to get in my lane. "Go ahead, lady," I said, out loud, to no one. The exit for Sunset was coming up. Had she put on her signal by mistake? If she didn't switch lanes soon, I was going to pass her, and no one behind me was going to be nice enough to let her in. She didn't even know how good she had it. I rolled down my window and stuck out my arm to gesture at her to go ahead already. Exhaust fumes blew in like hot ghosts. By the time the Corolla finally pulled ahead, I'd lost sight of the moving van.

My phone rang. It was Mollie.

"Girl," she said.

"*He* asked *me* to move in," I said.

"Where are you right now?"

"I'm in the car! I'm on my way!"

"Oh my God," Mollie said.

"What?"

"You're homeless."

"I'm not *homeless.*"

"This is how it starts. Everyone thinks it could never happen to them, but many Americans are just one financial setback away from losing their housing. . . ." Mollie volunteered with a nonprofit in her neighborhood that counted those experiencing houselessness while they were asleep. No problems ever got solved in California without data analytics. No problems ever got solved at all. She'd invited me to do the count with her, but she lived on the west side, so we never saw each other in person.

"You know I'm here for you, whatever you need, but my place is, like, well, you know how small it is," she continued. Mollie rented an illegally converted garage in Venice Beach, where she was documenting her fertility journey to single parenthood on Instagram. Her apartment didn't even have an indoor shower.

"Don't worry," I told her. "I won't ask to move in with you."

"It's normal to be in shock right now. You're experiencing a trauma. Whatever you're feeling, it's normal to feel that way."

"Nothing about his life will change!" I screamed. My hands gripped the wheel at ten and two, like I was learning a lesson. Luke risked nothing and I had to start from scratch. Before Mollie could answer me in her therapy voice, I told her I had to go.

I took the Hollywood exit, and at the light, I felt around

in my purse on the passenger seat until I found my vape pen.

Aside from Mollie, all my other girlfriends had little kids. What was I going to do, become a live-in nanny? At my age? The only people I knew with bedrooms with en suites to spare were Luke's rich friends—they would not have described themselves this way, but I had looked up their real estate on the internet and I knew what they were worth. Had they by now seen the Reddit post, and were they sharing it in a group text, adding laugh-cry emojis for punctuation? *I felt as an empath how demoralized she was when she stopped wearing actual pants.* Did they pity me, too? I wasn't about to ask them for any favors.

Then there was my mother. I took a long drag off my pen. If things got really bad, I could call Mary. But I wasn't that desperate yet.

When I arrived, the van was already parked in Luke's narrow driveway. The back was open and two guys in white T-shirts were carrying my mid-century modern teak credenza down an aluminum ramp. There was no room for me to park. "Hey," I called out the window as I did a slow drive-by. "Excuse me. Hello?"

One of them looked at me, a curiosity. They set the credenza down in the driveway.

"Do you guys mind holding tight for a few minutes before you start bringing anything into the house? I just need to call someone."

"We've got another job after this one in Atwater Village."

"I'll pay time and a half. I'll pay cash. Please!" I yelled.

I'd donated six black garbage bags of clothes, plus most of my dishes and kitchenware except for a box of favorite coffee mugs. My old bed frame and mattress were trash. I gave away my bedding to a domestic violence shelter Mollie recommended. I washed and scrubbed and dusted my entire apartment—from the cobwebs in the ceiling corners to the marinara stains on the kitchen baseboards—so I could get my full deposit back. It was spotless for the benefit of a stranger.

I double-parked on the street, put my hazards on, and called the only person who could help me.

Craig picked up on the first ring. I pictured him sitting there, king of a once-magnificent kingdom, waiting for my call. I hadn't seen him in twenty years.

"Dayna?"

"I've been thinking about your offer," I said. I squeezed my eyes shut so hard I saw stars.

"And?"

"I'll do it," I said. I didn't have to tell him why I changed my mind.

Then I went inside to rescue Owen Wilson.

Craig Deckler lived in a ten-thousand-square-foot compound designed in the 1920s by a famous architect who took his inspiration from the ancient Mayan temples where human sacrifices were made to feed the gods. High in the Los Feliz hills, it stood apart from all the other mansions, an imposing fortress, bleached like bone. The Deckler House had been used for decades as a film set, as a stand-in for a lavish palace on another planet in sci-fi movies, or a vampire manor on TV. It was a multimillion-dollar family heirloom.

Or it had been—until it began falling apart.

As I drove up Blackwood Avenue, a ruin rose before me. The patterned concrete blocks that encased the exterior, once immaculate, now crumbled like teeth in a bad dream. Leaves and vines climbed through the holes in the walls, trying to reclaim the site for themselves. Who knew what kinds of animals were sheltering in the cracked foundation;

the humans were losing their battle against nature. Most noticeable of all was an enormous L-shaped steel frame that kept the south wall from collapsing and crushing its downhill neighbors.

The last time I'd been here was 2001. The deterioration was striking. As I approached the ornate front gate that separated the estate from the world, I felt my hands go numb on the wheel, my body issuing a warning to turn around and go home before it was too late. But there was no home to go to. The Lopez Bros. moving van was close behind me.

I'm here, I texted Craig.

Be right there, selfportraitat13

I blinked at his text. After all these years, this was how he still saw me: as the handle I'd given myself to wear, at a time when the internet was more like a masquerade ball than a networking mixer.

When we met, I was a college freshman, and Craig was in his thirties. He found me through the blog where I posted the self-portraits I took with my digital SLR and a long shutter release cord. At the time, I was obsessed with Nan Goldin, Cindy Sherman, Claude Cahun, and, most of all, Francesca Woodman—she was half Jewish, like I was. As a teenage girl, she was already posing nude in the cemetery. She took self-portraits at RISD with clothespins clamped to her breasts and the flesh of her stomach, her head missing from the frame. In Italy, she posed in a white leotard at a strange anatomy museum where wax women lie in glass boxes like fairy-tale rejects, their guts splayed for viewing. She staged two blurry girls reaching toward each other through a hole in the crumbling wall of an abandoned factory. Francesca made the condition of being a young woman look like a mystery that was better to explore than solve.

At twenty-two, she jumped to her death. The long exposure time on so many of her black-and-white photographs gave the impression that she spent her brief life trying to tell us something about ghosts. She left her fans behind with questions we could never ask her. We made a cult of Francesca.

I named my blog after her *Self-Portrait at 13*.

On Saturday and Sunday mornings, when my classmates were sleeping off their hangovers, I searched for empty rooms where I could shoot. I carried my tripod around campus and posed in wooden bathroom stalls wearing Mary Janes and bobby socks and sprawled atop chem lab tables in unlocked classrooms and kneeling the wrong way in a chapel pew like a heretic. To obscure my face, I flipped my long dark hair forward, like a veil, and tied a vintage silk scarf so it looked like my head was on my body backwards. Or I cropped my head out of the frame. Instead, I highlighted my bare shoulders in a silk slip, a slice of pale hip above my low-rise skirt, a bruised thigh against a wrinkled bedsheet.

Your work reminds me a lot of Francesca Woodman, Craig said in his first comment. Have you heard of her?

Had I heard of her? His comparison of my work to hers was the skeleton key that unlocked me.

Every day, I got through my classes, the charade of socializing with girls I believed I had nothing in common with, so I could go back to my dorm room and talk to Craig. The Dayna who went to class was an avatar of the real Dayna who lived online.

From the comments section, we progressed to emails and instant messaging late at night. I felt like I'd earned Craig's attention by being worthy of it; he wasn't one of my professors, tallying my participation points. Craig could have been talking to anyone. He wanted to talk to me. He told me he worked in marketing for the third most popular search engine and that he owned stock in the company. He told me that his house in LA was used as a set in sci-fi and horror films. Was he married? I never asked.

I gave him my address at school and he mailed me a book of the fashion photographer Deborah Turbeville's haunting photos of an empty Versailles and another book of Man Ray photographs. He'd flagged *Minotaur* with a sticky note that had one word: *uncanny*. It was a black-and-white optical illusion. A woman's nude torso, arms overhead, biceps flexed, became the face of the monster from the labyrinth: her nipples its eyes, her concave stomach its gaping mouth. The woman's head is missing from the frame.

Have you ever had an exhibition? Craig asked. The word *exhibition* made me think of the word *exhibitionism*, which made me blush.

What do you mean?

Of your photographs, he said.

Of course not, I thought. *Where would I have an exhibition? At the café that does open mic nights every Thursday?* Imagining people I knew in real life examining enormous pictures of my body was even more embarrassing than making friends on the internet.

I started typing *no,* and then changed it to "not yet."

It would be an honor for me to curate your first show. We can have it here, at the house. You'll come.

I said yes to the exhibition like a dare. Craig scheduled the show during my summer break and sent me a list of the thirty photos he thought we should print. Together, we narrowed the list down to a dozen. He took care of getting the prints made and purchasing frames and said we would work out the expenses later—I had no idea if this was standard or not, but I tried not to ask questions that would cast me as naïve.

It was only when I was standing outside LAX, shocked by the sun and haze, waiting for Craig to pick me up, that I started to feel jittery and ill, like having too much caffeine on an empty stomach. Based on the stereotype of desperate lonely men who chatted with younger women on the internet, there was a good chance I was about to meet a strange and awkward person. What if he was even older than he'd said he was? What if he had some kind of repulsive tic? I would be polite and kind, I decided. Imagining myself acting gracious and benevolent toward some loser was more comfortable than forecasting what I would do if I found Craig attractive.

I sat on my suitcase, feigning casualness in my plastic sunglasses, wearing my camera around my neck.

When he pulled up to the curb at LAX in a beige '80s Mercedes, I handed him my suitcase right away so he wouldn't have his hands free to hug me or even shake my hand. Craig smiled tightly, without showing teeth, like I was not what he had been expecting either. Without our chat window, I couldn't read his thoughts. While he put my suitcase in the trunk, I focused my lens: He was tall and broadshouldered, with wavy dark hair and a subtle cleft chin. He was dressed up in a dark three-piece suit, like a gentleman from one of the old novels they assigned at school.

I climbed into the passenger seat. After Craig pulled away from the terminal and merged into one of the lanes leading to Sepulveda, the car trunk flew open. "Shit," he said. And then, "Excuse me." He stopped in the middle of a lane of traffic and ran to shut the trunk.

"This kidnapping is not off to a great start," I joked when he got back in.

Craig laughed and his whole face relaxed. I felt like I'd won a prize. When he turned to look at me, I lowered my sunglasses to let him see my eyes. I noticed he wasn't wearing a wedding ring.

Neither of my parents knew where I was; after they divorced, it was easy to lie and tell one I was with the other. They didn't even know about my photography. My mother would have been scandalized by the images. Either she would have called them pornography or asked me why I had to hide my beautiful face. Mary valued beauty above any other virtue; from a young age, she taught me to carefully manage mine, the way other parents teach their children how to save money for the future. My father was a psychotherapist, and I was waiting to show him my work until I had achieved something—like this show—that he would recognize. Then he would view my self-portraits as art, I thought, instead of analyzing what it meant that his daughter was posting seductive photos on the internet.

When I saw the house on Blackwood Avenue for the first time, from a distance, I gasped.

"Your house was on *Buffy*," I said.

"You didn't believe me," Craig said.

"I thought maybe this was all an elaborate ruse, to, like, lure me into your dangerous lair."

Craig raised his eyebrows. "And yet, here you are."

I expected a grand entrance, but instead found myself following Craig up a dark, claustrophobic staircase and through a narrow hallway to the main floor of the house. The living room was two stories tall, framed by huge columns of stone blocks, and lit up with natural light from the large picture windows that overlooked the dizzying city below. An enormous wrought-iron chandelier hung from the ceiling. I didn't know anything about architecture, but the dramatic contrast between the choked entrance and the vaulted heights of the living room seemed like a mistake—and because I was so young that I thought I knew everything, I said so.

"It's called compression and release." Suddenly his hands were on my shoulders, his thumbs kneading and dissolving the tension below my neck. He took his time. His hands were warm and strong. I couldn't move.

"The architect wanted you to feel constrained," Craig said, squeezing, "before the relief."

Then he let go.

And with that touch, the atmosphere changed. Craig was someone else inside the house than he was outside of it. So was I. I couldn't wait for him to touch me again.

This house will make you do things, I thought.

Craig showed me to a guest room that was decorated entirely in Pepto-Bismol pink, from the patterned wallpaper to the curtains to the canopy bed.

"I'll let you get settled," he said.

As soon as he left, I was hungry to document everything. I photographed the glass perfume bottles and tasseled atomizers and lacquer trays on the vanity. I took a small white jar of a hand cream called Esoterica and assembled a still life with an hourglass, an old hairbrush, a crystal ball paperweight, a strand of pearls, and a blue bra from my suitcase. To impress the kind of people who collected art, I'd packed the most expensive dress I owned, from my high school graduation. But the house was already working its influence on me; emboldened, I put on a vintage black silk slip over the blue bra, an outfit I'd previously only worn in private. I propped my camera on the dresser and posed flat on my back on the canopy bed, my high-top Converse sticking out over the edge, the shutter release remote in one hand. I was channeling the bedroom scenes in *The Virgin Suicides*, all the sisters stuck inside together, not allowed to leave, fated to die.

When I was finished, I wandered into the dining room,

where a graceful woman was covering the table with platters of cheese and crackers and cold black grapes. Her dark hair was pulled back from her face to emphasize her eyes, which were a startling shade of sea-glass green. She wore simple, delicate jewelry that looked expensive. She couldn't have been much older than me, but there was a large gap in taste between us.

Her silent assessment of my outfit was enough to signal her disapproval.

"I'm Craig's stepsister, Paula. And this is my husband, Lucien Delacroix," she said, articulating each syllable like I was supposed to recognize the name. The short, serious man was arranging wine bottles in a large silver bucket of ice. It was the first time I'd met a couple where the wife was taller than her husband. *He must be rich*, I thought.

"Thank you so much for coming," I said.

"This is our house," Paula said.

Mortified, I poured myself a glass of white wine from a bottle that was mercifully open and went to the long hallway where my photos were framed, staged, and carefully lit. I felt Craig behind me, watching me look at myself. When I turned around, he took my picture. *That's not how it works*, I thought, flustered.

"You lied to me," I said.

"About what?" His eyes narrowed.

"You never told me you live with your sister."

"I'm sure I did."

"No," I said. "I would have remembered." Learning this fact made me shuffle the deck of cards in my head about who Craig was, and how he lived. He'd been boasting to me for months about where he lived—was the house even his? Or did it belong to his sister and her husband? Were they just letting him stay here because he had nowhere else to go?

Craig insisted he'd told me, but even if he hadn't, he promised their living arrangement wasn't unusual for LA. A lot of properties had guest houses. Craig had his own apartment in the separate chauffeur's quarters.

The living and dining rooms quickly filled with dozens of guests—I was stunned by how many people had come to see my photographs, until I realized most of them were there for a rare glimpse inside the famous house. Whenever anyone asked me a question about the architecture, I referred them to Craig and refilled my wineglass. Craig also hadn't told me he was charging an entrance fee that would go toward repairing damage caused by the Northridge earthquake. The house was the main character that night. I was just a curiosity inside it.

Craig sold all twelve of my prints, and split the proceeds with me. I made more money that night than I'd ever made in my life. Standing beside him next to the swimming pool, spinning from all the wine, toasting our success high above the sprawling city, I felt like this was only the beginning of my future. I imagined adulthood as a string of successes I would collect, like charms on a bracelet. My exhibition was the start of a dazzling chain.

"You really think I can be an artist?"

"You already are," he said.

I moved closer, until the sides of our bodies were touching. An eternity passed until finally Craig put his arm around my bare shoulders. I was holding my breath, waiting for him to kiss me. That wasn't why I'd come here—I hadn't even known what he looked like until he picked me up—but ever since we arrived at the house, there was a charge between us, something at once forbidden and inevitable.

"You must be tired," he said, without looking at me.

"I'm wide-awake."

He removed his arm and we went inside. There was

Paula, wearing blue gloves, on her hands and knees, violently attacking a carpet stain. I knew Craig couldn't just follow me into my room, not in front of her, so I said good night and then lay half awake for hours in that pink bedroom, waiting for him to open the door. Overnight, the bed became bigger and emptier. In the lonely dark, I felt like a child. Craig never came to my room. He never escalated the stakes in our game, and I didn't know how to do it myself.

When I got back to school, I imported all the self-portraits I'd taken in that pink bedroom into Photoshop. As I started editing the one of me lying on my back, I decided to make it a diptych. The first photo was just a girl in a canopy bed. In the second version, I duplicated the image and added a shadowy black figure, larger than a man, near the closet door, watching the girl on the bed. Something had happened to her between the first image and the second. I adjusted the saturation and burned the edges so the photos looked like they were taken decades ago. Hours passed in a blur. It was the first piece I'd ever made that wasn't only about me. It was about us. It was my best work.

But every time I thought about posting it to my blog, I froze. After the exhibition, more people were following me, waiting to see what I would do next. If this was my best work, I'd have to post something even better after the bedroom photos. Better and better and better. I made lists of ideas, but they were all derivative and stale. No campus setting came close to the drama of the Deckler House.

I didn't show my photographs to my father, but I did call to ask him about a situation one of my "friends" was in. She was a very talented singer, I said, but after she played her first solo gig, it went so well that she lost her voice. She couldn't sing at all. And singing was what she loved.

"It sounds like performance anxiety," he said.

"What should she do?"

"I'd be happy to talk to her."

"Thanks, I'll let her know," I said, unwilling to drop the mask.

Instead of telling Craig about my performance anxiety, I shut him out. I avoided his messages.

Dayna, is everything okay?

Have I done something to upset you?

Can I call you? I'm sure we can clear this up. If it was something I said, I'm sorry.

I miss you.

You never should have encouraged me, I wanted to say. *You ruined it.* Instead, I went to the next party I was invited to, drank until I could not be held responsible for my own decisions, and then slept with my roommate Carrie's on-again, off-again hockey player boyfriend, Russell. That was on September 8. A few days later, Russell and I were watching disaster footage on TV. We were inseparable after that. Carrie never forgave me, but Russell was the cure to what ailed me. He gave me a place to be every night that wasn't mediated by a screen. He was easily impressed—all I had to do was remember his diner order or give him a synonym for "important" when he was writing a paper. Based on the kinds of movies he liked to watch, I thought my photography would confound him. I dreaded showing him that side of me. When I realized I could keep my photos private, I felt weightless and free—the way he looked skating on ice.

I could have given Craig the courtesy of telling him I'd decided to quit photography, but I worried that would make him look bad in the eyes of his friends who'd taken a risk and bought my prints. He might try to talk me out of it. A disappearance seemed cleaner. I set all the posts on my blog to private. I created a new email address, without telling Craig. I killed my avatar.

After graduation, I moved to LA to write for *Entertainment Weekly*, covering celebrities whose job it was to always be posing. I was like a baggage scanner at the airport; I could see the darkness that famous people hid underneath their shiny surface, and I developed a skill for forming quick intimacies with sources, to get tips and leads about who was cheating, and whose fortune was running out.

From my cubicle at the magazine, I followed Craig from a distance. The company he worked for filed for bankruptcy; it was one of the casualties in the dot-com boom. Paula's husband, Lucien, dropped dead from a brain aneurysm shortly after my exhibition. Their house completely fell apart. The destruction was biblical in proportion: A decade after the earthquake, there was unprecedented rainfall, and the 27,000 concrete blocks that made up the house's exterior soaked up the water like sponges, causing them to crack and crumble. Insurance wouldn't cover the damage. Hollywood stopped calling, and Craig and Paula lost the income stream that their family had long relied on. Neighbors complained to the LA County Board of Supervisors that the landmark status should be revoked unless they repaired the retaining wall. They couldn't afford to.

A few famous actors stepped up to start a foundation and purchase the house, make the repairs, and reopen it to the public as a museum, but Craig wouldn't sell.

Each time I thought about reconnecting with Craig, and admitting I'd never been able to stop thinking about the house, or him, I didn't know how to explain why I'd disappeared without saying goodbye. The years made it harder, instead of easier.

After my most recent layoff, Luke had encouraged me to post on LinkedIn and ask to be "kept in mind" for any "opportunities."

That's when Craig Deckler reappeared in my life. He sent me a link to a piece in the *Los Angeles Times:* "Who's Profiting from the Hype House Gold Rush?"

I am, Craig wrote cryptically. We can. At the end of the message, he gave me his phone number.

I never showed Craig's message to Luke. I thought I had more time to job search after Luke asked me to move in with him. Instead of asking for more details, I'd replied politely to Craig and said it wasn't a good fit.

Now here I was, standing at the locked gate of the Deckler House.

I checked my face in my phone's camera; I didn't want to look like I was trying too hard, but I also didn't want to look as furious as I felt. I hit my vape and quickly pulled a couple of pieces of dark hair down from my ponytail to frame my face, just as I saw Craig walking to meet me at the gate.

"Wow," Craig said.

"Hi, Craig."

"You look exactly as I remember."

"You, too," I said. If anything, he looked even better than I remembered. Time had intensified his charms. His hair was still thick and wavy, only graying at the temples. Dark, mournful eyes. The long lines around his mouth framed his familiar close-lipped smile, which gave the impression he knew more than he was saying. He was wearing a blazer over a white T-shirt, and thick, black-framed glasses.

Craig opened the gate for the movers behind me, who were unloading my boxes from the truck onto silver dolly carts. If he was curious about how I'd advanced so quickly from accepting his job offer to moving everything I owned into his guest house, he didn't say so.

Cash. I'd promised the moving guys cash. I emptied my wallet, but it wasn't enough. Before I even had to ask, Craig took out his wallet and gave me everything he had. I stared at his hands as he counted the money. No wedding ring.

Once the movers were gone, I could finally collapse on his couch. The décor inside the guest house was minimal, white and gray, anonymous but comfortable. Craig didn't have any artwork or personal photographs on the walls. The kitchenette was in the corner of the living room. There was a two-burner stove but no oven. A ladder led to the sleeping loft. Once I unpacked some of my boxes, I told myself, the room would feel bigger, brighter.

I unzipped Owen Wilson's carrier, even though I knew he wouldn't come out yet. Not until he felt safe.

"You have a dog?"

"I have a rabbit," I said.

He stared at the mouth of the carrier as if a strange beast lay inside.

"Is that a problem?" What was it with men and rabbits? *I can leave*, I thought. *I'll take my son and go.*

"Not a problem," he finally said. "Just unexpected." He went to the kitchen to pour me a glass of cold juice.

"Where will you sleep?" I asked.

"In the main house," he said.

"In the hype house?"

Craig laughed. "In the hype house."

I held the cold glass to my forehead as he told me how the whole thing worked.

Craig ran the house like a company town. Everything was included but nothing was free. Craig earned rental income from the creators, a significant cut of all their brand deals, plus a "management fee." Once a month, he cut each creator a check for what they were owed, after expenses. He had a virtual assistant in the Philippines who handled emails and paperwork and bookkeeping. The creators in the top-tier hype houses were getting record deals, movie roles, TV shows, and clothing lines. One family had made so much money on their teenage daughters that they launched their own venture capital fund.

"Just a few months ago, Paula and I were preparing to give up and sell the house, but now there's a chance we can hang on to it. It's this platform. Don't ask me to explain how it works, but there's nothing like it."

"What made you think of me? Why am I here?"

"It's all a kind of performance, isn't it?" Craig asked. "For the camera."

As I followed Craig up the suffocating staircase and into the vaulted living room, I time traveled. It was like sightseeing inside my own memory. The house had a way of moving you through it, directing you where to go. It remembered me as much as I remembered it. Inexplicably, my ears started ringing.

My new colleagues looked like disaffected students on a field trip to a marvel of architecture they couldn't give two shits about. Two white girls in light-colored jeans with the knees ripped out were sitting on the living room floor, their long hair middle-parted and falling over their faces like privacy booths for scrolling their phones. Two boys in hoodies were lying on their stomachs on the red Turkish rug, arm wrestling, when Craig and I walked in. No one acknowledged my existence.

"Hi, everybody." I waved and one of the young women shot me a mean-girl stare that made me wilt inside like I was fifteen again. It was only then that I realized she was filming the arm wrestling on her phone. *Sorry,* I mouthed, and then turned my full attention to the competition. The sandy-haired boy was grimacing and wincing with the effort of flexing, but he was losing his leverage as his arm lengthened; his dark-haired opponent had expertly rolled his hand on top of their death grip, and after a few more seconds of struggle, he clinched the win.

As soon as it was over, they both sprang to their feet and unzipped their hoodies to reveal neon-pink T-shirts advertising an energy drink I'd never heard of called JUVENIS. The mean girl climbed up on the arm of the sofa to get a better angle of the T-shirts. She gave them a thumbs-up. Breathless, the competitors shook hands and patted each other's backs like Olympic athletes on the medalists' podium.

What was I doing here? They were talent and production and marketing. They could do it all. They didn't need me. In the media industry, everyone over the age of thirty was expendable. Everything I'd lived through—the phrase "bikini body," Beanie Babies, presidential scandals, rollerblades, dial-up modems, the recession, the rise and fall of American Apparel, eyebrow trends—was irrelevant to their culture. I was a human museum.

"Jake Cho," the champion said, walking right up to me, extending his winning hand; his grip was warm, firm, professional. When he touched me, the static in my ears stopped. He was about a foot taller than me, with moody '90s heartthrob hair that he was constantly touching to sweep away from his eyes.

"Dayna Lev," I said. "Congratulations."

"Dayna's moving in with us," Craig added. "She's the one I told you about."

"What's your niche?" Jake asked.

"My *niche*?"

"I can't find you," said the girl who was still seated on the floor, staring at her phone. "What's your username?"

My mouth went dry. "Oh, I'm not a content creator."

"She's being modest," Craig told them. "Dayna knows all about content."

"Can she make us go viral?" the other boy asked.

"Of course she can," Craig said. Maybe he thought wearing those glasses gave him the edge of authority, but watching the way he spoke to them, I better understood why I had been summoned to the house. Craig needed a translator. Neither of us had kids, but I was closer to their generation. Their generation didn't want our expertise. They wanted us on our knees, worshipping at the altar of their youth.

"Anyone can go viral," Jake said. He was talking to them, but he was looking at me. "It's about being consistent in your niche to grow your core audience and *then* you can make a strategic play for their attention to generate revenue, as long as the users don't feel you've lost what made you authentic in the first place. Right?"

I stared back. "One hundred percent," I said.

My tour guide to their local culture, Jake went around the room and introduced everyone: His arm-wrestling partner was Sean Knight from Little Rock, Arkansas. Instead of a handshake, he gave me a hug, like this was a family reunion. I wasn't sure if the large silver crucifix necklace he wore was religious or ironic. The girl who'd filmed the match on her phone was Sean's girlfriend, Piper Bliss. If I were casting for the role of Piper, I could have my pick among thousands of young women who all moved to LA with the same dream. Her beauty didn't distinguish her. What set her apart was her naked resentment. Either she didn't want to be here or she didn't want me to be here. She clung to Sean, although I wasn't sure how he could stand her.

The fourth member of the quartet was Morgan Bokelberg. When she stood up from the floor, I saw that she was almost six feet tall. She was wearing a purple *Rugrats* T-shirt and a huge pendant necklace made from the head of a baby doll, with rhinestones for eyes. When Morgan smiled, the light made her braces sparkle.

They were all looking up from their phones now. It was my turn.

"I've worked in the industry for some time," I said, hoping that a vague gesture in the direction of Hollywood would win me some points. I swallowed. "I'm sure I have a lot to, uh, learn, but I hope that my professional expertise will mean," I glanced at the brand name on Jake's chest, "much more exciting things ahead than JUVENIS."

Craig started a round of applause. Sean and Jake fist-bumped. I sucked my vape.

In the privacy of my new apartment, I touched my phone and saw sixty-two unread messages. The Reddit post continued to spread like a virus through my contacts. People I hadn't heard from in years were taking this opportunity to let me know they were following my public humiliation. I'm so sorry. I don't even know what to say. One former co-worker simply wrote: Yikes!

I gave Owen Wilson his dinner, and then I downloaded the app I had been avoiding, as someone born in the twentieth century. I was planning to follow each of the creators who lived in the house, but before I could even locate the search button, the platform began serving me videos.

I watched a silent slow-motion horror movie, captioned "ur parent's house after day drinking," that followed a young woman in a tube top as she opened a refrigerator to find only raw vegetables and condiments. I watched someone with short emerald hair rise to the challenge of "you can't just twerk to every song" by twerking to "Iris" by the Goo Goo Dolls. I couldn't believe what these people were willing to put on camera—acne, filthy kitchens, hula-hooping to pay off student loan debt. A woman on her honeymoon in Bali cried over a flight cancelation while her wife comforted her.

Afraid to like any of the videos, or leave a comment that would reveal a piece of my soul to the machine, I searched "Sean Knight" and found that he shared one account with Piper; their bio read "you only yolo once." Jake alternated between posting tributes to '80s and '90s movies and posing shirtless. Morgan's bio said "bopo maximalista." Her content was attention-grabbing because she dressed her voluptuous figure in the kind of mismatched whimsy that I associated with toddlers. Craig's creators were so different that they rarely cross-promoted.

I lost feeling in my left hand from holding the phone. I could scroll until dawn; Luke wasn't there to tell me to put my phone down and come to bed. It was like measuring one serving of candy and realizing no one will know if you finish the bag.

I almost wished I had caught Luke in the act of a more spectacular betrayal: Another woman's perfume on his expensive V-neck. A knock at the door, and it's a reality TV star holding a baby, saying, "He's yours." Degrading porn on his laptop. A cannibalism kink. *That* would make viral content.

What if, when I'd walked through the front door of his house earlier that afternoon, I'd been holding my phone, filming him in corpse pose on his yoga mat, a small organic cotton beanbag over his eyes. Text overlay: "pov ur boyfriend chilling after dumping you."

I shook my left hand to get the blood flowing and traded my phone for my laptop. I googled the familiar keywords "Deckler House Los Angeles" to see what media attention Craig had gotten so far for his hype house.

The first result was from *Rolling Stone:* "Fans Believe That Missing Influencer Is Latest Sign That This LA Mansion Is Definitely Cursed."

On r/Blogsnark, a popular influencer gossip forum, fan theories are brewing surrounding Becca Chambers, a tarot card influencer with two million followers who abruptly stopped posting from the Deckler House, a Los Angeles icon with a strange and deadly history.

Originally built for silent film star Gypsy Deckler in 1924, the house gained notoriety in 1959 when its exterior was used in the campy horror film *House on Haunted Hill*. Frederick Loren, played by Vincent Price, throws a party and offers $10,000 to any party guest who can survive twelve hours in the house. After the film's release, local teenagers tormented the home's owners, George Deckler (Gypsy's nephew) and his wife, conducting strange initiation rites, daring one another to ring the doorbell or throw a brick through a window, trying to instigate a reply from the ghosts inside.

George Deckler started to patrol the property at night with a German shepherd and a shotgun, and that was enough to quell the chaos outside. Inside the house was another story. By combing through public records and obituaries, fans have discovered that George, his first wife Marion, his second wife Viola, and his stepdaughter's husband all died inside the Deckler House. Add in all the natural disasters that have caused the house to physically decay over the past thirty years, turning it into an eyesore for Angelenos, and the Deckler House seems like the last place anyone would want to stay.

But this year, Craig Deckler, son of George, and the third generation of Decklers committed to keeping the house alive, invited applications from influencers across the country who wanted to live and work inside the house. Like her predecessors in *House on Haunted Hill*, Becca arrived at the gates with dreams of fame and fortune, unable to foresee what the house had in store for her.

On Blogsnark, there are dozens of stories of fans receiving messages from Becca's videos that they say are too accurate to dismiss as coincidence or a lucky guess. For example, one user wrote, "She knew the last thing my grandma said before she died!" The forum has become an online support group for anyone who feels misunderstood by friends and family members who don't believe them when they say that one of Becca's videos changed their life.

Some fans are searching for a connection between Becca's final video, about the Lion's Gate Portal opening on August 8th, and the rumor that the house was originally built with stones looted from the Pyramid of the Magician in the ancient Mayan city of Uxmal. Others have dedicated themselves to interpreting the relevance of the Eight of Swords card that Becca references in that same video. For someone who was previously posting as many as five times a day, some fans believe there could be an esoteric explanation for why she would suddenly stop. "Maybe she was afraid to tell us what she saw in the cards," one user wrote.

Neither Craig Deckler nor Becca Chambers could be reached for comment.

I recognized the byline on the story: Meg Frank. We used to work at *Entertainment Weekly* together. She was several years older than me and was always in her car or at a lunch, chasing stories, while I worked from the safety of my desk, fielding tips and emailing sources and writing blog posts of celebrity news that broke first on TV. Meg was exasperated by my aversion to phone calls; I'm sure she thought I'd never make it as a journalist. Now here she was, writing the kind of story you could write without ever leaving your desk. All you had to do was read the comments section and come up with a headline that would get enough clicks to save you from losing your job in the next layoff round.

Meg wasn't out covering Skid Row with a photojournalist. She wasn't on the team of *LA Times* reporters who won the Pulitzer for investigating a university cover-up of medical misconduct. She was combining internet conspiracy theories with Los Angeles lore, knowing that her coverage of this story would spur *more* conversation in online forums, *more* stories. There was no other explanation for the credulity she afforded the anonymous commenters. *She knew the last thing my grandma said before she died!* The Meg I used to know knew better.

Wasn't it obvious why someone like Becca would apply to live here? She was young and ambitious. The Deckler House was oozing atmosphere. It made her famous. Wasn't it possible she left for a more prominent hype house? Maybe a bigger manager had poached her from Craig. Maybe she was negotiating offers before she resumed posting. Maybe she was working on a huge secret campaign.

At random, I clicked one of Becca's videos that was embedded in the *Rolling Stone* article. Her face was cropped from the frame. The focus was on her long white acrylics, as she shuffled a deck of cards. There was a caption across the top third of the video that read, "a secret they've been waiting to tell you." Hashtag channeledmessage. Hashtag spiritual-awakening. A pink Himalayan salt lamp was plugged in on the table behind her. There was a candle burning in a glass jar. Pulsing music played in the background. The first card she drew, the Knight of Cups, meant *I want you.* The second card, the Ace of Wands, meant *And I won't stop.* The final card, the Lovers, meant *Until you're mine.*

The video was eleven seconds long. I watched it three times in a row, in a kind of trance. *I want you. And I won't stop. Until you're mine.* As skeptical as I was of the astrology-psychic-tarot-numerology-past-life-regression-therapy belief system that passed for religion in LA, there was also a teenage girl deep inside me pulling my sleeve, asking, *What if it's true?*

I closed my laptop. It was past two in the morning. This was how people got addicted to the platform. They kept scrolling until they got the message they wanted to hear. They mistook code for clairvoyance.

I would not only have to learn the platform, but master it—quickly. I'd be working on commission; I only earned money when the house did. If I could figure out how to change the narrative that writers like Meg were telling about the house—if the story became one of triumph instead of disaster—I could use this experience to land my next job. I could prove I was still young enough to pivot. I wasn't yet extinct.

THE NEXT MORNING, I shooed two raccoons who were washing their tiny disgusting hands in the swimming pool after their dawn garbage raid.

"I want to see your process," I told Sean, "and that will help me gather information, so I can make recommendations for improvement."

"Basically, we emulate." He pulled up a video on his phone to show me, of a young woman in a bikini climbing on her boyfriend like a human jungle gym. It had been viewed more than two million times.

"You get ideas from what the other couples accounts post," I said. "I get it."

Sean frowned. "Kind of. I mean we make the exact same video. If something goes viral for another couple, we copy it, so the algorithm shows it to the same audience. Same audio, same lighting, same text on-screen."

"The same *text* on-screen?"

"*Everyone* does it," Piper said. In the shade of the evergreens, she shivered in her bikini.

"Just for now," Sean said. "We emulate other videos in our niche to grow our audience, and one day, when we're big enough, we're gonna be able to do whatever we want. We can be ourselves." He fired up Piper's bare arms with his hands. "Ready, babe?"

Sean secured his phone to a five-foot-tall tripod and then got into position, feet planted, upper back rounded, bracing himself, the strongman in the freak show.

To re-create the viral video, Piper was going to have to jump on Sean's back, then climb like a little monkey around to his chest, heave her torso over one of his shoulders, and then hang upside down with her face near his ass until he pulled her through his legs for a final cling. Once the challenge began, her feet could never touch the ground. They had to do the whole thing in one take.

On the first try, Piper got as far as his waist and then hopped down in frustration.

"I can't do it," she said. "Why did you pick this one?"

"Here," I said, pulling out my phone to find the original video.

There was a text from Craig: How's it going?

Extremely well actually!! I said.

"Watch it again," I told Piper. "See, Sean can hold you while you put your hands on his shoulders and press yourself up."

Reluctantly, she agreed to try again. And again. And again. Sean was in his element. He was like a dog that needed to be exercised to the point of exhaustion during the day so he could sleep at night. By the time they were able to complete the entire sequence in one fluid motion, they were both glistening with sweat. I was standing behind the tripod, watching. With Sean cradling her butt in his arms, Piper turned to the camera and laughed so hard her snaggletooth showed. For that one second, she stopped performing, stopped watching herself from the outside. They needed more moments like this, I thought. Their real selves perforating the imitation.

"Maybe it's two videos," I said.

"What is?" Sean asked.

"You'll post the video that copies the original. But I think you should also stitch together all the times you had to stop and start over. The outtakes. But end it with Piper laughing. And then we can see which one gets more views."

I left them alone to edit and went back inside the house to find Morgan. There had to be another way to grow their audiences without churning out copies of copies of copies. I remembered what I'd noticed the night before when I was scrolling: They were never in one another's videos.

In the hallway, I passed a dark-haired woman carrying a laundry basket. At first, I mistook her for an elegant housekeeper.

"Paula, right?"

"Yes?" Her pale skin was stretched tight across her face like a canvas.

"You don't remember me, but I was here a long time ago. For a photography show. I'm Dayna."

"Ah, you came back," she said. "They usually don't."

Before I could stutter a response, she turned to go upstairs. Morgan's voice was so loud that I could follow it like a beacon. She was in the pink bedroom, wearing a bathrobe and a turban, sitting at the ornate mirrored vanity, doing her makeup on camera while she explained a mysterious Taylor Swift album that was never released. I hovered in the doorway, pierced with the memory of the long night I'd spent in that room. Some invisible force kept me from crossing the threshold, entering Morgan's territory. I waited for her to stop filming before I spoke.

"You're a fashion influencer, right?" I would not humiliate myself by trying to pronounce "bopo maximalista" aloud.

"Yeah?"

"Have you ever styled someone else in the house?"

She shook her head. I showed her a photo of Leonardo DiCaprio wearing a blue Hawaiian shirt. She raised her eyebrows.

"For Jake?"

"It's the movie's twenty-fifth anniversary," I said.

She put down her pink makeup sponge and went straight to her closet, which went on and on and on. She had an entire wardrobe department. She pulled every short-sleeved button-up shirt she could find and threw them on the bed.

"Will he let me do his hair?"

"I'll ask him."

Morgan pointed in the direction of Jake's bedroom and I vaped before I knocked on his door.

He answered with his earbuds in, in the middle of doing biceps curls.

"I'm sorry to interrupt you, but I—"

"I've been waiting for you all day," Jake said, switching the dumbbell to his other hand. "Saving the best for last?"

I laughed. "It's the anniversary of *Romeo and Juliet*. If you let Morgan dress you up and do your hair, then you'll be in her video, and you can give her a shout-out at the end of yours. That way, your followers find her and vice versa."

"What's the hook?"

"The hook," I repeated.

"What I say at the beginning, so they don't keep scrolling."

"Like a question," Morgan shouted from her room. She was listening to us. "Like, 'Is karma real?'"

"Is love a tender thing," I said. I walked past him and took a piece of paper and pen from his desk, to write down the lines for him to memorize.

"How do you know this?" Jake asked.

"I know a lot of things," I said.

Back in Morgan's room, Jake tried on one shirt after another. The blue one that was most similar to Leo's was so tight on him that he couldn't button it all the way.

"Leave it like that," I said.

Morgan artfully placed pieces of hair around Jake's face like she was arranging a bouquet.

He handed me his phone to film him as Romeo: *Is love a tender thing? It is too rough, too rude, too boisterous, and it pricks like thorn.* Jake didn't recite it like a lovestruck actor—he delivered it like he was about to launch into a pitch for powdered greens. I bit the inside of my cheek to keep from laughing. Then he rattled off some trivia about the Baz Luhrmann movie. He thanked Morgan for styling him for the anniversary video and she popped on camera—still in her bathrobe—and waved. Then he told his audience to click the plus sign to follow him for more "classic" movie content.

The collaborations would grow their followings, but I was limited by how many creators Craig had. The biggest hype house had nineteen residents. We had four.

We're going to need more bodies, I texted Craig.

Once I was alone in the guest house, I obsessively toggled from Piper and Sean's account to Morgan's to Jake's, refreshing their profiles, waiting for the view counts to rise.

When the numbers plateaued, I cringed. All my instincts had been wrong.

Sean knew better than I did—his video with Piper strictly copying the other couple's viral video got exponentially more views than my outtakes idea. Jake's *Romeo + Juliet* anniversary video hardly broke six thousand views, and his fans felt betrayed.

whose in the bathrobe Jake?? not your girlfriend I hope?

maybe it's his sister

his SISTER?

Jake I think as a community we deserve an explanation
AND an apology

There wasn't a single reference to the movie. I hadn't turned the nostalgia dial back far enough. Jake's fans were even older than I was. They didn't want Leo DiCaprio meeting their eyes in a fish tank; they wanted Patrick Swayze to lift them overhead in a lake.

I emailed screenshots of Jake's comment section to Craig's virtual assistant, Annabelle. She was the closest thing I had to a co-worker. I told her I worried I'd made a mistake by having Jake and Morgan collaborate on a video, and asked if she thought we should take it down. She lived in another time zone—by the time she replied, would it get worse? Why hadn't Jake warned me this would happen? Why had he trusted me? Just because Craig told them I knew how to make them go viral?

Craig had been wrong to bring me here. He'd overestimated what I could do and there was only so long I could fake it.

Go ahead, I thought. *Quit. Move in with Mom. Enter the raccoon-feeding phase of life.*

But maybe I could buy myself enough time to get better. There had to be something our house had that the other houses did not.

My son was licking his paws and washing his face, in his little self-care routine.

"What's our unfair advantage?" I asked him, stealing a phrase from one of Luke's consulting calls.

He stopped grooming to stare at me, nose twitching.

Come over to my house, I texted the group. I have something to show you.

When the four arrived, I was waiting for them on the couch. "I'd like to introduce you to Owen Wilson," I said.

"No way," Jake said. "He looks just like him." Instinctively, he took out his phone to snap a picture.

"Wait," I said. "Don't post that yet. This is my child, so I'm very protective of his image on social media."

"He doesn't have his own account?" Morgan asked as she sat down next to me. She was wearing Care Bear pajamas.

"Nope."

"Whoa," Sean said. "Crazy."

Morgan stroked O.W.'s head between the V of his ears with a single finger. His adorable nose twitched.

"I'm searching to see if the name is already taken," Jake said.

Piper hung back by the door, arms crossed, skeptical.

"The reason I wanted to introduce you all to O.W. is because I had an idea for a little friendly competition," I told them.

Sean grinned and rubbed his hands together.

"What kind of competition?" Morgan asked, worried already.

"The first person to increase their follower count by twenty-five percent gets to use Owen Wilson in a video."

I could tell by their faces that this was the first time they'd done math since high school.

"But that could take, like, weeks," Piper said.

"It's good to have long-term goals," I said.

"I don't know," Morgan said. "My parents told me that competition is destructive to self-esteem."

Jake took the rabbit from my lap and cradled him in his long arms. "I already know what I'm going to do when I win," he said.

OLIVIA

When I was little, my parents took me to a museum with a dollhouse exhibit. It wasn't an ordinary dollhouse: The rooms inside weren't connected by a floor plan, or even by the same time period. Each shoebox-sized room was like a stage set, framed behind glass. I wasn't allowed to touch the rugs or see if the rocking chairs really rocked. I had to stand on a carpeted step to peer inside at the tiny staircases and the tiny chandeliers, the tiny paintings and the tiny fireplaces. The doors led nowhere. Fake sun flooded the parlor. The spinning wheel stood still. By the fifth or sixth room, I was restless. *Where were all the dolls?*

"Who lives here?" I whispered to my mom.

"I'm not sure," she said, reading aloud the gold-plated caption at the bottom of the frame, even though I could read it myself: *English Dining Room of the Georgian Period, 1770–90.* "I think you're supposed to use your imagination."

My dad brought his face very close to mine and spoke quietly. "Imagine you were sitting at the dinner table eating your roast beef and you looked up and there was a huge little girl looking in your window. With one finger, she could destroy your whole world. Wham."

I jolted with a thrill of fear, picturing myself as both the girl at the table and the monster at the window.

Now here I was, the doll at the gates of the dollhouse. I took the time to get the angle right so the Deckler House rose, monumental, behind my right shoulder in the selfie. It looked just like the photo on Wikipedia, except now I was part of history, too.

I kept my sunglasses on and made a kittenish *oh* with my lips, which were puffy and burning from the bee venom gloss. By the time I got the shot I wanted, I was sweating.

I made it. All the way from Minot, North Dakota, I wrote in the Instagram caption. *Emerson says once you make a decision, the universe conspires to make it happen.* I added a sunflower emoji and a fingers crossed emoji and an upside-down smiley emoji and a string of yellow hearts. Most of my followers were people back home, who only wanted to see me do well, after everything that had happened. I didn't post the photos I took of the busted side of the house that looked carved out like a jack-o'-lantern, the dark holes ready-made for a rabbit warren or a possum kingdom. The people who believed I was making a big mistake by leaving home, I knew what they'd say: *you pitching a tent in there, Olivia? haha*

The application had asked for links to all my social accounts, among other things: where I fell in the birth order (only child), my attachment style (anxious), how much time I estimated I spent on my phone compared to my peers (above average / mostly lurking), how many sexual partners had I had (prefer not to answer), and what wild animal I thought best represented my personality (I said a bison calf—in the Badlands, they have signs everywhere telling tourists to keep a safe distance, but inevitably some blue state idiot will try to kidnap one of the calves and bring it home in a Subaru; touch me at your own risk).

The front gate was locked. It took me a minute to find the black box with the doorbell. Inside the box, a yellow Post-it note said, DO NOT RING THE BELL WE MIGHT BE SHOOT-ING. I texted the number listed and held my hair off my neck, praying for a breeze. Children did not ride bikes in the street here. No cars passed. Even the palm trees held their breath.

I'd found the application in one of the forums where fans posted their Becca theories. I dare someone to actually apply for this lmao, the person who shared the link wrote.

How desperate would you have to be?

On a scale of 1–10, with 1 being "engaging in self-harming behaviors" and 10 being "thriving," how would you rate your emotional response to stressful situations? the application asked. *What do you know how to do better than anyone else?* I could have kept going, translating myself into drop-down menus and ten-point scales for hours.

"Olivia?" A petite woman with long brown hair and a face like a pretty fox met me at the gate.

"So nice to meet you," I said, extending my hand through the bars.

"Wait," she said, laughing, as she opened the gate. Once we were both on the inside, she shook my hand. "I'm Dayna. Your producer." She was wearing black skinny jeans and a dark blouse with a high neck and ruffled shoulders. Up close, her olive skin was surprisingly smooth, like she was using a filter.

I awkwardly tugged at the hem of my cutoff shorts. I was wearing the wrong clothes. I could see that now, through context clues.

"Do I have time to change?"

"We were actually expecting you at noon," Dayna said.

"I know. I'm so sorry. It was the bus. Well, more than one bus." Three buses.

"Wow," she said. "The bus." I didn't know what she meant by that, but I followed her through the front door and into a small stone vestibule that was cool and dark like a tomb. The close walls of the staircase squeezed me so tight I had to carry my duffel bag in my arms. It was tricky packing according to the instructions I'd been given. I had to pack for what was essentially a three-month sleepover at a stranger's mansion. No previous experience in that department. But if I failed the screen test, I'd be lugging all this stuff back home on the bus. Too much luggage seemed overconfident and I didn't want to jinx it. There was nothing left in North Dakota to go home to.

I didn't realize I was holding my breath until we summited into a living room with high ceilings and tall stained-glass windows. Huge stone columns framed a long, dramatic hallway; the columns were inscribed with patterns I didn't know enough to decode. There was the same level of detail in décor that I'd seen in those miniature rooms at the museum, but now every piece of furniture was my size. At one end of the living room, there was an enormous fireplace beneath a glass mosaic of a peacock. The firebox was so big, I could have crouched inside it. The carpet was dark red, the color of old blood.

Whoever designed this house is dead, I thought.

"Are you okay carrying all that?" Dayna asked after I'd already carried everything.

"I have a lot of upper-body strength," I said so she wouldn't feel guilty for not helping.

"Let's go see Craig," she said.

His office was the first door off the main hallway. Dayna never answered my question about changing my clothes and I didn't want to ask again. I thought about removing my cropped sweatshirt, but what I had on underneath seemed even more inappropriate.

"Hey," she said, to get him to look up from his laptop. "This is Olivia from South Dakota."

I smiled politely, but Craig didn't see me. He was looking at Dayna.

"Join us," he said to her. He was wearing a white dress shirt, the cuffs rolled to his forearms, and a dark suit vest, like an actor in a period piece, playing the country doctor who delivers the bad news.

"I can't," Dayna said, "but I'll talk to you tonight?"

Craig nodded.

After she left, I wasn't sure if I was supposed to put all my bags down or keep standing there until I was given further instructions.

Behind his desk, the wall was covered in framed photographs of the house, up close and from a distance, in black and white and color. Some of them were taken inside the house, of a younger Craig posing with women who looked like models or actresses, wearing glamorous dresses draped off the shoulder and slit up the thigh. I was too far away to recognize any of the faces.

How many other girls was I up against? I had arrived at the house ready to do anything. I just needed Craig to tell me what it was on my application that made me captivating and then I could just do that, on repeat, like an animal, until I found what I was really searching for.

"Please sit," Craig said, gesturing toward a chair in front of his desk.

Relieved to have a command, I unloaded my bags on the floor. I could feel the red marks on my shoulders where the straps had dug in.

"Thank you," I said.

"So," he said.

"Yes," I said.

"You're the crier."

"That's me." I tried to sound cheerful, but I was taken aback. Out of everything I'd put on my application, that's what he noticed?

He shut his laptop and raised his eyebrows, expecting me to fill the silence.

I waited for him to ask me about what it was like where I was from, or how my flight had been. I could have told him about the RVs I saw parked under the overpasses and the tents on the sidewalk, or described the desperate woman with the infected foot I saw on the bus, a sight that I doubted he'd ever had to witness. When you owned a house like this, you could stay inside forever, and only let the beautiful in.

Craig said, "Whenever you're ready."

"You want me to cry right now?" I swiped at the sweat above my lip with the back of one hand.

People assumed that actors had a special button they could push inside their mind for tears, but crying took real concentration. Wearing lashes had been a mistake; they were a distraction as I squeezed my eyes shut and scrolled my mental catalog of triggers. I could think about all the dogs waiting in cages for adoption, or when Emily in *Our Town* goes back to her twelfth birthday after she's already dead. Breathing helped. If I panicked, it made crying even harder. I remembered the video I'd seen of the baby who'd been in an accident, how the doctors and nurses stood along the hallway of the hospital while his gurney rolled past, and his mom kissed him goodbye before they took his organs to save another baby. Sometimes I wondered if the platform showed the same sad videos to everybody or if the ones delivered to me were personal.

I focused on the image of the mom kissing her baby

goodbye until I felt that familiar sting in the back of my throat and a subtle vibration between my eyebrows, and when I looked at Craig, my lower lip was trembling and my eyes brimmed with tears.

I blinked and one fell down each cheek. At the end of the video were photographs of the baby—before the accident—laughing. On-screen, the text said, *Four lives saved!*

"Very good," Craig said, "that's enough." Like I'd made a mess. There wasn't any Kleenex, so I wiped my nose on my sleeve.

Had he asked all the girls who auditioned in his office to cry? Was I "very good" compared to other criers, or was my crying unlike anything he'd ever seen before, and that's what made it good?

"Your room is upstairs," Craig said. "It's small, but it's only two thousand."

"Wait," I said. "I got the job?"

Craig cleared his throat. "Technically, no. You won't be an employee. You read the article we emailed you?"

"Of course," I said, even though I couldn't. It was behind a paywall.

From one of his desk drawers, Craig produced a contract and I quickly skimmed the numbers: I had ninety days to grow my audience to a million. They would find brand partners for me and deduct a management fee and my monthly rent from the income that I earned for the house. What happened if no brands wanted to work with me? Would I still have to pay rent?

I had $422 in cash in my backpack.

"Do you have any questions for me?" Craig asked.

Where's Becca? That's what I'd come all this way to ask. That's what anyone in my position would ask the man in charge: *What did you do to Becca?* Some of her fans thought she'd burned out, channeling all these messages for us—but who was forcing her to post all that content in the first place? Craig. Did Becca owe him money? Was he stopping her from posting, as a punishment for some transgression? But to make money, wouldn't she have to post? We couldn't find her in the background of the other creators' videos either. When we posted comments asking about her, those comments got deleted.

I had to find her. She was the only one who could help me. But I also had to be careful about where I looked and who I talked to until I knew who to trust. Unlike Becca, I was a nobody. If I disappeared, no one would look for me.

"Do you have to be twenty-one to sign a contract?" I asked.

"Eighteen," Craig said. "You're over eighteen, aren't you?"

I nodded. "Nineteen." I signed *Olivia Grace Dahl* in cursive.

Officially, I was inside the house. I remembered what my dad had told me at the museum, all those years ago.

With one finger, she could destroy your whole world. Wham.

I left my bags in the living room and wandered, unsupervised, down the long hallway that divided the house into chambers. To my right was a series of closed doors. Every window on my left overlooked a different landscape—city, valley, desert, palm trees. The house carried me like a conveyor belt to the kitchen, where I found the doors that led out to a terrace with a pool. The water shimmered a sick shade of green in the sun and the stone tiles around the perimeter were cracked and crumbling. No one was swimming. At the far end of the terrace, in the shade of a few tall pine trees, they were rehearsing. Even with their backs to me, I recognized them.

In a lime-green corset top and an orange beanie, Piper

was the figurehead at the front of the ship, unfurling her delicate arms and tossing her black hair to the music like she loved it and then shutting her body back up like a shell, a shell with perfect boobs, to subtly bounce once, twice, and then pause. There was a series of additional bounces at the end, but it required counting and coming in on an off-beat, and the boys ruined it and they had to start over. Jake was tall and aloof in dark sunglasses; Sean was shirtless and golden, flexing his pecs for the camera. Morgan hunched behind the tripod, directing.

"Hey," I said, waving as I approached. I knew everything about them, but they didn't know me at all. I didn't want to come across like a creepy fan. I wanted to seem like an equal. Or at least like I had potential to become an equal.

Piper turned around. "Hey," she said. She was wearing the same shorts as me.

"I think we have the same shorts," I said.

"The what?"

"The same shorts?"

"I doubt it."

I looked to Morgan to referee, but she was looking down at her phone. "I'm Olivia," I said.

"Jake," he said, shaking my hand.

"You're the new one?" Piper asked, squinting at how little I was giving her to work with.

"Olivia, I need a neutral opinion," Sean said. "Be honest. Do I look skinny?" He rotated to the left and to the right so I could behold his six-pack from multiple angles. Was this a trick question?

"Dude," Jake said.

"You look huge," I said.

Sean grinned and gave me a high five; it felt like acing a test.

"Literally what do I tell you every day," Piper said.

"But Olivia doesn't know me."

"Sean, you have body dysmorphia," Morgan said, bored.

I peeled off my sweatshirt and tossed it by the pool, to prove I was willing to show skin, too, if that's what it took.

"I've never seen a pool this color before," I said.

"That's the raccoon pee," Sean said.

No one laughed.

"Can someone teach me the dance?"

Piper turned to face me, but wouldn't let me mirror her. Another test. When she shimmied right, I shimmied left. When she tossed her hair from side to side, I looked her right in the eye. Then she turned around and we did the whole thing for the camera. This time, when Jake missed the beat, we rolled with it. It was a mistake with low stakes. It was the best day of my life.

When we were done, Piper took her phone from the tripod to add the hashtags and post the video to her account.

"What's your niche?" Morgan asked me.

I wasn't prepared for her question. Should Craig have assigned me one? Was it in the contract? I wasn't a comedian, a baker, a skateboarder, an interior designer, a pet owner, a guitarist, a painter, a makeup artist, or a lifestyle vlogger. I wasn't #thatgirl.

I almost said, "I'm an actress."

But then, in the strange, still heat of that afternoon, the sun went behind a cloud and a dark shadow fell across the face of the house.

"I'm an orphan," I said.

Morgan reached out and touched my hair.

"You're very pretty," she said. "Can I style you?"

Everything in Morgan's bedroom was pink: the paisley wallpaper, the lace window curtains, the comforter on the canopy bed, even the upholstery of the stool where I sat at the mirrored vanity, hair pulled back from my face with a silk headband that Morgan gave me. *Mid-Century Bedroom of Southern California, 1960–70.*

"For the aesthetic, were you thinking 'dirty' or 'haunted,' or do we want, like, 'crying clown'?" Morgan frowned and dragged one finger down her cheek in the path of a tear.

"Haunted, I think."

Morgan was my artist and I was Morgan's art. She set her phone on a tripod aimed at my reflection in the vanity. As she contoured my cheeks into hollows, I wondered if my own room in the house would look like a stage set. Did every bedroom have its own color scheme? Would I have to decorate it myself?

"Did you do all this yourself?" I asked.

Morgan paused what she was doing and gave me a gently pitying look in the mirror.

"Oh, you don't know the lore."

That wasn't true. I knew a lot about the house from the internet.

"What lore?"

Morgan started at the beginning. The house was built for a silent movie star in the 1920s, but she was never able to have children, so she left the house to her nephew George in the 1950s. At the time, he was married to his first wife, Marion.

"First wife?"

"This was her bedroom," Morgan said. She gestured at a framed oil painting on the wall, of a dark-haired woman at an easel. She was holding a paintbrush in her left hand, poised to fill in a blank space, shaped like an egg, on her canvas, but she wasn't looking at the canvas. She was staring intently at me, the viewer. There was something about the empty oval that unsettled me. The woman in the painting was holding the oval in her right hand. It protruded from the canvas, violating the boundary between art and reality.

"They kept the room exactly as she left it. After what happened to her."

"What happened to her?"

"Whenever the house was used in a movie, there would be all these actresses, right? Beautiful women. Young women. George thought he could just have anyone he wanted because the house served them to him, like a buffet. Look up." Morgan delicately sponged dark circles under my eyes.

This was all being recorded, but the final video would be in hyper speed. They would see our mouths moving but they wouldn't know what we were talking about.

"People cheated in the olden times because open relationships hadn't been invented yet," Morgan explained. "Marion could deal with the cheating as long as she didn't hear about it, but things got serious with an actress named Viola. George said she could move into the house with her daughter. When Marion said no, George said she was being selfish; they had nowhere else to go."

"How do you know all of this?"

"You'd be surprised how much people say in front of me because they don't think I'm smart enough to understand. They treat me like I'm just a little kid playing dress-up."

"I think you're smart," I said.

Morgan smiled at me in the mirror.

"Marion was right. She was being replaced. George was a doctor, so he was like, here, take this phenobarbital. Marion took the whole bottle of pills and a bottle of vodka and got in the bathtub."

Morgan abruptly stopped what she was doing and put one hand on the wallpaper, near the painting. She closed her eyes to concentrate. "We haven't forgotten you, Marion," she told the wall. "We're keeping your room for you. As long as we don't lose the house."

The skin on my arms prickled. "What's wrong with the house?"

Her eyes flew open. "That's why you're here, Olivia."

"To save the house?"

"To make money for Craig. It's all for the renovation. The house has belonged to the Decklers for almost a hundred years. He can't give it up."

I did the math. Collectively, we were paying at least $10,000 a month in rent. How much more did he need before our services were no longer required?

"Close your eyes," Morgan said, and misted my face with setting spray.

In the gold-framed vanity mirror, I melted my face into the shape of a sob. I looked absolutely wretched.

"It's perfect."

Morgan opened a vintage brown and brass steamer trunk filled with pale silk nightgowns and polyester blouses with high collars, plus belts and scarves and sunglasses. I put on a white blouse with underarm stains and a jumper that was too tight to zip all the way up, with a baggy men's cardigan thrown on top.

"Don't move," Morgan said while she cut the elbows out of the sweater with a pair of scissors.

"Are the clothes Marion's?"

"Some are hers," Morgan said. "Some are Viola's. George married her after Marion died." She glanced at the wall, as if to see if Marion was listening.

I pulled on knee-high argyle socks and buckled a pair of cheap black canvas Mary Janes.

"You still need a prop," Morgan said, "something to carry with you, like an old suitcase."

"A bundle on a stick?"

"Classic." We fashioned one out of dish towels and a Swiffer stick and then we were ready.

Morgan texted Jake to meet us outside so he could film her filming me for her own account.

In the opening shot, I walked up the street to the house, bundle over one shoulder, stopping at the gate. The sun was in my eyes, but I tried not to squint. Close-up on my face at the gate. Once nervous, once hopeful, once pulling on the bars. It was the most relaxed I'd felt since I arrived at the house. Having a role to perform was a vacation from scrutinizing and criticizing everything I said and did and thought when I was stuck playing the role of myself.

"What's her niche?" Jake asked Morgan.

"She's an orphan," Morgan said. "We're filming her first day at the orphanage. Black and white."

"Dope." He flashed me a smile of approval that made me shimmer.

When we went back inside, the setting sun was casting dramatic shadows from the stone columns along the long hallway. I walked slowly, dragging one hand along the wall like I was unsteady on my feet. Then I collapsed.

"The orphan is, like, a metaphor for the alienation of adolescence, right?" Jake asked.

It hadn't occurred to me that being an actual orphan could be a metaphor, but that sounded smart, so I said, "Exactly."

Jake said I could watch him while he edited the video on my phone. We sat on the floor of the hallway, shoulder to shoulder. His fingers moved so quickly, I could hardly follow the steps, but I didn't want to ask questions and break his focus. For the music, Jake searched "sad vibe audio." When he was finished, he showed me how to play a preview. It looked so professional—like a twenty-two-second movie.

"It's a little long," Jake said, handing my phone back to me.

"But it's aesthetic," Morgan said, encouragingly.

I changed my generic username to @littleorphanOlivia. Then I posted my first video. Immediately, I refreshed my account, waiting for the view count to go up.

"How long does it usually take to go viral?"

Jake and Morgan exchanged a look.

"Try not to look at your phone," Jake said.

Morgan nodded. "Yeah. Try to stay distracted."

Behind her, I noticed Dayna leaning against a stone column, watching us and vaping. With one arm, she cradled a rabbit. "Grab your stuff," she said, "and I'll show you to your room."

I followed her up another dark staircase; it seemed like they were stowing me away in the attic. My room was as small as a dorm room, with a twin bed, a dresser, and a small closet. Nothing like Marion's room. This must be where George once kept his servants. The only window faced the back of the property, where there was a separate guest house.

"That's where Owen Wilson and I live," Dayna said. "You can call me on a tin can."

"Okay," I said.

"I'm joking," she said.

"Am I allowed to pet him?"

"Sure," she said.

"Owen Wilson," I repeated, before I could forget. "Hello, Owen." I scratched the top of his head and ran my hand over his soft reddish fur. Then I lay down on the bed and closed my eyes, suddenly overcome with exhaustion.

"I'll let you unpack," Dayna said.

I didn't even hear her leave. I slept without dreaming, like a long black screen between movie scenes.

When I woke up, I was starving. I followed the voices downstairs to the kitchen and watched what everyone else did first. Sean weighed a raw steak on a kitchen scale and entered the data in his phone before he seared it in a pan. Jake opened the freezer and rifled through his options, all equally unsatisfying. "Whose is this?" he asked, holding a pizza made of cauliflower. When no one claimed it, he preheated the oven. I considered asking if I could share, but Jake was over six feet tall; the Jake-sized serving was an entire pizza.

At the sink, Piper pulled her long hair into a topknot and put on an apple-green apron that made her look like a '50s housewife. After she washed her hands, she began to assemble an elaborate salad in a huge wooden bowl. She washed and dried the red leaf lettuce in a salad spinner. She added pre-shredded kale from a bag, roasted beets cut into quarters, and crumbly white cheese. She left the sink to toast chopped pistachios on the stove in a tiny pan. I realized she had her phone in a stand on the counter. She was filming her meal prep.

Morgan was eating handfuls of trail mix straight from the bag, periodically pausing to pick the seeds from her braces.

Quit waiting for people to help you, I thought. *Help yourself.* In the pantry, I grabbed a box of cereal. From the open shelves above the double sink, I chose a pretty lemon-yellow bowl and filled it to the brim. Like we were players on the same team, Jake passed me the milk from the fridge before I even asked for it.

At home, we always waited for one another before we started eating, but here it seemed like everyone started eating whatever, and whenever, they wanted. I slid onto the barstool next to Sean, who was cutting his steak.

"You don't have to keep wearing that," Piper said.

"Wearing what?"

With one finger, Piper drew a circle around her face. "It's kind of freaky."

I'd forgotten I was still wearing the makeup. "I'll take it

off," I said. I concentrated on my cereal like it was an oracle. Hardly anyone had viewed my first orphan video. Part of me wanted to check my phone for an update, and another part of me didn't want to confront the disappointment.

"Babe, be nice," Sean said to Piper, with his mouth full.

"I'm always nice," Piper said.

"I'll leave a comment on your video," Morgan said, intuiting my despair. "That will help boost engagement. 'What happens day two at the orphanage,' question mark, question mark, question mark, surprise eye emoji."

"Thank you," I said.

While his pizza baked, Jake went through a stack of mail, ripping up envelopes before he even looked to see what was inside.

"Are you sure you don't want to save those for the FBI?" Piper asked.

"What are they?" I asked.

"Jake's fan club," Morgan explained. "One of them figured out our address and then it was all over. She told all the others."

"They're moms," Sean said.

"You make it sound so wholesome," Piper said. She licked lemon juice off one of her fingers. "It started when he did that video without pants on and it went viral."

"*Risky Business*," Jake said. "The classic scene. With the white socks?"

I nodded. All I had to do was memorize the keywords so I could search it later when I was alone: *Jake, no pants, white socks, risky business.*

"Tell her how much money they send you," Piper said.

"That's okay," I said, pouring more cereal into my bowl so I wouldn't have to look Jake in the eye. It was none of my business. Jake didn't have to tell me. I didn't have to know.

"The most I've ever made from a Live is two thousand dollars," Jake said, like two thousand dollars was nothing.

"And they send you an allowance," Piper said.

"And they send me an allowance every month. They pool their money together. I told them they didn't have to. I think they want to. And then I, like, say their names in my Lives so they know I appreciate it."

I was so distracted trying to envision someone like my aunt or my high school drama teacher, Ms. Larson, sending money to Jake every month so he would say her name and make her feel special that I didn't notice the woman standing behind me in the kitchen.

"What do you think you're doing?" she snapped.

She was tall, gaunt, even older than Dayna, dressed in all black and pearls. Her brown hair was pulled back so tightly, I could make out the shape of her skull.

"Nothing." I felt my face turn pink.

"That is a *decorative* bowl. It's antique. It's *special*."

"I'm so sorry. I didn't know. I'll wash it by hand and put it back," I said, but it was too late. She had already cleared my place and was pouring the milk down the sink and running the hot water. Jake stepped to the side, out of the way. *Yikes*, he mouthed behind her back.

I picked up my phone like there was something essential inside it that demanded my full attention.

There was a text message from Morgan that said, that's Paula

Paula?

Viola's daughter

okay but how was I supposed to know not to use the yellow bowl? I replied. I wished everything in the house was labeled like an exhibit, so I knew what I was allowed to touch without having to ask.

the bowl was Becca's favorite

My arms broke out in goosebumps. Of all the bowls in the kitchen, what were the odds that I'd be drawn to that one? When was the last time Becca had eaten from it? Had she ever posted the bowl in one of her videos—could that explain why I had chosen it from the shelf? I felt a tiny thrill at the connection between us. I was getting closer.

I stood up from the counter and announced I was going to bed. It was nine P.M. No one argued or begged me to stay. They were likely relieved. Now they could talk about me behind my back.

As I climbed the stairs, I opened the app on my phone. The dancing video from this afternoon had over eight thousand views; the orphan video had eighty-two. The only comment was from Morgan.

In the small windowless bathroom, I scrubbed my face and watched the dark makeup run down the drain. In the mirror, my cheeks were pink and there were whiteheads on my chin.

I locked myself in my room. While I scrolled videos of hot girls walking, manifesting their dreams, and blending single-serve beverages, I ate the room-temperature string cheese and sleeve of peanut butter cookies I had in my backpack. If I failed at this, where would I go? Everyone back home thought I'd moved to Hollywood to become an actress. If I went back to UND, I'd be the girl who tried to get famous, whose head got so big she thought she was better than where she came from. They didn't understand why I was really here.

I was living in my aunt's basement when Becca's video came up in my scroll. At the beginning it said, *if you're seeing this, it's meant for you.* I kept watching. There was a spread of tarot cards on a table and then the text on-screen changed. It said, *Someone is missing you in heaven. They have a message for you.*

I tasted hot tears in my mouth, mixed with peanut butter cookie. In bed, I turned my camera on selfie mode and sucked in my cheeks and tried to make my face sexy and pouty like Piper. Through my tears, I looked lumpy and stupid, like a baby. I returned to scrolling, searching for a trending dance I could learn quickly. It wasn't too late to change my niche.

I found a video to copy from a creator with six million followers, and propped up my phone on my dresser. I watched the video over and over until I had the choreography memorized—what my hands had to do while my hips were doing something else and when I had to grab the crotch of my pants and spin in a circle—and then I was ready to record. The lighting in my room was terrible. My hair looked stringy and gross from how Morgan had styled it for the orphan video; when I put it up in a ponytail, my acne was more noticeable. I kept my hair down. My nose was red from crying. The first take wasn't awful, but I knew I could do better. If it took me all night, I would stay up all night.

All at once, I felt a warm surge of energy, like the first time I'd ever tried a shot of liquor. Coursing through my body was the sudden impulse to go wild. I'd thought I was a doll, but I was really a marionette. The house pulled my strings.

I discarded the recording and started over. It was only on the third take that I realized the original creator was also lip-syncing while she danced. I had to go back and memorize the words. I started the recording from the beginning, mouthing the lyrics: *insecure much? unsure much? keep shipping us (oh oh oh) you rupture me.*

Either I could perform the dance, or I could lip-sync, but I couldn't do both at the same time without messing up. How had that other girl done it? How many hours had she practiced? Maybe I wasn't cut out for this after all. Now I was crying again.

insecure much?

After my next attempt, I watched the video preview the way Jake had taught me and tried to be objective, imagining I was a stranger watching a video of a nineteen-year-old girl dancing to the hit single "u ruthless," openly weeping through the lip sync.

Instead of saving the video to my drafts folder, I accidentally hit the button to post. Immediately, I recognized my mistake. A timer in the upper left-hand corner told me what percentage of the video was finished processing. There was no undo button. I felt like I'd swallowed a fist.

When my video was finished uploading, I watched the whole thing again: halfway through the fourteen-second choreography, Little Orphan Olivia wiped her snotty nose on the back of her hand.

The first comment came almost immediately: wtf did I just watch??

I heard Paula in my head: *What do you think you're doing?* That's exactly what my aunt would have said. What if she saw this?

Surely there was some way to delete the video. And if I couldn't figure out how to do it myself, I would be brave and go back downstairs and knock on bedroom doors until I found someone who could help me undo what I had done.

But when I looked again, there were a thousand views. I refreshed: sixteen thousand. The bulb in the table lamp flickered off and on. I was going viral for crying. The attention flooded over me, a salty wave.

your beautiful
me every day at school
boys don't know what pain we go threw
she's just like me fr
are you okay?
Jesus died for you
she fake
this made me cry
it will get better bb

DAYNA

Owen Wilson had an accident. Outside his litter pan, I found a dark stain on the soft mat inside the rabbit enclosure. This had happened before at Luke's, when O.W. had a UTI. *Please don't have a UTI*, I thought. I hoped the accident was just a result of acclimating to a new environment. Or he was marking his territory. He'd done that at Luke's before, too.

"Mommy is a girlboss now. She doesn't have time to take you to the vet," I told him, in the embarrassing singsong I only used when I was certain we were alone, as I scooped him up and kissed his precious little head. If he was becoming incontinent, if he started sitting in pee, it could damage the fur and skin on his hindquarters. I checked his butt and decided to give him a dry bath. All my rabbit-care items were in a yellow diaper bag with a fluffy white bunny print I'd gotten as a gift. I found the baby-safe cornstarch powder and gently laid O.W. on his back on a towel on the floor. The key was to keep him calm. If he sensed my anxiety, he might struggle to get up. I sprinkled the powder in between his

legs and around his tail and gently rubbed it in before wip-
ing it away with a dry washcloth. Even if his long ginger
mane reminded me of those old photos of bearded Civil War
generals, he was a baby. He was an old man and a baby at
once. Benjamin Button. I needed him to live forever.

When you asked kids what they wanted to be when they
grew up, they all wanted to be YouTube stars. They never
said, *I aspire to become a middle-aged rabbit owner.* I had never
wanted a rabbit once in my entire life. It was Mollie's idea.
She was always rescuing the vulnerable and then telling
you about it, trying to con you into becoming a better person. She'd already donated one of her kidneys and said she'd
give the second one away if they'd let her. Owen Wilson, for-
merly known as Parsnip, was a class pet who ended up at a
no-kill shelter in Pasadena. He captured Mollie's heart on
Facebook and she asked me if I would consider fostering. I
said absolutely not. Mollie said she understood my hesitation,
then sent me an article about people who die from loneliness.

I was close to Mollie because we were the last two child-
less women standing out of the clique of girlfriends I made
when I moved to LA after college. When I wasn't working,
my social life was like a reality TV show: me and a bunch of
other women dressing up to go out and be the center of a
dramatic arc; our male co-stars were mostly off camera,
scared of us. We cried in public. We overshared for the reaction shot. We started book clubs as an excuse to drink wine
and gossip. At industry events, we were each other's plus-
ones. We went to the beach and wondered aloud why we
didn't go to the beach more often. With six of us, there was
no shortage of material. I didn't think our show could ever
get canceled. I thought we were committed to remaining
interesting to one another. *Someday,* I used to think, *I'll pick
up photography again, and I'll take everyone's portraits.* I always assumed there would be more time to be ourselves.

And then I blinked and everyone had boyfriends. I blinked again and there were three bridesmaid dresses hanging in plastic in my closet. Friend four eloped without telling us. Blink blink. It was just me and Mollie walking the beach, but instead of watching the sunset I was squinting at a picture of a four-year-old on Instagram who had her mother's eyes. No one celebrated their birthdays anymore—they just invited me and Mollie to parties for their kids. The parties started at twelve-thirty P.M.

This is how I became a rabbit owner.

Taking care of O.W. allowed me to reassure myself that I was not a selfish person. I was not making a mistake I would regret later. I was just making choices. My choices were just as valid as theirs.

After O.W. was groomed and back in his enclosure for bedtime, I microwaved a frozen meal and sat in front of my laptop. I responded to an email from Craig's assistant, Annabelle, about a sleep-tracking app that was interested in sponsoring Piper and Sean; another brand was offering to send Morgan free samples of a stick you could rub inside your thighs to keep them from sticking together when you walked.

Tell them we don't work for free, I wrote. Do THEY work for free?

When I wasn't supervising the shoots, I was spending hours a day bingeing content about how to game the algorithm by changing the camera angle every few seconds, targeting hashtags, and looping, so that users watched the same video on repeat, juicing the view count. Sometimes I would spend all day perfecting a single video, and it would get 800 views. Meanwhile, Olivia went viral for making a mistake. Tears streaming down her cheeks, she posted a video about *Curiosity*, the moon rover who sang "Happy Birthday" to itself, all alone, "an orphan." It was viewed more than 500,000 times; the comments section was filled with users telling Olivia that *Curiosity* roved Mars, not the moon.

Working all the time kept me from dwelling on Luke. For two weeks, I'd been running on adrenaline and the incentives of a job well done—not only to get paid, but also to prove my own relevance. That all my effort made a difference.

Since Craig refused to download the platform to his phone, citing security concerns, the only way he could see the creators' videos was if I sent him the links to watch in his web browser. I sent him one of Morgan doing Olivia's makeup to match the cover of a book; another of Sean pranking Piper by filling her face serum bottle with yogurt. When Jake and Piper took my suggestion to team up to re-create a moment from *Dirty Dancing*, the video traveled on the currents of controversy. Jake's fans were jealous of Piper; Sean's fans were outraged that she would dance with another man.

Craig and I easily found our way back to our old routine, talking through screens, via keyboards, at night. It felt illicit and safe at the same time. Because I first crawled inside the internet when my parents were getting divorced, I still associated chatting online with splitting my outer self from my inner one, like peeling the rind from the fruit. It was the secret social life I carried on while everyone else was sleeping. Chatting wasn't like texting, which was efficient yet superficial. Chatting was long and sinuous, a labyrinth.

Genius, Craig typed in our chat, in response to the *Dirty Dancing* controversy.

Jake and Piper deserve most of the credit, I replied. It took us two hours just to figure out that lift.

It was your idea. Wasn't it?

Yes.

Brilliant, Craig said.

After the last few years—surviving months of interview rounds to get a coveted spot at some buzzy new digital media venture that promised to "meet the moment," only to be laid off when management decided to pivot and relaunch with twenty-four-year-olds who gloated in their "some personal news" posts, unable to foresee they would fall victim to the next reorganization—I had nearly forgotten how it felt to hear the words *genius* or *brilliant* about my ideas.

Is there anything you need from me? he asked.

It was after midnight. I was already in bed. The only light in the room was the blue glow of my laptop screen.

Come over, I typed. I shut my laptop before he could respond, and climbed down the ladder from the loft.

O.W. was asleep in his habitat. I vaped as I watched out the window, waiting to see his tall, dark figure cut across the motor court from the house to my front door.

"Hi," he said.

"This isn't what you think it is," I said. I'd thrown a kimono over my pajamas.

"How do you know what I think it is?"

"Come in. I'm making tea."

Craig pulled two mugs from the cupboard and I got our tea sachets from a bottom drawer. It was as if we'd done this dance a hundred times before. I thought of those old billboards: *If you lived here, you'd be home by now.* When I stood up, the kettle was boiling. He poured the hot water into my mug and we went to sit on the couch.

"Are you comfortable here?"

"Yes," I said. "Thank you." I lightly squeezed his shoulder. The reason I'd invited him here was so the house wouldn't overhear our conversation. That was superstitious, but I felt steadier here, in the guest house, than I did in there. Here, I felt like I was the one in control.

"I didn't know if I would ever see you again," Craig said.

I watched the steam rise from my mug. All I had to do was explain why I'd disappeared on him twenty years ago, after my photography exhibit. How I'd felt rejected when he didn't come to my room and then found a boyfriend my own age who took up all my time. So predictable! Once that was out of our way, we could laugh and forgive each other. But there was a childish part of me, even all these years later, that blamed Craig for taking photography from me. Coming to this house was supposed to be the start of my career as an artist and instead it was the end. The exposure halted me. I couldn't post once I had a bigger audience. He stopped me from becoming who I could have been. I began to wonder if I'd taken this job not only out of desperation but because I thought he owed me.

"My boyfriend dumped me," I said instead. "The day I was supposed to move in. That's why I'm here."

"Ah. So I'm the safety school?"

I smiled. "Well, I don't know how safe it is here."

"What do you mean?"

"Some people think the Deckler House is cursed."

I expected Craig to laugh, but he just sipped his tea.

"This is what I wanted to talk to you about," I said. "I thought doing more collaboration videos would show who we are, as a collective. But we still haven't received a single offer from a major brand that wants to sponsor the house— I mean all the creators, not just one or two."

"And you think the house itself is preventing that from happening?"

It sounded ridiculous when he put it that way. "No," I said. "I mean that if the house has a bad reputation, maybe bigger brands are scared to work with us."

Craig set his mug down on the coffee table and turned to

face me. "So let's dispel the myth. Let's show everyone what it's like to live inside a piece of modern art. Get people invested in the restoration."

I shook my head. "You mean post more about architecture? I don't think that's what our audience cares about."

He stared at me intently. "I know why you came back, Dayna."

"Because my boyfriend broke up with me?"

"You came because of the house. That's why they all come. To see inside the house. But not everyone comes back."

"You mean some of them just leave," I said.

Craig nodded. "Not everyone is as strong as you are," he said, putting one hand on my bare shin. I hadn't known I wanted him to touch me until he did. I put my hand over his so he would stay. "But now we have a unique opportunity to show the Deckler House to the whole world. More people can experience it than ever before."

"Uh-huh," I said. I didn't say, *But how can they really experience it if they've never been inside?* I didn't want to argue. A warm drowsiness overcame me. We were sitting so close that I could rest my head on his shoulder.

"I'll let you get some sleep," Craig said, standing. He put our mugs in the sink before he left, and I felt something in between pleasure and ache—a flicker of longing.

AT BREAKFAST, PIPER was filming shirtless Sean at the counter as he cut pieces of banana into a blender. He tossed the last piece in the air and caught it easily with his mouth like a golden retriever. Olivia was dressed in her generation's uniform of high-waisted jeans and plain white T-shirt, eating an omelet with a knife and fork, a cloth napkin spread across her lap. Morgan was practicing her latte art.

"Can I make you one?"

"Please," I said.

Jake was multitasking, watching something on his phone with his earbuds in while he ate a dry waffle with one hand and took notes with the other.

I raised my latte in the air. "Hey," I said. "Um, good morning, hello. I have an announcement."

Piper still had her phone up. I couldn't tell if she was filming me or if she was so attached to her phone she had forgotten she was holding it.

"I have crunched all the numbers, analyzed all the metrics, and we have a winner."

They all stared at me.

"A winner in the contest. To grow your following?"

"Already?" Morgan asked.

"You all have been working hard. Posting two to three times a day. Collaborating with each other on videos. I recognize and celebrate all your effort. But one of your accounts has experienced explosive growth over the last few days and I want to reward that, in some small way." Jake locked eyes with me; he was anticipating my next words, trying not to break into a smile. He took his earbuds out.

"Olivia," I said, turning my head. She paused mid-chew. "In just a couple weeks, you've gained 63,000 followers. That's incredible. Congratulations. I think we have our winner."

"What?" she asked.

"The rabbit," Morgan told her. "You win the rabbit."

"Orrin Wilson?"

"Not to keep," I clarified. "But to use in one of your videos."

Suddenly, Piper threw her phone on the floor. Based on Sean's disturbed reaction, the phone belonged to him. "That isn't fair," she said, raising her voice. "Olivia wasn't even here when you told us about the contest! How can she win a competition she didn't even know she was competing in? This administration is corrupt!"

I tried to keep a straight face. Maybe Olivia hadn't moved in when I announced the contest—I couldn't remember—but even if Piper was right, why didn't they tell Olivia as soon as she got here? They spent all day and all night together, didn't they? My surprise turned to anger. Did Piper think she had a competitive advantage by excluding Olivia from the contest? If Piper expected everything in her life to be fair and just, then this was a lesson she needed to learn sooner rather than later.

"Whoa," I said, raising my hands palms forward to de-escalate, like I'd seen in a documentary about cops. "I didn't even get the sense you *wanted* to win."

"You don't know *anything* about what I want!" Now Piper was crying. She picked up the glass blender and looked like she was about to throw it, too, but then reconsidered and put it back. Sean tried to put a hand on her shoulder and she violently rejected his touch.

Jake cleared his throat. "Hey, coach, I gotta admit I'm with Piper with this one," he said. "It's unsportsmanlike conduct."

I gritted my teeth.

Sean seemed unsure what to do with Piper as she stood there hyperventilating, humiliated by her own vulnerability, her fragile chest pumping, snot running into her pretty mouth. I wanted to tell her about the future: how in five years, she would not be able to remember why she was crying now, over a rabbit who didn't even belong to her. I wanted to give her the long view. *In five years, you won't even be speaking to these people*, I thought.

"Let's all take a deep breath," I said.

No one breathed.

When it dawned on Olivia that they all thought she'd won the prize by cheating, her eyes ballooned. She looked to Jake to confirm the truth, but he wouldn't meet her gaze. So Olivia turned to Piper. "You can have it. You can have my prize."

"I don't want Dayna's stupid fucking rabbit either," Piper said. Then she hiccuped.

Drawn by all the noise, Craig found us in the kitchen. He looked like he'd just gotten out of the shower; his hair was damp and wavy and he was still buttoning his shirt cuffs. When he met my eyes, I flushed.

"Everything okay?"

"Everything is brilliant," I said. I stood completely still, daring anyone to challenge my version of reality. "We were just working out the schedule of filming with Owen Wilson so everyone gets a turn. Jake, do you want to go first?"

Help me, I silently pleaded.

"Works for me," Jake said.

Craig wasn't listening; he was looking at Piper with concern as she shivered and blotted her face with a paper towel. Men always got so uncomfortable when women cried; they saw tears as some secret weapon against which they had no defense. Nothing they learned by playing war with other boys in the woods prepared them for our tears.

"Olivia was teaching Piper how to cry," I explained.

Olivia knew enough to play along. "Honestly, she did a lot better than me when I first tried," she said. "But you should drink some water so you don't get dehydrated."

Sean took the cue and poured his girlfriend a glass. Piper glared at me. I had to get out of here.

"Walk with me," I told Jake.

On the short walk to the guest house, I realized how little thought I'd given to awarding the prize. Rabbits aren't playful and indestructible like dogs. They're sensitive to threats. As prey, they can see what's coming at them from a distance, but not what's right in front of their faces. It's possible for a rabbit to die from fear. Their skeletons are so fragile they can break their own backs by trying to flee constriction.

What was I thinking—that I would just hand over my baby and let him be used as talent, unsupervised? I knew better. I was going to have to be there, with each of them, as they made their Owen Wilson content, watching for any hints of distress or discomfort.

"Did you grow up with pets?" I asked Jake.

"I wasn't allowed to have a pet."

"That's too bad."

He shrugged and responded to something on his phone as I unlocked the door. In the daylight, I felt exposed by my own living habits. The two mugs from last night were still in the sink. I'd left a glass of ice water sweating on the coffee table without a coaster. My pajamas were still on the floor of the bathroom. I saw my habitat through Jake's eyes.

"He's not a cat," I explained as I picked up O.W. from his enclosure. Jake followed my instructions exactly and held him with his hind legs tucked inside the crook of his arm and one hand on his torso, so he felt safe so far from the ground. Owen Wilson typically disliked men, but he was calm as Jake slowly stroked his scruff.

"If he starts squirming, it means he wants to get down. You can't ignore his signals."

"No problem."

"If you're going to make a *Royal Tenenbaums* video, he'll need a Stetson and a fringed jacket."

Jake tilted his head back and laughed. His teeth were so white.

"No? Too obvious? *Bottle Rocket*?"

"Too much work," Jake said. "I'm just going to stream with him. I'm saving up for my first feature."

"Your first feature," I repeated.

"Film," he said.

"That you're directing?"

"It's all good," he said automatically, as if I'd apologized. Owen Wilson started wiggling and Jake crouched immediately and gently released him on the floor. He hopped under the couch.

"Let's give him a few minutes," I said, gesturing for Jake to sit across from me. "You were telling me about your movie."

"If you ask most creators what they're going to be doing in five years, they have no idea. But I have a five-year plan. I'm writing the beat sheet now. When I can show my parents that I can make a movie, they'll understand that what I'm doing is real."

Jake leaned back in his chair to stretch his arms overhead; when his shirt lifted, I couldn't help but look at the strip of smooth, soft skin above his waistband. He checked his Apple Watch. "I'm supposed to start the stream at noon." It was 11:58.

"You already announced it?"

"Yeah, I posted something on our walk."

"Do you mind if I ask how old you are?"

"Twenty-two," he said. "How old are you?"

"Thirty-two," I said, without thinking. I wasn't prepared for the question—at my age, who ever asked anyone their age? At my age, getting carded at Erewhon was a compliment.

"A millennial," Jake said. "I knew it."

I gestured at my collection of succulents, which I had arranged on top of my credenza, the only piece of furniture from my old apartment.

"Your parents don't believe what you're doing is real?"

"My parents think I just started my senior year at UCLA," he said.

I flinched. What would his parents think of me—of what I was doing with their son? I didn't want to think about what we were doing from their point of view.

"Are they paying your tuition?"

"They think I have a scholarship," he said.

O.W. hopped out.

"Do it now," I said, "before he goes back in."

We quickly figured out a place to prop his phone so his hands were free to hold Owen Wilson. I showed him the pile of soft blankets inside the enclosure where he could put him down should he start to get uncomfortable. And then I brought up Jake's profile on my own phone and entered the stream, to watch Jake the way his fans watched him.

"How's everybody feeling today?" Jake asked, which seemed to me like a pretty generic opening line, but his fans took the question seriously, like they'd been waiting all day for someone to care enough to ask. @shannon_from_the_island was waiting for her biopsy results and she was nervous, given her genes. @TrishaRose77 said one of her littles was home sick and they were watching Jake together. @maddysmom was experiencing some annoying side effects from her new meds. Rapidly, Jake acknowledged them all by name, and responded to their disclosures with an astonishing mix of empathy and positivity. A geyser of heart emojis erupted continuously from the bottom right corner of the screen. His attention was like a drug.

"Hopefully I've got something that will brighten your day a little bit," Jake teased.

Take off your shirt!!!!!!

hahahahahaha

your too cute

You look handsome & huggable.

Love you both ways.

I can sit here all day!

There were a thousand women watching, and the comments were coming so quickly, I could hardly keep up. Jake didn't engage the horny ones. I watched him gently lift Owen Wilson the way we'd practiced and turn him to face the camera, and then I turned my focus back to my screen, to follow their reactions.

Jake, you had a baby??

You didn't tell us!

What's his (or her?) name?

this is so sweet!

how old is she?

is he a rescue??????

can you say my name out loud please?

Jake leaned down to kiss the top of O.W.'s head.

"His name is Owen Wilson." That's all he had to say. They couldn't believe it—what a perfect name for the rabbit. What a perfect pet for Jake. He was a natural.

I'm crying

I think I just ovulated

This was when the donations started pouring in: thousands of roses, some donuts, a coral reef that took up half the screen. I didn't know the monetary value of each gift, but Jake probably had a rough mental tally going.

"I have a family to support now," he told them with a straight face. So brazen. He was going to milk these women. There was a competitive nature to the tipping; Jake read the names aloud of his biggest donors, and that made the other women jealous. From the stream of comments, I learned that they were not only giving him gifts on the platform— they were also sending him cash directly, which they referred to as his "allowance."

When O.W. wanted down, Jake set him on the blankets and showed the women whatever they asked for. *We want to see you stroke him*, they said. They wanted to see his tail. They wanted to see Jake put things in Owen's mouth. Jake was their camgirl. He performed on command for cash.

No wonder Jake hadn't told his parents what he was doing. After all, I'd never told mine about my self-portraits. We'd each found a corner of the internet where we did not have to be our parents' child. It was normal, I told myself, to seek independence from your family. It was the American way. Only Jake had figured out how to turn his rebellion into revenue.

I WAS CLIMBING the secret staircase to Griffith Park when a call from an unknown number interrupted the podcast I was listening to, about a cold case in Norway from 1970 involving an unidentified woman found burned to death in an icy valley. The ringtone startled me into answering by accident.

"Hello?"

"Dayna Lev?"

"Yes?"

"This is Mindy Bliss. Piper's mom. Do you have a minute?"

With those words, I was rudely transported away from the eerie clues contained in the dead woman's clothing labels and back to my irritation from earlier that morning. *Here we go*, I thought. I braced myself for what was coming: an explanation of her daughter's special circumstances (anxiety? ADHD? Tourette's? dyslexia?) and a request for accommodations, like I was a teacher who'd judged an assignment on its merits instead of on Piper's valiant efforts to overcome her unique limitations.

"You've probably seen a lot of things about Piper on the internet," Mindy said. "But I wanted you to hear the full story from me."

I had no idea what she was referencing. To me, Piper was a mass-produced commodity. Every hype house had one. She was interchangeable with any of the thousands of young white women with glossy hair, flawless skin, tiny waists, and juicy asses they earned through mind-boggling squat variations. There was an entire genre of videos dedicated to what to read, drink, and wear if you wanted to be *that girl*. The problem, as I saw it, was that Piper had nothing that differentiated her except her bad moods.

"This is off the record, right?"

"Off the record for what?"

"Craig gave me your number. He said you were an entertainment journalist."

"Wait." I stopped her. "Are you Mindy Bliss, the mommy blogger?"

Mindy groaned. "I've published two *New York Times* bestsellers and produced six seasons of a show on home organization, but I'm still just a mommy blogger? It's infantilizing and sexist. Do we call men 'daddy bloggers'?"

"I'm sorry," I said, even though it was hard to think of any men who earned a six-figure income posting photos of their children. "I didn't mean to strike a nerve."

"Maybe you can see a little where Piper gets it from." Mindy laughed.

"Anyway, I'm not a journalist anymore," I said. At the top of the next flight of stairs, I sat down under a canopy of bougainvillea and vaped.

Mindy and I came from different countries on the internet; while she was blogging about potty training Piper, I was posting Fiona Apple lyrics underneath high-contrast black-and-white photos of my collarbone. But she was a trailblazer. Many other women were able to build careers writing openly about motherhood because of what Mindy started doing in the early 2000s.

"Five hundred thousand people watched Piper grow up from the time she was a baby," Mindy told me. As one of the first bloggers to pivot from banner ads to branded content, Mindy was ahead of the curve. Advertising revenue from dog food and diapers and weight loss brands paid the family's bills and financed all-inclusive resort vacations and filled Piper's college fund. At the peak, she was earning $50,000 a month. I was surprised she named the figure, but Mindy wanted to give me an indicator of just how successful she was.

"When the whole world shut down, Piper taught me how to post videos," Mindy said. Piper appeared in a few of her mom's videos, but she took off as a star on her own. When Piper had a few million followers, she was invited to move into the hottest hype house in LA: twelve young adults living together in a mansion in Thousand Oaks. The pool had its own slide.

"Hold on," I said. "What do you mean, 'when Piper had a few million followers'?" She and Sean had a fraction of that now.

"On her first account," Mindy said. She sighed. "I blame myself for a lot of what happened. I got carried away. When Piper moved out, there was nothing to hold my marriage together. I didn't know how to be a private person anymore. Or maybe I had been forced into some kind of private person retirement and I wanted a comeback. I actually missed having people follow my life. Follow *me.*"

"You live-blogged your divorce?"

"Worse. I did it on camera. I didn't even think about how it would affect Piper because it wasn't *about* her." The more humiliating details she revealed—about her husband Maury's erectile dysfunction, their dead bedroom, the road trip he took with his buddies while she was going through painful pelvic floor PT—the more people stood by the side of the road to gawk at the car crash. It became a kind of compulsion, to leave nothing undisclosed.

"I was kind of in a fugue state," she admitted.

At the hype house in Thousand Oaks, Piper started acting out. She filmed her rebellion. As Mindy narrated, I opened the platform on my phone. I found Piper's old personal account, and I scrolled back until I could match the visuals to what Mindy was telling me: Piper got sloppy drunk and made out with her best friend at the house, Soraya. She added bisexuality to her bio. She filmed herself bingeing the snack food she had once promoted as a child on Mindy's blog—that was part one. Part two was her throwing up in the toilet while Soraya filmed. Piper shaved her arm hair on camera. She asked Maury to pick her up at the house and take her to get her belly button pierced; when the piercing got infected, Soraya drove her to urgent care.

"I was dead to her," Mindy said. "She wanted nothing to do with me. She wouldn't answer my texts or my calls. She'd chosen Maury."

The public followed this bizarre mother-daughter story in real time. Each time one of them did something, the other one reacted.

On Piper's eighteenth birthday, Soraya took her to get an ankle tattoo that said "Daddy's Girl." Mindy hated it. She posted a defiantly cheerful mother-daughter photo of them together in their Suburban, and a Blogsnark poster pounced on it, juxtaposing the fake-happy photo with a picture from Piper's own Instagram account of her new tattoo, mocking

Mindy's delusion. The internet was Team Piper. The comments were filled with sympathy for the teen who had grown up in the spotlight "without consent." They speculated about how Piper would frame her parents' divorce in her college application essays—would she say it taught her how every story has two sides, or that adversity makes us stronger?

"And then the *Us Weekly* article came out. Maury was dating Soraya. Someone inside the house leaked it to a reporter."

"Holy shit," I said. I stopped looking at my phone. My imagination took over: Maury's visits to the house where his daughter lived on the lavish set of a teen soap opera. The grand gestures that rendered him heroic. The desperation to feel desired once more. How did he ask Soraya for her number? How did they see each other privately without Piper knowing? I googled images for each of them, by affiliation: "Soraya hype house"; "Mindy Bliss husband." Then I could undress them in my head and smash them together like paper dolls.

Of all the videos, the one that disturbed Mindy the most was of Piper trying to cut out her own tattoo. She could barely describe it to me. It was quickly taken down for violating the platform guidelines, but not before she watched it twice.

There was one more person left to hurt.

"For forty-eight hours, Piper posted nonstop about Soraya's betrayal. It escalated very quickly. Soraya became the source of all Piper's pain. She wanted Soraya to feel the hurt that she did. She wanted to punish her."

"What did she do?"

Mindy took a deep breath. "She took all the sympathy and concern that people had for her because of me and she weaponized it. She knew everyone was watching her now. She gave out Soraya's cell phone number. And she said something like, 'If you ever cared about me, if you care if I live or die tonight, call Soraya and tell her she's a shitty friend and a fat bitch who only pretended to be queer for the follows.'"

I squeezed my eyes shut. "And people actually did it? They called her?"

"The harassment lasted for weeks," Mindy said. "Even after the video was taken down. It was too late. It was all over."

"What did you do?"

"I drove straight to the house to pick her up, but by the time I got there, she'd already been kicked out. Everyone was on Soraya's side. I don't know who Piper stayed with. She's only started speaking to me again recently. I think Sean encouraged it.

"I think she wanted attention and I wasn't"—Mindy's voice caught in her throat—"I wasn't able to give her the attention she needed at that time." She let out an enormous sigh. "The point of me telling you all this is so that you can understand why she needs the rabbit."

"Say that again?"

"Piper doesn't talk. After she left Thousand Oaks, she stopped speaking on camera. I'm sure you've noticed? She's gone mute. She'll post dancing videos, but everyone is a dancer. She started over with the couples account, but I told her that she still needs to rehabilitate her personal brand. She thought the rabbit could help."

"Piper thought my rabbit could help her rehabilitate her brand," I repeated.

"Right," Mindy said. "It was the best conversation we'd had in a while. I told her that I still get emails and comments from people asking how she's doing. When she's ready, I want to be a part of her life again. I won't ever post anything again without her permission."

I realized Mindy wanted to use Piper in her content again. Who was Mindy Bliss if she wasn't the mother of Piper? Maybe their reunion was a scene we could stage inside the house. Maybe Mindy's audience—older, wealthier, more obsessed with real estate—was who Craig wanted me to reach.

"So you've never seen inside the Deckler House?" I asked.

OLIVIA

Craig's office was empty. I kept the door open so I would hear footsteps if anyone came near. There were no windows in here, so I turned on the desk lamp. The wall behind his desk was a gallery of framed photographs; the other two walls had dark bookcases filled with albums and scrapbooks, abstract marble statues, an old tobacco pipe, and a mirrored tray with a crystal bottle of amber liquor and a matching set of glasses.

I didn't know how much time I had.

The photographs were arrayed in chronological order, beginning with faded prints, smaller than postcards, of the house under construction. There was one black-and-white headshot of a young actress in a floppy hat, her eyes darting coyly to the left, and another of a man in a tuxedo, autographed, *My best wishes always, Vincent Price.* There was a candid shot of a serious young woman in sunglasses and a headscarf, her face out of focus, sitting on a picnic blanket, holding a smiling baby. Then an entire row of color photos from the '60s and '70s, with a man in a dark mustache posing with beautiful women like a proud hunter of game.

"George," I whispered, and pressed my fingertip to the glass to make his self-satisfied face disappear.

In the bottom row, George was standing beside teenage Craig, who was in a dark suit, looking miserable. A funeral or a wedding, I couldn't tell. The last picture, in the bottom right corner, small enough to miss, was of a teenage girl in a black slip and dark eyeliner. She was scowling.

Becca wasn't hanging on Craig's wall. I was pretty sure that all these photographs were taken before either of us were born.

I slumped in Craig's desk chair and took a selfie. I imagined posting it to the forum, in the same thread where someone had dared anyone to fill out the application for the Deckler House. *Guess where I am*, I'd say. But I could never do that. Someone in the house might see it.

His laptop wasn't here, but I could search the bottom drawer of his desk to see if I could find Becca's contract—maybe even her application to live in the house. There were files for each of us: Jake Cho, Piper Bliss, Sean Knight, Olivia Dahl. But nothing labeled with Morgan's or Becca's names. I checked again, to make sure I hadn't missed a file folder.

A delicate white spider was crawling across the top of the desk. I froze. I'd never seen a spider that color before; she stood out, bright against the dark wood. I watched her slip inside one of the bottom drawers and I followed. It was a miscellaneous drawer of disorganized notes and old mail. Against all that white paper, I lost the spider. I shuffled things out of the way to see where she had gone. That was when I saw the three orange prescription bottles at the bottom of the drawer.

Suddenly, loud bells began to ring throughout the house. Had I triggered an alarm in Craig's office? Were there hidden cameras in here? Could he see me? My hands started shaking. I only had time to see that the prescriptions were all in Becca's name before I put them in a pocket of my long dress and ran out into the hallway.

When the bells played through their song a second time, I realized it was the doorbell. I'd never heard it before.

"Dayna?" I called. "Do you want me to get that?"

No one answered.

The doorbell, I remembered, was outside, at the locked gate, beside a sign that said not to ring it. Maybe the visitor had already tried texting the phone number on the sign. Maybe it wasn't a visitor—maybe it was another creator, here to audition.

I descended the dark, winding staircase, touching the pill bottles in my pocket to make sure they were real, and approached the gate, where a middle-aged woman in dark leggings and an oversized white button-up stood, taking pictures of the house with her phone through the bars. She was wearing a vinyl tote bag on one shoulder.

"Can I help you?"

"Yes, you can," she said, smiling. "I'm a member of the California Historic Properties Commission. Are you a resident?"

"Of California?"

She pushed her sunglasses to the top of a pile of frizzy blond hair. "Of this address," she said.

It sounded like a trick question. "Um, may I ask what is this in regards to?"

"I'm here for my annual meeting with the homeowner."

"Craig Deckler."

"That's right," she said, pleasantly surprised.

I opened the gate, and once her view was unobstructed, she took several more pictures of the façade.

"Would you mind?" she asked, holding her phone out to

me. She scrunched and fluffed her hair and then posed, un-smiling. I took a few shots before she stopped me and told me to raise the camera higher, to flatter her neck.

"You must be really into architecture," I said.

"I can't believe I'm actually here in person."

"That's what I thought, too, when I first got here."

She followed me up the stairwell to the main floor of the house. I showed her to Craig's office and said, "Please make yourself at home."

Had I shut his desk drawer? I couldn't remember. If anything in there was in disarray, I now had someone else to blame.

There's a woman here to see Craig, I texted Dayna. She would know what to do.

In the dining room, I crouched behind a black lacquer screen and took out the prescription bottles. I looked up the names of each of the drugs: olanzapine for seeing or hearing things that other people do not, fluoxetine for depression and intrusive thoughts, and lorazepam for anxiety. I'd been prescribed lorazepam, too, but I hadn't taken mine in months. Not after what happened. Every bottle was full. Becca wasn't taking her medication—or maybe she was, until she stopped. Did Craig take it from her? Why would he want her to stop taking her medication?

When I reached a dead end, I opened the app and replied to the comments on my most recent video.

Are you literally an orphan?

Yes

For real?

Yes

Is this a hoax?

No

Are you a real orphan how do we no what happened to your parents you seem too old to be an orphan?

I didn't know how to respond to this one.

What happened to your parents?

I killed them. It was my fault they were dead. No, I couldn't write that.

I heard one of the boys yelling from the terrace at the back of the house. I put the bottles back in my pocket and ran.

Jake was in his red swim trunks, his back to the pool, arms raised, while the woman tried to get close to him. Sean was guarding Jake's body, blocking her access, filming the whole thing with his phone. The stranger had her phone raised, too.

She was trying to get a selfie with Jake.

"You can't be here, Sue," Jake said. "This is where I live."

"Just one picture and then I'll leave. I swear."

"He told you no," Sean said. "No means no."

Sean noticed me standing by the door, but Sue's back was toward me. She couldn't see me. She didn't know what I could do.

In the sunny haze, the water was a still, soupy green.

"After everything I've given you!" Sue yelled. "You're just an ungrateful brat!"

"If you can't control yourself," Sean said calmly, "we're going to have to call law enforcement."

I thought that sounded very professional, the way he said *law enforcement*, instead of *the cops*. Sean was smart—he never would have let a stranger waltz right inside the house because she said she was from a "commission." I wondered how many times Jake had been in this situation and how far this woman would go to get a piece of Jake, if she had already gotten this far. Would she try to kiss him? Put one of her old veiny hands on his butt? Unbutton her shirt and ask him to autograph her boob? Hold a Ziploc bag to Jake's mouth to steal his sweet breath?

Before Sue could take another step closer, before I let myself consider the consequences of my behavior, I ran full speed at her body and toppled her into the pool.

The first thing I felt was the blast of the chlorinated water up my nose, followed by the shock of the cold, close to pain, throughout my body. Wearing a long dress was like swimming inside a tent. The wet fabric was dragging me deeper. My feet reached for the bottom and found nothing, oblivion. We were in the deep end. The thought flashed through my mind that this would be an incredibly stupid way to die. When I forced myself to open my eyes, the water was a cloudy bottle green, dotted with dead bees and pine needles. I swam in the direction of the light, but just when I was about to surface, I felt a hand on my skull, shoving me down. I waved my arms underwater until I elbowed my enemy—I hoped it was her crotch but I wasn't sure—and then I used my remaining strength to crawl to the opposite end of the pool, my constricted legs as useless as an injured mermaid tail.

"You bitch," Sue spat in my direction the second I finally surfaced. With her thin hair wet and plastered to her scalp, she looked like an evil eel. I sputtered and coughed. Sean was filming the whole thing.

"Who the hell is this?" Dayna asked. She was standing next to Sean, vaping.

"This is one of my followers," Jake said. "Olivia let her in." He was holding the pool skimmer pole like it was a baseball bat, ready to swing.

In the shallow end, I could stand and catch my breath. My eyes burned from the chlorine—or the raccoon urine. Hard to be sure. Sue was dog-paddling, trying to collect all the items that had spilled from her bag when I shoved her into the water. A sunglasses case, several prescription bottles, a tin of mints. Her car keys and phone were at the bottom. She'd have to dive.

I put a hand inside my pocket. Those weren't Sue's prescription bottles. My phone was also gone. It would be easy to retrieve the bottles if I had Jake's pole, but I was too humiliated to ask for his help. *Olivia let her in.* I waded in deeper, closer to Sue, to grab the bottles before she did.

"Don't go anywhere," Dayna told her. "Not until I understand what's going on."

"Let me know if you want me to call the police," Sean said. "I have it all on camera."

"I am a citizen of the United States of America. I can go wherever I want," Sue said.

"This is private property," Craig said. Although he'd arrived late to the catastrophe, we all turned to him for direction. Paula stood beside him in a black dress and big black sunglasses.

I took a deep breath and dove back under for my phone. Sue's pink quilted wallet was down there, too.

"Here," I told Craig when I came back up, handing him the wallet.

He opened the wallet and removed the ID so Paula could take a picture of it. They worked in sync, as a team.

"Sue Gambino, we have your information," Craig said. "We know where to find you if we decide to press charges for trespassing."

Her sopping wet shirt clung to her lumpy body as she climbed the ladder. Sue paused to wring out her wet hair into the pool.

"And what if I want to press charges for assault? What's *your* name?"

"Don't answer that," Craig told me. He handed Sue her wallet.

"I'll show you out," Paula said.

Before Sue left, she bent down to get a good close look at my face. "See you on the internet," she said.

Dayna helped me out of the pool and wrapped me in towel after towel, like a mummy. My teeth wouldn't stop chattering. The sun had disappeared behind a dark cloud. When I lay back on a deck chair, I saw that my sneakers were swollen and soaked, probably ruined. Dayna got on her knees and gently removed each one. Craig hovered above her, watching. No one said anything to me; they were probably calculating my punishment. I didn't even want to think about what I'd done to my phone. I watched Sean try to show Jake something on his phone and Jake brush him off. Then Jake threw the pool cleaner like a javelin in the direction of the evergreens.

"I'll take Jake to the police station," Dayna said. "We can go in my car."

"No one's going to the police," Craig said.

"That woman is stalking Jake. She knows where he lives. Where we all live."

"We can't get the police involved."

"It's my fault. I'm sorry I let her in; she told me—"

"Why did you let her in?" Dayna asked.

"She told me she had a meeting with Craig." I felt so stupid. Sue hadn't known Craig's name until I gave it to her. It wasn't like college, where they gave everyone an orientation packet in advance and I read the whole thing cover to cover; I knew what constituted plagiarism and I knew the signs of affirmative consent. But here, I only learned the house rules when I accidentally violated them.

"It's okay," Dayna said. "You didn't know."

"Do I have to go home?" I asked Craig. I didn't even know where that would be.

"Don't worry," he said, patting my towel-swaddled leg. Another wave of guilt crashed over me.

"This isn't about Olivia," Dayna said to Craig in a low voice. "This is about protecting Jake. Jake should file a police report. He needs a restraining order."

"Once you file a police report, it becomes part of the public record. And who has access to the public record?"

Dayna blinked. "The press?"

"Correct. And once the media finds out about this story, Jake's name gets linked to Sue Gambino. Her connection to Jake is stronger than ever. She has a link to Jake that none of his other followers have. He'll never be able to shake her. And as a bonus, Mr. and Mrs. Cho will be thrilled to learn what Jake has been doing for the past three months."

At this, Jake groaned and put his head between his knees like he was going to pass out.

"But this happens all the time to celebrities. Celebrities have stalkers. What do they do—if they can't get a restraining order?"

"They get a German shepherd," Craig told her.

Dayna's face went white. "No. You can't. If you get a German shepherd, I'm leaving."

"I'm going to blow chunks," Jake announced. Dayna rushed over to help Sean take him inside. Craig followed them.

When I was finally alone, trembling in my cold, damp cocoon, I opened the bottle of lorazepam, took a pill, and swallowed it dry.

"New orphan look?"

I stood in the doorway of Morgan's bedroom, holding my soaked dress and sneakers, trying not to drip on her décor.

"I'm the last survivor of a shipwreck," I said.

"Or a plane crash on an island."

"I outran a tsunami. Where were you?" I asked Morgan. "Didn't you hear us outside, yelling?"

"Orthodontist." She flashed her teeth at me. "What happened?"

"Basically, I ruined everything. I'm a natural disaster. I don't know if Jake will ever speak to me again. Sean took a video." I was too numb to cry.

"Oh no." Morgan moved a huge pile of clothing off a chair and onto the bed so I had somewhere to sit.

"My phone fell in the pool. I can hardly—" All the apps were wiggling on the home screen. Futilely, I poked at them to make them stop. What was I going to do without my phone? I hadn't even gotten my first sponsor yet. How was I going to buy a new phone?

"Give that to me." She turned it off, wrapped it tightly in a silk scarf, kissed it three times, put it inside a zebra-print bucket hat, and took it into her closet. "The house will take care of it."

"The house will take care of it?"

"The house knows you can't post content without it."

I felt woozy from the pill. I welcomed the sensation. Whatever Morgan said seemed within the realm of possibility because the realm was dilating.

"What else did you ruin?" she yelled. She was so deep inside the closet that I lost sight of her.

"My shoes," I mumbled. "These are my only pair." I could hardly keep my eyes open. There was the sound of something clattering to the floor in the closet and Morgan said something sharp under her breath. I didn't have the energy to check if she was okay. Drifting off in the chair, I dreamed I was a spider, crawling inside the pupil of Becca's eye. The eye was in the middle of her forehead. I thought, *I didn't know how easy it was to get inside.*

When I woke up, my towel was unwrapped. Morgan was pulling a dress up my bare legs, like I was her doll. I crossed my arms over my bra at the same time I noticed the tripod.

"Are you filming this?"

"Relax, Olivia. I was only trying to help you. You're so tired."

"I can dress myself."

I waited for her to take the hint and turn around, to give me privacy. I zipped up the vintage orange dress myself. It had embroidered flowers down the front and fit like it was made for me.

"You know, actresses can't be self-conscious," Morgan said. She was looking out the window. "When you do costume fittings for movies, you'll have to change in front of people. They might write it into the script that you take your top off, like what happened to Sydney Sweeney."

I put on the knee socks and penny loafers she'd pulled for me.

"I'm not acting, Morgan. This is my real life. You can turn back around. What are we doing?"

"Wait! I knew it would fit you!" She squealed and pushed record on her phone. "Say what you just said again."

"What are we doing," I said, flat.

"We're going shopping."

"I don't have any money."

"Cheer up, little orphan. I'm taking you to Goodwill."

I expected Morgan's car to be as unique as her bedroom, but she drove a green Subaru Outback with 116,000 miles on it, a hand-me-down from her aunt, when her aunt bought a new Subaru Outback. Inside, it was boiling and smelled like a wet dog.

"Sorry the AC doesn't work," she said.

"It feels good." I was still defrosting. I rolled down the passenger window and stuck out my arm to soak up sun. On the radio, Olivia Rodrigo was singing about crying all night on her bathroom floor. A plastic flamingo danced on the dashboard. As we drove down Blackwood Avenue, a hot wind blew my hair off my face.

"Sometimes I forget how good it feels to leave," Morgan said.

I felt it, too. I took a deep breath and marveled at how easy it was. Maybe it was the lorazepam, but I didn't have the tight pressure in my chest that was my constant fear of messing up, failing, and getting exiled back to North Dakota. No one was watching me. I instinctively reached for my phone before I remembered it was in the closet. Instead, I found a pair of Morgan's round wire-framed sunglasses in the cup holder and put them on without asking. The lenses were Capri Sun gold. In the passenger-side mirror, I looked like a glamorous stranger.

"How did you know I'm an actress?" I asked.

"What?"

"In your bedroom, you said I'd have to change in front of people if I was in a movie."

"You told me you were an actress."

"No, I didn't."

"Then I must have read it in your application." Morgan put on her left turn signal and checked her mirrors.

"You read my application?"

"I help Craig with that kind of stuff. You think he knows where to find creators for the house? He's not even on the platform." Morgan laughed.

"Well, how did he find you?"

At the next red light, Morgan turned to look at me. "I'm here because of Becca."

"So am I," I said. "Look, I have goosebumps."

So did Morgan. She held her arm right up next to mine. "We can only talk about her when we're outside the house."

"Why?"

"Craig told us not to talk about her or make any content

about her. I think he's mad that she left. Now we all have to pretend like she never existed or something."

Morgan pulled into a spot in the Goodwill parking lot.

"Is that because Craig . . ." I thought of the photo of George with all those women; the fact that Craig had it hanging in his office. "Do you think Craig and Becca were . . ."

Morgan made a disgusted face and then seemed to reconsider. "I actually hadn't thought of that before."

"Really?"

"It would just be so . . . gross," Morgan said.

"Maybe he was in love with her," I said.

Maybe that's what all the drugs were for. To sedate her. Override her objections. I wasn't ready to tell Morgan about the prescriptions I'd found. How did I know she wouldn't take them from me? Or tell Craig I was in his office?

"You've seen her final video?" she asked.

"Only three hundred times."

"I know she had a conversation with Jake the night before she posted that video. He was the last one of us to see her."

"Were Becca and Jake a couple?"

As soon as I said the words, my imagination filled in the details. The house was like a dorm. Piper and Sean were already together and Morgan didn't seem like Jake's type. That left Becca, with her long, dark hair. She seemed shy and a little awkward, but she had a quiet intensity that made her a pretty riddle. If it were a movie, she wouldn't understand that Jake was flirting with her and he would have to tell her: *Becca. I like you.*

"They could never be a couple," Morgan said. "Not with Jake's fans. You have no idea."

I had some idea. Maybe Becca wanted to go public with their relationship—like Piper and Sean—and Jake told her no? I knew how obsessed Jake was with his account, his following, his income. He had much more to lose than I did if his followers turned on him. If Becca was getting in the way of his goals, would he ask her to—what? Stop posting? Leave the house? Did he break her heart that night, tell her it was over? Did she threaten to go public anyway? Did she demand too much? Was Jake ever angry with Becca in the way he was angry at Sue? Was that why she looked so upset in her goodbye video?

"Have you heard from Becca? Has she tried to contact you at all?"

Morgan shook her head. "Maybe she wanted him to miss her. But I miss her, too."

The Goodwill was a huge warehouse with floor-to-ceiling plate glass windows facing the parking lot. Racks of jeans and dresses stretched on and on to infinity. A mom in bike shorts and a sweatshirt was holding a toddler on one hip and sorting through the women's tops. The toddler was sucking fruit from a pouch.

"I love your style," the woman said as we passed. I realized she was talking to me. "Did you get that dress here?"

I looked at Morgan.

"Say thank you, Olivia."

"Thank you," I said. "This is my stylist."

"Do you have a card?"

Morgan took out her phone to show the mom where to find her on the internet. When the woman registered how many followers Morgan had, she asked for a selfie she could share with her group chat.

As soon as we were in the jeans aisle, we doubled over laughing.

"I'm treating you to a Goodwill makeover," Morgan said. "You can thank me later, in your Oscars speech."

I held my arms aloft like a forklift and she piled her finds on top. Pencil skirts and peasant blouses and little black dresses and one bright teal blazer with built-in shoulder pads and black velvet trim. Every decade was given equal consideration. Whenever she saw a designer label she recognized, she whispered its name. "Comme des Garçons, $14.99," she said, awestruck. It was a long black skirt with a single black suspender that went diagonally over the shoulder and across the body.

"I'm not sure where I would wear that," I said.

"Doesn't matter," Morgan said, throwing it on top of my stack.

Alone in the fitting room, I felt a little panicky. How would I know what to pair with what? I tried to put together an outfit that Morgan would wear in one of her "get ready with me" videos: cropped red plaid pants that zipped on the side with a fuzzy black tube top and black combat boots. I looked like the mall version of punk. I looked twelve.

"Ta-da," I said weakly when I came out.

"A for effort, but try less matching!" Morgan said. "Or it looks like a costume!"

Try less matching. How many times had I tried on something in my bedroom and come downstairs to ask my mom if it matched? When she said no, I always changed. She was the last person I'd gone shopping with. We went to Old Navy before I left for UND. More than a year ago. That's where we got the white dress that I about drowned in.

I wished I could text her now, to tell her I met a famous influencer in Los Angeles who told me to "try less matching." I knew which emojis she would text me back.

"Try the teal blazer with the Comme des Garçons skirt," Morgan called to me from the other side of the door. "Same boots."

I followed her instructions and pulled my hair into a messy high ponytail. In the mirror, I looked older, bordering on intimidating in the boots.

"Can I see?" she asked.

I opened the door.

"It's perfect."

"It's only twenty-two dollars."

"A baby bison," Morgan said. "That's what you wrote on your application. The animal you're most like. What did it mean? A baby bison?"

"I'm more dangerous than I look," I said quietly.

"What are you," she said, "like a criminal or something?"

"Are you going to try anything on?" I asked, desperate to change the subject.

She stood up and followed me into the dressing room. "I wasn't sure if you were cool about sharing," Morgan said, unbuttoning her jeans before I even shut the door. I backed up against the wall opposite the mirror to give her more space to change. Before I took off the skirt, I pulled on a pair of pants so she wouldn't see my underwear. I unbuttoned my blouse with my back turned. I was sweating. I could hear her undressing as she dropped her bag, her shirt, and her bra on the floor.

"Which one should I try first?"

When I turned around, she was completely topless, holding a gray men's suit vest up in one hand, and a white spandex tank top in the other. I tried not to stare at her breasts, which were angled upward, like small ski slopes, with pale nipples at the top.

"Both," I said, stupidly. "I mean together."

"Your face is all red."

"No, it's not."

Morgan's head fell back as she laughed. Her breasts jiggled slightly.

"I'll wait for you outside," I said.

"Olivia," she said, holding the top of my arm. "Don't leave me. You're the only friend I have now." Her eyes were dark and serious. She was daring me to flinch.

I swallowed. "Okay."

I watched as she pulled the suit vest on and slowly buttoned it—the buttons were on the wrong side, she said. I watched as she shimmied out of her shorts. Her legs went on forever. I'd seen her try on clothes in her videos, but this was different. She wasn't performing for the camera; she was performing for me.

She turned to look at herself in the mirror in the vest. "Nah," she said, and removed it.

Now she was down to just her peach thong. Her lack of self-consciousness made me feel like there was something wrong with the way I'd been programmed.

Morgan climbed into a red cocktail dress with stiff taffeta sleeves and asked me to zip her up. I stood right behind her and pulled. The zipper was wide and silver and decades old. Morgan was almost half a foot taller than me.

"I don't know if I can get it up over your, uh—"

"*Pull*, Olivia," she said, sucking in.

I stood on a chair and reversed my hand grip so I had more leverage. She squeezed her shoulder blades together to make the fabric give. Finally, I was able to zip it all the way up.

Morgan turned to the side to check herself out. The fabric of the dress was so stiff that it corseted her waistline and pushed her boobs up toward the square neckline. A long slit ran up her left thigh.

"I can barely move," she said, "but I look hot."

"So get it," I said.

She turned. Our faces were so close. "How do you think it looks?"

"I think you'll be able to make content with it."

She frowned. "You don't think I look sexy in it?"

"I think you look extremely sexy in it."

"Sexy to the male gaze or sexy to the female gaze?" Her voice was so loud that I was worried that customers in the other dressing rooms could hear us.

"Female?" I guessed. I climbed down from the chair.

Morgan tilted her head to one side. "Do you like me, Olivia?"

"Of course I like you."

"Why?"

"Because you're the only one who talks to me."

Satisfied, Morgan touched the top of my head like I was her pet.

Craig stopped us the second we walked past his office.

"What's going on, Morgan?" he asked. But he was looking right at me. *He knows*, I thought.

"We went shopping," Morgan said.

"What is *this*?"

"This is Olivia."

He frowned. "I asked you to be respectful. That's all I asked. A minimum of respect. You're a guest in my home. This is not a dress-up game. This is not a game at all."

I scanned the wall over his shoulder to see if any of the pictures on the wall were crooked. Maybe I left a fingerprint on George.

The photograph of the woman holding the baby. I was wearing her dress with the flowers down the front. Morgan had dressed me in Marion's dress. It was exactly my size.

"I'm so sorry," I said. "After I fell in the pool—"

"What have you been keeping all her clothes for?" Morgan interrupted me. "If you don't want anyone to wear them? You wanted us to come live in your house, right? You didn't want it to be empty and sad? The house only comes to life with *us*. That's what you *said*." Her face was all red.

"Her clothes do not belong to you. If you can't follow the rules, Morgan, I'll have to move you to another room. I'm sure Olivia would be happy to trade with you."

"I'm not giving up my room," she said. "I'm paying for it."

"I'll take the dress off," I said. "It's no problem."

Morgan stormed out with all our shopping bags and I followed her back to her bedroom.

"I never thought he would see you in it," she said. "He doesn't get it. He's too old."

Before I took off Marion's dress, she had me stand in the corner, against the wallpaper, so she could take my picture. Against my back, the wall felt unusually warm. I was exhausted and hungry after a long day, but Morgan was relentless. Her eye was a camera. She never stopped looking.

Finally, she went into the closet to get my phone for me. I put the prescription pill bottles and my old dress and shoes at the bottom of one of my shopping bags.

"See if it works," she said.

The screen glowed, alive. Instinctively, I opened the platform first.

There was a new comment on my most recent video from @user888273912, who wrote, I know what happened to Olivia's parents

I felt lightheaded. The comment already had twenty-one likes. When I clicked their username, there was no bio. No videos. Nothing. They were following 632 accounts and no one was following them.

Prove it, I replied to the anonymous user.

"Olivia?" Morgan asked.

"It works," I said.

DAYNA

We sat in a horseshoe in the living room. I propped my laptop on the coffee table.

"Hi, Dad," I said. At first he was a grainy face, sitting in the dark, but then he turned on his desk lamp, which gave his skin a warm yellow glow. He was completely bald on top now, with a gray goatee and round wire-framed glasses. He looked like Ben Kingsley with that same tight, sweet smile. On top of his checked button-up, he wore a wool sweater vest. Behind him, a row of walnut bookcases. It was so good to see him and at the same time so terrible to see him on a screen—a reminder of the distance between us.

"Can you hear me?"

"We can hear you."

Once the tech was working, I took a seat on the couch between Olivia and Morgan. Across from us, Sean had a protective arm around Piper. Jake sat alone.

"Well," he started, "I'll say this is a rather unusual setup for a peer support group, but effective psychotherapy requires risk-taking, and that applies to me, too. I have to take risks as a practitioner. So when Dayna asked if I would visit your artist collective, I took a risk. I said sure." *Artist collective.* That was his translation of the phrase I'd given him: "collab house."

When he paused, I rushed to fill the silence.

"So much has happened," I said. "It's hard to even know where to start."

He smiled at me. "Dayna, I hereby release you from facilitating the group. That's why I'm here," he said. His teasing was gentle, but I got the message. I remembered the time I took a beginners' swing dancing class and as soon as my partner's hands met mine, he said, *Oh, you're one of those women who like to lead.* I tried to relax into the couch.

"I'll start by simply introducing myself. My name is Walter Lev and I've been practicing psychotherapy for fifty-four years. I wrote the very first book on group therapy and I've become an expert in the field. You're wondering what this old guy is doing on Zoom, but I haven't retired because there's nothing I'd rather do than explore the condition of being human. And I look forward to getting to know each of you."

"Nice to meet you, Dr. Lev," Jake said. "I'm Jake."

"Here's what we'll do. I know you all know one another already, but let's go around the circle and you can tell me your name and the feeling, or the emotion, you're bringing to the group today. Jake, would you feel comfortable starting?"

"Uh, sure. I guess the emotion I'm feeling is frustration. Like I'm in a trap? I know which Jake they want, and I know how to perform the Jake they want. I know what professionalism is. But the more I give them what they want, the more they think they know me. They feel close to someone I invented. Which makes me not want to be myself even *more.*"

"And when you say 'they,' you're talking about . . ."

"My audience."

I stifled my instinct to jump in and explain how Jake was so popular that there were other young men trying to copy his charisma, recording videos where they put their face right up to the camera and said, "Good morning, angel," preying on lonely women with fantasies of feeling treasured. But the copycats were lazy and unoriginal. It was just shtick. They didn't spend days scripting and producing a multipart video essay on kissing in K-dramas. They could never be Jake, which only made Jake's Jakeness more valuable.

"Depressed," Piper said.

"And your name is Piper," Sean added.

"And my name is Piper."

"Piper, can you help me understand how depression feels?" He was good with them. He was patient. He really listened. I felt a spark of envy.

When my parents divorced the first time, I was in high school. He left us the old farmhouse and rented a town house. I begged to go with him, but he had his work. All my mother had was me. *She needs you.* He probably said the same thing to both of us. The only way she knew how to love me was by passing on her arcane diet and beauty rituals. We had steamed vegetables—no butter, no salt—every night for dinner. I started having nightmares for the first time since I was a child. I was desperate for him to ask me about my life, and all the overwhelming sensations that came from existing inside the body of a teenage girl, but my problems were minor-league. He had patients who were delusional, suicidal, in psychosis. He told me about his most unusual cases, and I understood that they were my competition for his attention. From him, I learned to become a listener.

"Well," Piper said, "it's like I go to work every day and

all these strangers get to judge my performance and some of them are like, she doesn't deserve to be famous, she's only famous because of her mom, and some of them ask me why I haven't killed myself already. Then I go to sleep and wake up and do it all over again. How would *you* feel?"

"I think I would feel pretty lousy," Dad said. "So you said depressed is how you're feeling today, and it also sounds like there might be some anger there, too."

"Maybe."

I had the impulse to vape, but I didn't want my dad to see.

"I'm Sean. Body stuff."

"Could you tell me a little bit more about that?"

Sean cleared his throat. "Body dysmorphia."

"What does that term mean to you?"

"Like not feeling big and strong enough. Worrying about what other people see when they look at me. Comparing myself to other guys. Even when she tells me I look big." Piper rubbed his back.

"My name is Olivia and everything I do is wrong." Her voice was flat, her face expressionless.

Before Dad could respond to Olivia, Morgan said, "Don't you think depression and anxiety are just natural by-products of late-stage capitalism?" She was hugging a pillow. "Morgan."

"How are you feeling right now, Morgan?"

She pulled the laptop closer to her. "You know when you have a necklace and the chain is really delicate and it got tangled in your jewelry box and you're sure there's a way to untangle it—it's just going to take time—but you're sitting there on your bedroom floor, pulling apart the little knots and all it does is make more knots? And you wish you could ask your mom because she would know what to do?"

Piper was nodding.

"Thank you, Morgan, that's a powerful metaphor. Dayna?"

"Yes?"

"The artists have all been vulnerable; I know how hard that is to do in front of a stranger. It might be helpful if the group heard how you're feeling, too."

They all turned to look at me. As I'd listened to them describe the pressure they were under, the burden of expectation to be who their audiences wanted them to be, I felt a surprising amount of sympathy. But this was the price of celebrity. When I worked at *Entertainment Weekly*, we had a running joke that after a band broke out, their sophomore album was always about the dark side of fame.

I wanted to warn them that their lives would not get any easier from here, but in fact would only become harder, more complicated by piling obligations and regrets and failures, compounded by the threat of their own insignificance, and that was why it was important to develop strength, resilience, and flexibility. That's how I had ended up here: not because it was my first choice, but because I could adapt to change. I didn't expect the world to change to accommodate me.

But I was the therapist's daughter; I had to give the therapist's daughter answer to the prompt.

"I'm feeling a little bit guilty," I said, "for something I did. I held a contest, but it wasn't fair. I should have thought it through. I can take my responsibility for my part. I guess I thought a competition would be motivating, but it actually hurt the group. And for that I'm sorry."

Dad nodded and wrote something down. Then he asked if I had a timer.

"On my phone," I said.

"Wonderful. Please set it for twenty minutes. I'm noticing that there are some intense emotions in the room today, so I want to give everyone the opportunity to journal about what they're experiencing."

"And then we have to read it out loud in front of everybody?" Piper asked.

"Sharing is entirely optional."

"Are we allowed to write a poem?" Morgan asked.

"It's your journal and you can write whatever you wish."

When I looked at my phone, I saw the text from Craig:
I have something for you

I made sure everyone had enough notebooks and pens and then I went to meet Craig in his windowless office. I slouched against the doorframe, vaping, while he finished the email he was writing.

He raised an eyebrow. "Tough day?"

"I'm not depressed," I said. "I'm just having an allergic reaction to late-stage capitalism."

Craig laughed. "You've been talking to Morgan."

As soon as the nicotine hit my brain, I felt a blissful rush of reprieve. For a second, nothing mattered. I didn't have to hold anything together. I didn't have to impart any life lessons. I felt loose, pliable. A little reckless.

"Come here," Craig said. "I have something to cheer you up." He leaned back slightly in his desk chair.

I obeyed and went to stand behind him, leaning over his shoulders so I could read the email that his assistant, Annabelle, had forwarded.

I read the beginning aloud: "I found your house through @littleorphanOlivia. Is she really an orphan? My grandfather Giuseppe Scaccabarozzi was an orphan also, after the war."

"I wanted to be here when you saw it," Craig said.

"Wait," I said. "House of Scaccabarozzi wants to work with us?"

I hadn't thought of the label in years. They peaked in the 1970s with colorful crocheted jumpsuits, but it was a family-owned business and there was so much drama and infighting in the '80s that *Saturday Night Live* made a sketch about it. The family name became a punch line.

I continued reading: Sofia, the granddaughter of the founder, was trying to steer her family in a fresh direction. She saw what Gucci and Burberry and Loewe were doing on the platform and recognized the opportunity to reach a younger audience. Our "iconic property" was essential; House of Scaccabarozzi wanted a dramatic setting to highlight the work of their brand-new creative director.

I realized why Craig was so excited. It wasn't just the money—it was the resurrection of the house as a film set.

Attached to the email were images of some of the pieces from their next ready-to-wear collection: body-skimming velvet in jewel tones, diaphanous tulle gowns with structured built-in corsets, chokers with celestial pendants, witchy thigh-high boots, a beaded bolero jacket, a dark wool cape. Black leather pants and brocade blazers for the gentlemen. For inspiration, Sofia had also attached an old photo of Stevie Nicks looking like Oliver Twist in a crimson velvet Victorian jacket and top hat, and another of Fairuza Balk baring her teeth in a still from *The Craft*.

Sofia was asking us to come up with a concept for a series of videos that would tie everything together: the house, the label's renaissance, all of our creators.

The commission I would earn—if Sofia greenlit our idea—was decadent. It was champagne over prosecco, cashmere over polyblend, first class over coach. Fantasizing about that much money was nearly erotic. If the campaign went viral, it would be game-changing for my portfolio. I'd never worked in fashion before, but it didn't matter—it was actually better that we were outsiders, all of us, because we weren't coming from an agency. There was no precedent for what we could or couldn't do.

"I wonder how competitive it is," I said.

Craig looked at me over his shoulder. "You mean how many other orphans is Olivia up against?"

I laughed. "Do we even know if she's really an orphan?"

"You spend more time with her than I do."

"You interviewed her," I reminded him.

"She's quite a good little actress," Craig said.

He wanted me to ask her.

"I wonder how many emails Sofia sent out," I said. "How many bids will there be?"

"How many houses are like ours? Let me show you something else," Craig said, minimizing his email window to show me a color photograph of the exterior of the house, taken as the sun set behind the city, with dramatic uplighting showing off the overlapping square pattern of the concrete blocks.

"When was this taken? Before the earthquake?"

"No, this is a rendering. Of what it will look like when all the renovation is finished. We're so close—if we land House of Scaccabarozzi, we'll have enough to begin."

"You keep saying 'we.'"

"Paula and I."

"Right," I said. "Of course." I brought my vape to my mouth.

Craig turned in his chair so that he was facing me. "You can stay as long as you like, Dayna." His eyes traveled down my body and back up to my face. I felt warm where his gaze touched me. "In fact, you seem to be tolerating it well."

"Tolerating what well?"

"Some women have told me that the house has a certain effect on them," he said. "And that's why they leave."

At the sound of my phone timer going off, we both startled.

"I have to go," I said, "but I'll work on a campaign idea. I'll make sure we have the number one orphan."

Morgan had volunteered to go first. She stood up and read her poetry aloud, pausing for dramatic effect at what I assumed were the line breaks. "I am your slave / From dawn to dusk / I labor so you can live / Inside the softest spots of me / Blooming like belladonna / Reminding me what doesn't kill / Us makes us viral."

At the end, she looked at us and smiled shyly, hiding her braces, anticipating applause. Jake gave her a few snaps and the others joined in.

"Pass," Jake said, holding his notebook to his chest.

"Pass," Olivia said.

"I wrote mine as a letter to Piper," Sean said. He ran a hand through the back of his hair, stalling. Piper had her hands over her face, peeking one eye through a V she made with her fingers.

"When you were getting canceled last summer," Sean read, "I slid into your DMs just to say hey, how are you doing, because I thought it might not be very good. I saw what other people were saying about you. I felt a calling to show compassion even if you never responded to me because John said, 'Let us love one another, for love is from God, and whoever loves has been born of God and knows God.' I actually didn't think you would respond to me. But you did."

He stopped reading to glance at Piper. She confirmed this with a nod.

"I couldn't believe you were talking to me," Sean continued. "You said it made you feel better just knowing there was someone out there who would listen. I gave you my number and said you could call me anytime, even if it was the middle of the night, not to hesitate. I told you, I'm here for you, and I still feel that now. All I want is to protect you and make you believe you are enough. I don't want anyone to make you feel less than. I pray for your haters."

At the last line, we all laughed. Piper hugged him and buried her face in his neck. Sean wasn't the most eloquent, but he was so earnest, it pierced me like an arrow.

"Does anyone want to share how what Sean said affected them?" Dr. Lev asked.

"I think it's really nice," Olivia said, tears streaming down her cheeks.

"Groups feel cohesive or—how shall I put this—a sense of togetherness when they have something in common. When they can form a sense of identity together. And what I've heard a little bit about from each of you this afternoon is that part of the challenge of being public figures is the sense that there's nothing you can do that will ever be enough. There's always going to be someone out there who's disappointed in you, or whom you can't please. And that must be profoundly frustrating."

I wondered if my dad realized that my job was to make them even more famous. After my conversation with Craig, I wanted to tell him, *I'm succeeding! I'm actually good at this!* But my dad wouldn't be dazzled by House of Scaccabarozzi, or my future commission. He hadn't raised me to be materialistic. He helped people in existential crises, asking themselves what life was for. I was so afraid to find out I was wasting my life that I was afraid to even pose the question.

"We have a few minutes remaining. Can anyone think of anything else you all share in common? An experience or a feeling or—"

"Becca," said Piper.

"Whoa," Sean said. "*Becca.*"

"Who is she?" Dad asked.

"She was one of us," Jake said. He looked down the hallway in the direction of Craig's office. "And then she left without telling us why."

"She *disappeared*," Morgan added, trying to shock my dad.

"No one knows what happened to her," Olivia said. "Right?"

Piper nodded.

They were all leaning in toward the laptop, wanting Dr. Lev to grasp this major event in their lives and help them process it. Even Olivia, who arrived at the house after Becca was already gone, was invested in solving the mystery.

That's when I knew what we were going to do for the House of Scaccabarozzi.

When I got back to the guest house, I called my dad. It rang four times and then the call went to voicemail. *You've reached the confidential voice messaging system of Dr. Walter Lev. I'm sorry I'm not able to take your call right now, but please—*

I hung up. He turned his phone on silent when he was in session.

Hi Dad thanks for today, I texted. I think it was really helpful for them. For me too. Let's catch up soon?

Owen Wilson followed me to the refrigerator, where I pulled out lettuce and cabbage for his dinner. "Mommy had a good idea at work today," I told him. I pulled out a plastic package of fresh basil I'd gotten for myself, and gave him a couple of leaves as a treat.

If I lived with Luke, I'd be driving home right now. After I found street parking, I'd have a human adult to describe my day to: the group therapy, the new campaign, the question of why Becca left and where she was now. Luke would be pouring our wine, sniffing and swirling as I spoke. The less he mirrored my enthusiasm, the more animated I would become, until I finally had to tell him how I wanted him to respond and he parroted it back to me. *He's a little on the spectrum.* That's what we said now, whenever we wanted to paint a more sympathetic portrait of the men who were good at making money but bad at listening to women.

At least Luke never talked over me. He always waited for his turn to speak, and when it was his turn, I listened like an Olympian. Like I'd been training all my life. I made eye contact and furrowed my brow in sympathy. I was Dr. Lev's daughter. My genetic inheritance was my listening face.

Do we even know if she's really an orphan?

Craig knew what I was good at.

I was buzzing with nervous energy, like a fly trapped between screen and door. I couldn't relax. I bent down and took six photos of Owen Wilson, trying to get the cutest angles of his ears. I texted the best one to Mollie, but she didn't respond right away.

I sent the same photo to Olivia and asked if she wanted to come over tomorrow morning and make her video.

Yes! she replied immediately. I have costumes! Thank you so much!

I made a pretty salad and took a picture of my plate that I sent to no one. I ate with my right hand and held my phone with my left.

On Instagram, I scrolled through the catalog of all the women I had ever known. The younger ones—my former interns, the assistant producers, the social media managers— still posted lifestyle content: monochromatic outfits and beverages, female friendships, tablescapes, engagement rings, little treats. They documented the lives they led when they weren't on the clock by imitating the most popular influencers who made a living selling them the lifestyle they were all unconsciously copying. Now that I had more experience on the platform, I could see how homogenous it all looked. How staged for the camera. We thought we were making choices based on our desires, preferences, and values, but really the platforms were driving our behaviors by rewarding us with likes for delivering content that performed.

The women my own age had all but disappeared. Instead of my friends, I saw dimpled toddlers in tiny duffle coats, hugging pumpkins. When I did see my friends, their bodies were usually hidden by flowing garments and they posed in a group, mid-sentence, eyes half closed. In their late thirties and early forties, their bodies were no longer works of art to adorn and perfect for the algorithm. Their bodies were beautiful machines. They had gestated little miracles and then locked their accounts, like walled gardens.

In the captions, things fell apart. The center could not hold. Women were quitting their jobs, getting antidepressants over telehealth, googling "adult women ADHD symptoms" in the night. Could we all acknowledge that our society did not value caretaking? We could. Did we remember that Oprah said women can have it all, just not all at once, and could we admit that we stubbornly believed we were the exception? Yes.

Can anyone think of anything else you all share in common? All these women were taking their turn sharing with the group, but not one felt like she was being heard.

Craig had said that not all women could handle the effect the house had on them. I could still remember the sensation I'd felt the first night I'd arrived at the Deckler House, all those years ago, like a flash of possession. The only person I'd ever tried to explain it to was my college boyfriend. I asked Russell if he'd ever been somewhere that made him feel like he was losing control and submitting to what that place wanted him to do.

"Maybe you should take a break from drinking," he said.

I'd shaken my head, embarrassed. I never brought it up again.

Had I altogether imagined it? Why couldn't I feel the house inside me this time—had I become desensitized to its influence with age? Sometimes, when I watched how quickly Piper and Morgan and Olivia could cycle from anger to tears to joy, it was like facing the multiheaded Hydra of my younger self. To become an adult, I'd slain her. The girls were still susceptible to getting flooded with feeling. They couldn't control themselves.

It was too early to go to sleep. I brushed my teeth. I applied lifting and tightening serum to my neck. I touched up my mascara and spritzed Velvet Haze on my wrists.

Some women have told me that the house has a certain effect on them. Craig would not have said that unless he'd heard other women describe what I'd once felt. Had the house left its fingerprints on Becca, too?

The door to his bedroom was half-open.

"Knock knock," I said.

From bed, Jake gestured for me to enter.

He was reclining against a pile of puffy white pillows, shirtless, smooth pecs flexing as he held up his phone. He'd pushed a black-and-white polka-dotted sleep mask to the top of his forehead. "Goodnight, ladies," he said to camera. Whatever they were saying in the comments made him laugh and he had to say it again: "Goodnight!" He pulled the sleep mask over his eyes and the bedspread over his body—somehow filming all of this with one hand—and tucked himself into bed. He continued to hold the phone, now aimed at his head on the pillow.

I waited for Jake to pop up and end the stream, but he remained like that, lying on his left side, motionless, full lips lightly touching, Sleeping Beauty. Minutes passed. I pulled out my vape and surveyed the landscape. His bed was shoved into a corner because half the room was taken up by his desk, which was like a mini production studio, with two monitors, LED lights, a microphone on a boom, and a dock for his headphones. On the wall opposite his desk, a retractable green screen pulled down from the ceiling like a window shade. His shoes were lined up on a rack from lightest to darkest. On the concrete wall behind the bed, he'd hung a *Rashomon* poster showing a bandit with a sword, a sad and desperate woman clinging to his arm.

Finally, Jake stopped the stream with his thumb, still blindfolded, and sat up.

"Sorry about that," he said. "Transitions are hard for them. They want to see that I'm really going to bed."

It was nine-thirty P.M.

"But you're not really going to bed."

"No offense, but you're the one who challenged us to get our metrics up. That equals doubling down on engagement."

"You're right," I admitted.

"One of them said she'd pay five hundred dollars to watch me sleep all night on camera."

"Sue?"

"I blocked her."

"Wise move," I said.

"Another woman."

"And?"

"Would *you* sleep on camera for money?" Jake asked.

"No," I said. "But no one wants to watch me sleep."

"You might be surprised," Jake said. He checked something on his phone and then decisively put it face down. He grabbed a purple hoodie that was balled up at the foot of the bed and pulled it on. "Sit," he said.

My options were the bed, the floor, or the gaming chair at his desk. I chose the chair and swiveled to face him in bed.

"Did Becca ever say anything to you about the house?"

"Like what?"

"Like a bad feeling she got when she lived here, or a weird impulse to do things she wouldn't normally do, anything like that?"

Jake crossed his arms and looked down at the bed, thinking.

"Well, she asked me to meet her outside," Jake said.

"When?"

"The night before she posted her last video. She asked me if I would rather lose all my followers but feel totally at peace and happy every single day or gain a hundred million followers if it came with a curse."

"What did you say?"

"I said I'd choose the followers, and that really upset her. I argued that if I had a hundred million followers, I'd be rich, I'd have access to the best health care. I could take care of my parents so they live to be a hundred. She said no, that's not how it works. I said, 'It's just a thought experiment.' She wanted me to agree with her, and when I didn't, she got mad at me. She really wanted me to avoid choosing the curse."

"Why did she ask you to meet her outside? So that the house couldn't hear your conversation?"

Jake smiled with one corner of his mouth. "You think the house can hear our conversations?"

"I've just heard that some people think the house is cursed or something. I mean, I've read it on the internet."

"Becca wanted to smoke weed and she didn't want Paula to smell it."

I laughed at myself. "Of course. Go on."

"I can't remember what came first, whether we got in a fight or we kissed. We were both, uh, high. I just wanted her to chill out."

"Was Becca your girlfriend?"

Jake hit his forehead a few times with his fist. "Did you read that on the internet, too?"

"I didn't read it anywhere."

"I don't think Becca had a lot of, um, experience. But she liked me, or she trusted me or whatever, so she thought she could get those experiences from me." How complicated it was to be Jake—to be an object of desire for so many women that he had to constantly draw and redraw the boundary lines around what he actually wanted.

"So, to recap, you saw her the night of August seventh, you played 'would you rather?' and she got mad at you, you kissed her, and you never saw her again?"

"*She* kissed *me.*"

"Sorry," I said. "Where do you think she went? What's your theory?"

"I think she freaked. It was too much pressure, knowing people were actually making decisions in their real lives based on her tarot readings. She got famous too fast. Morgan checked her room the next morning and most of her stuff was gone. It wasn't, like, a *crime scene.* Becca didn't have a car, so she must have called an Uber to take her to the airport. And then she went home to wherever she came from."

"You don't know where she came from?"

"She once told me her mom would kill her if she knew what she was doing, like it went against their religion. We bonded over that. We both had to keep secrets from our families."

"I noticed that none of you ever post about her."

"Craig told us not to," Jake said.

I blinked twice. "Why not?"

"He said it was better if we just continued posting as usual—not acknowledge that she left the house, or that we didn't know where she went. He made it seem like she told him where she was going and she didn't want any more attention. So we respected her privacy."

If Craig really did know where Becca had gone, that explained why there was no missing person report filed, no police investigation into her disappearance. Craig would do anything to avoid drawing negative attention to the house. As far as I could tell, there wasn't evidence of kidnapping or violence. But why would Becca tell Craig—and not Jake? Or Morgan? What made Craig her confidant? And how had Becca been able to maintain an air of mystery and a wall of privacy when she worked in an industry that required non-stop disclosure? If Becca didn't want to create content anymore, why hadn't she deleted her account? Why was Craig preventing them from posting content about the one topic guaranteed to get attention?

Questions ricocheted off the walls of my brain—they would all be answered soon. If my plan worked.

"I want to show you something," I told Jake, and climbed beside him on the bed. I pulled up the email from Sofia Scaccabarozzi on my phone.

His eyes went straight to the campaign budget.

"Whoa," he said.

"My idea is that we produce a series of videos that are all connected, as you all search for the truth of what really happened to Becca. You'll be wearing the pieces from the collection, and we'll stage the house like a Gothic mansion, with candles and dried roses and skulls or whatever. We can involve the audience—like Olivia can ask, 'Should I open this door? Or this one?' And to follow the story, you have to follow everyone in the house. One video will lead to the next. We'll call it Rabbit Hole."

The more I described what I saw in my head, the more animated I became; I was seeking his approval. It wasn't just that I wanted him to think the concept was cool—

I wanted to pass the test, prove that I finally understood what the platform wanted from us.

"And then, at the end, we find Becca?"

I drew a sharp inhale. His brow was furrowed; his question was sincere. In my imagination, I'd only visualized a fashion montage, set against the backdrop of the house. I hadn't actually thought about delivering real live Becca at the end. I hadn't thought through the ending at all. How could I promise we would find her? If she was out there, milking goats on a farm in Idaho, probably on the verge of betrothal to a nice young missionary, the only chance we had of reaching her was through the platform.

"I'd bet anything she's still watching us," I told Jake. After all, once I'd been inside the Deckler House, I could never forget it. "And if we make Rabbit Hole good enough, how could she resist playing along?"

OLIVIA

In a ruffled white jabot, Owen Wilson was Heathcliff. We had no moors, but we had hay. We had two centuries to get through before his nap time. Each video was different. For Oliver Twist, I filmed him at his water bowl and captioned it, "Please sir, I want some more." It was hard to think of a good costume for Jane Eyre, so I skipped ahead to Anne of Green Gables, since O.W. was a redhead already, and put him in a white pinafore. I'd made little rabbit-sized Harry Potter glasses from sculpture wire and a magician's wand out of a straw I painted black. I remembered what Morgan had said to me at Goodwill: *Try less matching or it looks like a costume.* But I loved a costume. Costumes were a way to make other people see you the way you wanted to be seen.

I let Dayna dress and undress him. He was her rabbit. I didn't want to scare him or make him uncomfortable.

"My son is a natural," she said, feeding him lettuce in between takes.

"What does he like?"

"He's an introvert. He likes cozy, dark places where he feels safe."

After the star hopped underneath the couch for his afternoon nap, I started editing. I re-created the *Never Let Me Go* book cover with a close-up of Owen Wilson's face. Dayna brought me a glass of water and a little white bowl of crackers.

"Thanks," I said.

"What about Rebecca?"

"Is that her real name?"

"Who, the dead wife?"

I started choking on a cracker. "What?"

"Oh, did you think I was—no. There's a novel called *Rebecca*. That's the name of the wife. But the narrator of that book is an orphan, too. I don't think the orphan even has a name."

I drank my water and avoided looking at her until I'd composed myself.

"Did you know Becca?"

"I moved in after she left," Dayna said. "I want to talk to you about her, but first there's something Craig wants me to ask you. It's sensitive. I didn't want to do it in the house."

Had he noticed the missing medication?

"In regards to what?" I asked.

"You don't have to tell me more than you're comfortable with, but I was just curious if, like, your username, littleorphanOlivia, if that is nonfiction or if—"

"Or if it's a hoax."

"Not a hoax," Dayna said. "More like a character. Craig thinks you're a very talented actress." She smiled, which gave me the creeps. I didn't want to hang on his portrait wall.

"I'm both," I said. "An orphan and an actress."

Dayna clasped her hands like she had just won a prize.

"Is that good?"

"Not at all," she said, frowning. "It's terrible. What happened?"

"You really want to know?"

Dayna nodded and grabbed a few crackers, settling in for the story. She was the first person to ask me what I did to my parents.

"If I wasn't really an orphan," I started, "I wouldn't be here, searching for Becca."

I MET PETER Hansen in the honors program. He was over six feet tall, with sandy hair and freckles, and hooded eyes that made him look like he knew something you wanted to find out. He'd grown up on a canola farm and was majoring in earth science, with a minor in sustainability studies. He had been on swim team in high school. There were so many girls in honors and only one Peter, which gave him an advantage. He wasn't my boyfriend—I knew I wasn't the only girl he was spending time with—but when we were studying together, and I had his undivided attention, I felt as fizzy and sweet as a root beer float. He kept saying he didn't get why I wanted to be an actress, like that was so beneath me, when I was so interested in science, in history, in politics.

"You're actually *smart*," he told me, as if I didn't know.

I could memorize quotes from dead presidents and global warming projections and save them to my cerebral hard drive. But what I loved about being onstage was that I could stop thinking. And just feel. When I was performing, a current ran through my body. I was an electric vehicle. I ran on a charge. In a live performance, there was no complicated history, and there was no anxious future. There was only my scene partner and what passed between us that day or night, never to be repeated exactly the same way again. That's how I felt with Peter, too. That a random confluence of circumstances had brought us together. The time we shared could never be replicated.

In the lobby of the theater after my scene study showcase in November, Peter met me with red and white carnations. I still had my stage makeup and false lashes on. He walked me through the freezing cold back to my dorm. The spruce and hemlock trees were blanketed in snow.

"Well? What did you think?" I'd played Masha in *The Seagull*.

"It was, uh, a little over my head," Peter admitted.

"Come on. You're actually smart," I teased.

"But you were good. I liked watching you."

I felt myself blush and I was glad we were walking side by side and he couldn't see me. Then he touched the arm of my coat and I stopped and looked up at him. When Peter kissed me for the first time, he held my face in his gloved hands. His lips were soft and warm, hesitant at first and then insistent. My body melted into his, a safe shelter from the bitter cold.

Over the next week, Peter stopped seeing Katie Jorgensen and Shelby Olson and Anna Parshall. I knew this because he spent all his free time with me, and when one of them texted, asking to meet up, he would show me what they said and what he responded, like a token of his loyalty. He didn't just ghost them, which I thought was respectful. I was in Peter's dorm room when Anna stopped by to pick up a book she'd loaned him. She was wearing a mask.

"Anna, chill," Peter said to her. "It's just us." We usually didn't wear them outside the classroom.

"You can never be too safe," Anna said before she turned her back on us and left.

An old fear flared inside me.

My senior year of high school, when the pandemic began, I had to start taking lorazepam for my anxiety.

My dad taught me to think for myself—not just follow the crowd. But thinking for yourself requires a lot of research. Sometimes you can know too much. When I did my own research, I found more and more reasons to worry: My dad was overweight and had diabetes and high blood pressure. My mom had lupus. If my dad died first, I'd have to take care of my mom. If my mom died first, I'd have to take care of my dad. Who would take care of me?

In my nightmares, they were in different hospital rooms, and I kept walking down a never-ending, brightly lit hallway, unable to find either of them in time to say goodbye. I would wake up crying.

Once I was on the medication, I was able to finish senior year in a numb dumb daze, staggering my way through Lady Macbeth, unable to feel her madness. I lost the ability to cry. I could still feel the pinch that preceded tears, but no release.

I thought about deferring my freshman year at UND so I could stay at home with my parents and protect them, but they pushed me to go. Whenever I had the premonition that something very bad was about to happen—*something wicked this way comes*—I was told to recognize and label that feeling as "anxiety."

My mom took me shopping for extra-long twin sheets, shower flip-flops, and a stash of over-the-counter pain and cold meds just in case. My dad got me Mace for my key chain.

There was so much to do when I got to campus that I didn't have time to worry. I was surprised by the relief that washed over me when I moved out—if I caught the virus, I wouldn't infect them. Maybe they were even safer without me. By the third week of classes, I had stopped taking my pills.

But by November, the case count was rising and the university didn't want us coming back to campus in between Thanksgiving and Christmas, to reduce the transmission risk. All finals would be conducted online.

"We won't see each other for almost two months," I worried. "You may not even like me in January."

"Why," Peter teased, "what's going to happen to you in January?"

I couldn't think of a clever comeback. Shelby would have known what to say.

"You know," I said.

"Know what?"

"How much I like you," I said. I couldn't look at him.

"How about I drive you home for winter break?"

I leaned in to kiss him and he returned my kiss with an urgent need. I didn't like kissing with tongues, but Peter did, and I liked Peter. His roommate was at football practice. Peter didn't seem sure what he was allowed to touch, so I lifted one of his hands and directed it under my turtleneck, on top of my padded bra. I wanted to give him something, but I was also nervous that he would explore under the bra and find out how little there was to give. We shifted from sitting on his bed to me lying on my back and him hovering above me, rubbing his hips against mine, still fully clothed. I ran my hands along the long length of his strong swimmer's back. I wished he would turn off the light but I also didn't want him to leave me.

"I don't want to do anything you don't feel like doing," he whispered. He sounded out of breath.

"I know," I whispered back.

We kissed for a little while longer, and when I felt him reaching under me to unclasp my bra, I sat up, pulled my shirt down, and said I had to go.

"I'll talk to you tomorrow," I said.

"Okay, Olivia," he said. He looked a little confused. Or crestfallen.

Good, I thought.

It was three hours to Minot in clear weather. Three hours in a car alone with Peter: It might be the last time I saw him until January. It would also give me three hours to make him think about how much he would miss me, to gradually convince him we should still see each other over break. It had to seem like his idea, not mine. He only lived an hour away from my parents.

I called my mom to tell her they didn't need to pick me up. I was getting a ride home.

"Oh really?" she asked. "What's his name?"

I sent her a picture I found online of Peter in his swimsuit, after a competition.

She replied with six hearts-for-eyes emojis. I lay in bed unable to sleep, thinking about how we would make it work: my career as an actress and his in regenerative agriculture. Maybe we could move to Minneapolis. Minnesota had a lot of funding for the arts. But did Peter's parents expect him to take over the family farm? I would have to ask him.

The next morning, Peter texted, I don't feel good.

No, I thought. *No no no.*

??, I replied.

My body hurts

Go to student health services, I told him.

Peter said he was going to try to sleep it off—it was probably just a cold. I usually put my phone on silent during classes, but I kept it on vibrate so I would know the second he texted me an update. It was hours before he texted me again: it hurts to swallow. I couldn't concentrate on anything all day. I kept replaying the same memories: Anna in her mask, Peter's tongue in my mouth. When I walked to the library and my nose started running in the cold, I wondered how fast I could catch it. Every time I swallowed, I searched for hurt.

I can't ride home with you unless you get a negative test, I told him. We were supposed to leave in forty-eight hours.

I've had a cold before.

Okay but my parents have underlying medical conditions. I have to protect them.

He didn't respond. If he was so sure he didn't have it, why wouldn't he get tested? The next day, wide-awake with racing thoughts at five in the morning, I put all the cold medicine I owned, plus a thermometer, in a shopping bag and walked across campus to leave it outside his dorm room. Did I think that if the cold medicine made his symptoms go away, we would know it was just a cold? Or did I hope that if he felt some relief from his symptoms, he would stop being such an asshole about getting tested?

Your an actual angel, Peter wrote when he found the bag.

When student health services opened at nine A.M., I got a rapid test. It came back negative, but what did that mean? It meant I could still have it. I could have it tomorrow or the day after that. I could have it whether I had symptoms or not and I could transmit it to my parents and then they would be hospitalized and then they would die and I would have to say something at their funerals. What would I say? That the fantasy of my future life with Peter had superseded my responsibility to care for my own family? Was I that selfish? My anxiety felt like a man sitting on my chest, try-ing to break my ribs under his weight. It felt like I wasn't getting enough oxygen. I couldn't risk it.

I was really anticipating spending time with you, I texted Peter, overthinking every word like a human thesaurus, but regretfully I've elected to pursue other options out of precaution. Maybe we can see each other over break?

Why cause you're afraid of catching my cold?

No

Then what's your deal

Peter, have you ever cared about anyone but yourself? My hands were trembling as I typed. Do you even care whether sick people live or die? Or are you a Nazi? It was the meanest thing I'd ever said to anyone in my life. As soon as I hit send, I felt like I was going to throw up. I wanted to see him. If I could just see him, I could explain everything! But I couldn't see him. That was the whole problem.

Your a crazy bitch Olivia. have a nice life!

I put my phone face down on my desk and squeezed my eyes shut so hard I gave myself a headache. The safest thing to do was to isolate myself from everyone. I would spend Thanksgiving alone. My parents and I could FaceTime. It was a small sacrifice. Next year would be better. In ten days, if I was still asymptomatic, we could reassess.

"I can't come home," I told my mom.

"Oh no. What happened?"

"I might have been exposed," I said. "Peter may have exposed me." Saying his name triggered a rash of anger.

"Your dad and I will come get you. That's what we were planning to do anyways!"

"No," I told her. "That's the whole point. It's too risky! I can't see you. Not for ten days."

"Are you having symptoms, Olivia?"

"You aren't listening to me!" I said. Why wasn't anyone taking this seriously? "I'm staying here. I'm staying on campus."

"Do the dorms stay open over break?"

"Hold on," I said. On my laptop, I started opening all the unread emails from the school. It took me less than thirty seconds to find out.

"They're closing the day after tomorrow," I said, and began to cry.

"Oh, honey," she said. "Are you still taking your medication?"

"In the car, I'm going to double mask and you and dad have to double mask, too. We have to keep the windows open. And when we get home, I'm going to stay in my room. I don't even know if I can eat with you guys. It's not safe. Okay?" In Minot, I would get tested again. I would wear a mask at all times.

My mom took a deep breath. "Let's take things one step at a time."

I heard my dad in the background, asking who she was on the phone with. "Olivia," she told him. "We're picking her up from school tomorrow. She's anxious," she whispered.

"Three hours in the car with both my girls? I'm a lucky dad," he said. "See you soon, honey."

The forecast called for freezing rain and sleet. I checked the Department of Transportation website for updates about road conditions.

During the ten hours I waited for my parents to make the three-hour drive to Grand Forks, I cleaned my dorm room and walked to Starbucks and back. I tried calling each of them and neither one picked up. I found my bottle of lorazepam and took one and then another, until I turned into a black hole. I wandered outside and made small talk about the weather with a campus security guard who couldn't even tell I was in outer space. When I was back inside my room, sufficiently numb from the cold and the pills, I reluctantly dialed my aunt, to see if she'd heard from them.

"I thought you were getting a ride home with a boy," she said.

"I was, but then I couldn't," I said. My tongue felt huge in my mouth.

"I'll call you back," she said.

I lay on my bare mattress and passed out.

By the time she called back, it was eight at night. She'd been calling all the hospitals. They'd been in a collision with a truck near Devils Lake.

"They're gone, Olivia," she said.

"What?" I was so out of it.

"I thought you were getting a ride home with a boy," she said again. Now she was crying as she reached through the phone for someone to blame.

"I was," I said. I was so out of it I couldn't even cry.

"OLIVIA, I'M—"

"You don't have to tell me you're sorry," I said.

"I *am* sorry. I don't know what else to say except how sorry I am."

"It's okay," I said. "It was my fault." It was a relief to confess. Now Dayna knew the truth about me. Telling the story wasn't nearly as painful as replaying the memory of my mom's voice, the way she said, *oh honey*.

"You can't blame yourself for this," she said, vaping.

Back home, people tried all sorts of tricks to make the guilt go away: They prayed with me; they prayed *for* me; they donated to charities in my parents' names and sent me certificates as proof; they named stars after Robby and Jennifer; they said everything happens for a reason but we don't always know the reason. Did they die so I could start over in this life, as @littleorphanOlivia, like playing a video game from the beginning with a new avatar, thinking that would make all the difference in whether I won or lost?

"You said that being an orphan is what led you to look for Becca."

I nodded. "My parents' will was set up so my aunt would

become my guardian if anything happened to both of them. After the accident, she sold our house, so at the end of spring semester, I had to move in with her. My aunt wouldn't make her kids share a room. So I got the basement."

"This woman is a piece of work," Dayna said.

"I downloaded the platform, and before I knew it, I was spending all my time there. One night I was scrolling and one of Becca's videos came up."

"Were you following her?"

"No, that's the thing—I wasn't following her. It was one of those *if you're seeing this, it's meant for you* videos."

Dayna's eyes went wide. She took another hit off her pen.

"Becca had a spread of cards on a table, and on the screen it said, *Someone is missing you in heaven. They have a message for you.* Then she randomly turned over the Judgment card and it meant, *You are shackled by internal judgments. Go get lost.*" I swallowed the lump in my throat. "It sounds stupid when I try to describe it—"

"It doesn't sound stupid," Dayna said.

"I watched the video over and over again, looking for the trick. She shuffles the cards—it doesn't seem like she planted that card there. Something made her pull that card. Also, why did the platform show me *this* video? I hadn't posted anything about my parents. How would the algorithm know my parents were dead? Right? What were the odds of it randomly showing me a video with a message from heaven versus the odds of my parents trying to tell me something *through* Becca? Then I thought, *I have to meet this person. I have to ask her to read my cards.*"

Dayna nodded.

"Becca wasn't following me back, so I couldn't message her, right? The platform started recommending all these other tarot and psychic accounts to me, but none of their videos made me feel the way Becca's videos made me feel. She's different. I know she is. When I saw that the Deckler House was looking for more creators, I thought, maybe that's what they meant by *go get lost*. Like *take a risk*. I didn't think I had a shot at getting in, but if I *did* get in—"

"I have to show you something," Dayna said. She pulled up an email on her phone and showed me photos of extravagant gowns. "House of Scaccabarozzi found us because of you. They love that you're an orphan."

"They want to sponsor me?" Before I could see how much money they were offering, Dayna put her phone away.

"They want to sponsor the whole house—if I can pitch them an idea that they like. I don't know how many others we're up against. But I want to help you look for Becca. You're not the only one wondering what happened to her. We build a whole campaign around the search. But make it fashion."

"Just tell me what to do," I said.

Outside, the setting sun lit up the orange sky. I'd been inside Dayna's apartment for hours. She said I'd made orphan content, and I'd made crying content, but I hadn't yet made any crying orphan content, and she thought that might be our ticket to winning the House of Scaccabarozzi job.

"People want to see the real Olivia," she said.

Dayna thought you could predict what the algorithm would reward. But the algorithm was ravenous. We just had to keep feeding it, before it forgot we were alive.

I entered the house through the back door and found Morgan in the kitchen, making little pillows out of dough on the counter.

"I'm making us dinner," she said.

"I think I'm going to just take something to my room."

"I'm making pierogies. You can help me!" Her phone was

propped against a vase, filming as she crimped the edges of the pierogies with a fork.

"I can't."

"Seriously?" She held up the fork.

"Next time."

"I've helped you with your content, Olivia." She pouted.

"Blame Dayna. She gave me an assignment."

I quickly made two peanut butter and honey sandwiches and grabbed a package of Oreos from the pantry. I didn't want cookies now, but future Olivia would, after what I planned to do to her.

Finally alone in my room, I opened Facebook on my phone for the first time in months. I ignored all my notifications and went directly to type my mom's name into the search bar. Once I was on her profile, I went into her photo albums, to travel back in time: from the last photo taken of all three of us, at my high school graduation at the State Fair grandstand, to a selfie of the two of us with pretzels the size of our heads at the mall food court, back through pictures of me bowing onstage as Emily Webb in *Our Town* my junior year, me and Mom holding Styrofoam cups of hot apple cider at the corn maze while I grinned with braces, Dad making a stern face in the car and pointing as we drove past the "Be Polite" billboard. The pictures of me as a little girl only went as far back as age ten. That's when she got on Facebook.

As I put the photos in chronological order, I watched myself grow up and I saw my parents age: the sagging skin around my dad's chin, the silver running through my mom's thick blond hair. I was so used to focusing on my own hair, my own skin, my own body, I didn't even notice that they were changing, too. No one ever mistook me and my mom for sisters. I had an old mom. I used to have an old mom.

After I picked "Pray" by Jessie Murph to go with the photo carousel, I wrote the text to go on top of the images:

Mom I thought I had more time with you
I'll never be able to take back what happened
I'll never be able to create more memories
But I pray someday
we'll see each other again

After I posted the carousel, I quickly ate a sandwich, to chew instead of feel, and then I started on my next video. A week ago, I would have obsessively refreshed, waiting for the views and likes to come in, so I could count them and figure out how I'd performed on the assignment. But now I knew there was no way to predict which video would hit. The only way to deal with the uncertainty was to keep producing.

What you've missed while I've been missing you, I wrote on the selfie I had taken in front of the house, the day I arrived. *I wish I could share my life with you,* I wrote on a screenshot of my first viral crying video; in the freeze-frame, my arms were lifted like a beggar's. *I hope you're proud of me,* I wrote on an image of Owen Wilson as Anne of Green Gables. *No one will ever understand me like you did.* Screenshot of my eyes closed, tears streaming down my cheeks.

By the time I posted the second carousel, the comments had begun to roll in on the first. **Story time! Story time!** they said.

Make them wait, I thought.

Inside my bedroom, the temperature rose, like I was under stage lights. I tried to open a window but it was painted shut. When I touched the wall, it was as hot as my little hand. I changed into shorts and a crop top. I put my hair in pigtails and then I did the strobe light trend, dancing like I was playing a drunk girl in a club in a movie, to all the things people say when your parents die. *Both of them?* I humped the corner of my bed, deranged. *I can only imagine what you must be going through.* I did a grapevine and clapped at the end. *There is a time for everything, a time to be born and a time to die.* Braless, I bounced up and down before the camera, grinning like a cheerleader for the winning team. When I played it back before posting, I looked like a slut.

This was how strangers would discover me on their For You page: grinding to my trauma. I was sweaty and out of breath. I ate six Oreos. To summon the same charge I had once felt onstage in front of an audience, I had to try so much harder. To feel alive, I had to hurt. The platform was less like a stage for a one-woman show and more like a gladiator arena where spectators came to watch the bloody extreme.

Olivia, Piper texted me.

Yeah?

Are you okay, she said.

This was not a question I had any interest in exploring. In the app, I pressed one of the "story time!" comments on the slideshow of my dead parents and clicked "reply with video."

"Funny story, from when I lived in North Dakota with my parents," I started. My forehead glistened with oil and sweat. Mascara was running down my cheeks. One of my pigtails was way higher than the other. There were little pieces of Oreo in my teeth. I noticed a whitehead on the side of my nose and another one coming in on my chin.

I stopped recording, deleted the clip, applied two pimple patches shaped like yellow stars, and started over.

"Funny story," I said quickly. I had three minutes to get it all in. "Freshman year of college I met this boy. I thought he looked good in a Speedo." At this, I burst out laughing. I stopped recording. I zoomed in on my face and pressed record. "I thought he wanted to be my boyfriend because he offered to give me a ride home for break. But right when we were supposed to leave, he got Covid! But he wouldn't get tested!" I started laughing a forced, hysterical laugh. I felt like the Joker; I'd watched the movie with Peter in his bed, on his laptop. "I didn't want to kill my parents by accident, so I called them to come pick me up and then they got hit by a truck!"

I'm coming upstairs, Piper texted.

I didn't even register what she was saying. I set it to the funny do-ba-do-ba-do-ba-do song and posted it. Now that I had begun exposing my life, it felt impossible to stop, like consuming a pint of ice cream and reaching the point when I knew I'd had enough, but I was so close to finishing, I just continued eating past the point of feeling sick.

The first video had twelve hundred views; the second had twenty-one thousand. The strobe light video was already up to sixty-seven thousand views and six thousand likes. No one would dare ask me again if I was really an orphan.

The door to my bedroom opened. Piper entered and softly closed the door behind her. She was dressed in a sweatsuit, her long dark hair pulled away from her face with a matching headband, carrying a mug. There was no time to fix my appearance—I knew how demented I looked from watching my own face on-screen. I ran my tongue over my teeth.

"Hey," she said quietly.

"What's up," I said, casual.

"I think I have those same shorts," she said.

I laughed.

"Shhh," she said.

"What?"

"It's late. Paula is probably sleeping."

I had forgotten about Paula. Had she been listening

through the walls to everything I said on camera? I didn't care if Piper watched my videos, but the thought of Paula or Craig or even Dayna watching me made me cringe. I wanted these videos to exist in a parallel undiscussed universe. Didn't we deserve a place for ourselves—without old people watching us?

"Want to take a break?" Piper asked.

"Not really," I said, sitting up tall. "I'm kind of on a roll."

"It will all still be there on the platform, like, waiting for you." She sat next to me on the bed and handed me the mug of tea. I didn't put my phone down for fear she would take it, but I drank.

The table lamp flickered on and off.

"What was that?"

"It happens," I said. "Touch the wall."

Piper frowned. "Is this a trick?"

"Just touch it."

"What the hell," she said. "It's like a factory in here. I don't know how you sleep."

"It's only like this when I make content."

My heart was beating in my chest like I'd just finished a mile run in PE. I reached for the orange pill bottle on my nightstand and took one of Becca's lorazepams. It was the only way I could come down. Piper didn't ask me what it was. She got up to look at the makeup and skincare products on top of my dresser.

When she came back, she started gently cleaning my face with a makeup remover wipe. It felt fresh and cold against my skin.

"I'm going to tell you a story," Piper said.

"Okay."

"When I was growing up, my mom was a blogger. A famous one. Her full-time job was making content about being a mom and about us—my brother and I. On the weekends, we would, like, pose for dog food ads and stuff like that. Sometimes my mom would write something that would make people mad at her and she'd be on her laptop all night, reading all the comments, and my dad would tell her to take a break and come have dinner with us and she'd say she couldn't. She was working.

"When people stopped reading blogs, my mom refused to quit," Piper continued. "She had to adapt. She started making content for other platforms. She was desperate not to lose her audience. And when I was sixteen, she took me to the doctor to get on birth control. It's what I wanted. I'd asked her for it. But I didn't know she was posting the whole thing on Twitter. It was right after the election."

"What do you mean, she posted the whole thing?"

"Like live-tweeting the OB-GYN visit. And saying she wasn't going to risk having a pregnant teen in a country that had elected a sexual predator who wanted to overturn a woman's right to choose. It went viral when I was in the stirrups. They invited her on *The View* to talk about it. I wanted to die. I was still a virgin."

I couldn't see Piper's face. She was seated behind me on the bed, combing my hair with her fingers, pulling pieces to French braid. I forgot about my phone, overflowing with attention, in my hand. My whole body melted.

"I understand why you want to post," Piper said, "and I'm not going to tell you not to. Just think about saving a piece of yourself. That they'll never see."

DAYNA

My phone rang shortly after breakfast while I was waxing my mustache. It was Luke. I didn't answer. Whether he was calling to beg me to come back or to "bounce" an idea off me or to ask what he was supposed to do with all the bunny care accessories I'd left behind, I did not care. Luke didn't leave a voicemail; he just called again.

Dayna pick up, he texted.

I'm busy, I said. I still had to do the left side.

Your mother is here. She has something to tell you.

I let out a long, low moan, which disturbed Owen Wilson. He hopped out of the bathroom.

I didn't call him. I called her.

"Mom?"

"Dayna," she said, in that syrupy voice that let me know she was putting on a show for Luke. Pretending she was normal.

"What are you doing?"

"I was returning some library books and I thought I would just stop by, see how you were doing."

Over the course of eight years, Luke and I had hosted my mother for dinner exactly three times. The first time, over peanut chicken skewers, she regaled us with a gruesome and tedious saga of an earache she was *certain* was caused by hatching insect larvae even though no doctor would confirm this, and the resulting, unresolved tinnitus. My mother had a unique talent for complaining about her life in a flirtatious register—she assumed you'd find her helplessness becoming, while you nodded along patiently, waiting for the whole thing to be over. At the end of the night, she pulled me aside to ask if I could spot her until her next alimony payment came in; I watched her put the cash in her Coach wallet. After that, she arrived at a low-key barbecue wearing a huge patch of white gauze on her face to hide the skin where she'd had a mole removed, and explained to our guests that without the mole, the channel to her intuition felt unobfuscated for the first time in years. The third time, she got so drunk on the cheap Chablis she'd brought that Luke had to drive her back to her apartment (she insisted that he drive her), while I followed behind in her old Saab, which smelled like the menthol cigarettes she smoked surreptitiously and Estée Lauder Beautiful.

There was no way she actually cared how I was doing. I wondered what she wanted.

"I don't live there, Mom."

"I know you don't, honey." She never called me *honey*. "I was just dropping by. People used to do this, you know. Be *friendly* to their *neighbors*."

"I'm not your neighbor—I'm your daughter."

"We both live in LA. If you ask me, that's a neighbor. But what do I know?"

Just invite her to see the house, I thought. End the awkwardness. Release Luke. She would love the house, I knew. She would want to move in. On the platform, she would fit right in with the other surgically enhanced septuagenarians dancing to trending audio in their California kitchens. I couldn't help but smile at the absurd image.

I told her I would text her my new address. "It's not far from Luke's," I said. "But text me when you get here. Don't ring the bell at the gate."

"What happened to your lip?" was the first thing she said when she saw me.

"I waxed it," I said.

"Put some vitamin E oil on that."

My mother was half a foot shorter than me, with a frail figure that had been elegant in the '80s, especially beneath a pile of costume jewelry, but now only telegraphed osteoporosis. Every day, she did an hour of calisthenics in her living room and ate grilled chicken she bought pre-cooked at the supermarket, dry. She permed her hair and dyed it the color of pennies.

"Luke is a very good-looking man," she said, apropos of nothing.

"Come on," I said. "I'll show you my apartment."

"I don't want to go in *there*," she said, looking at the guest house. "I want to go in *there*."

"I thought you just told me to put vitamin E oil on."

She rolled her eyes. "You look *fine*," she said.

I took her in through the kitchen entrance and down the long hallway to the living room so she could see the stone columns and the mosaic peacock and the view of the city from the big picture window. The door to Morgan's bedroom was half-open; I could hear her filming a video about ten different ways to style a pair of cowboy boots, whether you wanted to dress them up or dress them down. Olivia was alone in the living room, slowly spinning in circles with her phone at arm's length, trying to find the best light.

"Be careful, dear," my mom said. "You don't want to pass out."

"This is my mom, Mary," I said.

Olivia put her phone down and waved. "I'm Olivia."

"You must be an actress."

Olivia smiled. "I'm trying."

At the end of the hall, we reached Craig's office. I saw the wall behind his desk, completely covered with photographs of all the celebrities who'd visited the house, through my mother's eyes. Maybe he would indulge her with a recitation of all the movies that had been filmed here.

For the first time, I noticed that one of the women on his wall was me.

It was the photo Craig had taken when I was nineteen years old, standing awkwardly in front of my own work, my blue bra straps showing. My eyebrows were plucked into pinched black arches. I wasn't smiling—or wearing any expression that would have made me more appealing to my audience. I looked surprised to be captured.

"I can't believe you kept that photo of me."

Craig turned around to see what I was looking at.

"I have photos of all the prominent figures who have been to the house," he said.

"I always thought Dayna should have been an actress," my mother said. "With a face like hers."

"I'd like to introduce you to my mother, Mary," I said.

Craig raised his eyebrows. "I would have guessed identical twins," he said.

My mother giggled. "We often get that."

I rolled my eyes.

"Craig Deckler," he said, standing to shake her hand—a gentleman. "We've met before, haven't we? At Dayna's exhibition. It's a pleasure to see you again."

"No," I said, confused.

"What exhibition?"

"Of her photography."

My mother smiled graciously. She didn't even look at me. "Of course," she said to Craig. "Dayna's photography."

Desperate to change the subject, I said, "Olivia's parents are dead."

"That sweet girl?" Mom asked.

"I saw," Craig said, gesturing at his laptop.

"He's talking about some videos that she made last night, on the internet," I explained.

"I sent the links to Sofia Scaccabarozzi," Craig said.

"Perfect," I said. "And I have the concept, which I'll run by you"—I looked at Mom—"later this afternoon."

Craig nodded.

"Pleasure to meet you, Mrs. Lev," he said.

"*Ms.*," she corrected as she held out one hand, palm down, for Craig to kiss.

"Ms. Lev?" Craig turned to me, daring me to play along. I gave him my hand, too, like we were in some Regency romance, and he pressed it to his lips.

AFTER MY PARENTS' second divorce, when my mother absorbed the fact that she had spent my father's remaining patience and goodwill, she followed me to Los Angeles. *I've always wanted to live in the sun,* she said at the time. That was classic: acting as if she merely existed in the shadow of my father when really she was the hot star we orbited, helpless to her pull. I knew the alimony he gave her was also a gesture of generosity toward me—so I wouldn't have to bear the burden of supporting her. My mother had never worked. She wanted to be a faculty wife, but was born a couple decades too late for her dream role. She was neither a talented hostess nor a dedicated volunteer. She wanted to be invited to special occasions where she could flash her charm like a cocktail ring, without the expectation that she would ever return the invitation.

My father had once adored her. He loved her against his will and better judgment. She was his treasure.

I led my mother down the main corridor, past the master bedroom where Piper and Sean were shooting on a tripod propped in the doorway, squealing and laughing as they jumped from desk chair to messy bed to upholstered bench to chair, avoiding the pile of garbage and dirty laundry and brand swag on the floor, in a homemade parkour course. Piper was in a white bikini top and a pair of baggy gray sweatpants. Sean was wearing cargo shorts and a pair of tube socks.

Mom stood at the threshold for a minute to observe the monkey habitat at the zoo.

Then she whispered, "Craig is a very good-looking man."

"Uh-huh," I said, bracing for impact. Had she noticed Craig flirting with me?

"And no ring."

"He's my boss, Mom."

She turned to face me. Her green eyes were watery. "It's not too late for me," she said.

I felt my face crimp in surprise and horror.

"I hate when you do that with your face."

"What do you want me to do?"

"I know you think it's too late for me, but it's not. You'll make some inquiries for me." She squeezed one of my hands; her skin was cool and dry and smooth, like wax paper.

My father was an old man now, but he was twelve years older than my mother. It was hard to imagine my father dating at his age. But my mother was in her Nancy Meyers era—maybe she still had another shot at love. With the right person. It wasn't fair that an older man with a younger girlfriend was a king, while an older woman with a younger boyfriend was a desperate, pathetic predator—but still, my mother? And Craig?

You can't have him, I thought. *He's mine.*

We went out to the terrace—a beautiful setting for a wedding. Festoon the bougainvillea with fairy lights. Passed canapés. My daydream was interrupted by a raccoon leaning over the deep end of the swimming pool, fastidiously washing its hands.

"Son of a bitch!" I screamed while I banged one of the lounge chairs against the patio.

My mother clutched the neck of her blouse. "What are you doing?"

"There was a raccoon," I said. It had already scampered away, into the wild vines that had overtaken the cracked foundation and crumbling south wall of the house.

"You scared the living daylights out of me," she said.

I dragged two lounge chairs into the shade.

"Are you going to tell me why you were at Luke's this morning?"

"I wanted to see you," she said, reclining. Her bare child-sized shins stuck out beneath her khaki skirt; she wore beige leather slingbacks with old, worn soles.

"You could have called."

"Your father told me something very upsetting last night."

"What?"

"I couldn't sleep at all."

I squinted at her. "Why did he call you?"

"He doesn't want you to worry, but what about me? Your father has no regard for my equilibrium."

"Mom, what did he tell you?"

"He has pancreatic cancer." She pulled a crumpled Kleenex from her purse and wiped her nose. She wouldn't look at me. "What am I supposed to do? He knows how much I hate flying."

It was as if I'd stepped outside from a dark movie theater; everything was so bright it hurt. I stared out at the hazy city below the horizon, completely disoriented. *I'm in the wrong place*, I thought. *I'm not supposed to be here.* I was on the wrong side of the country, in a city where no one gave a shit about me, in a house that would never belong to me, speaking to the wrong parent, about the wrong misfortune.

"You're sure?"

"Stage four," she said. "Or three. Either three or four."

"Why did he call you?" I asked again.

She sniffled. "Your father pays my spousal support as long as he's working. If he retires, or if he—"

"I get it," I said, before she could finish.

My mother needed a rich boyfriend. My mother needed me to help her find a rich boyfriend.

"He wanted me to prepare myself, I suppose." She cried silently. Up close, I could see all the tiny red spider veins on her cheeks underneath her makeup.

I wondered when he had found out. When he was on the Zoom with all of us a couple of days ago—did he know then? Was he waiting for the results? What was he going to do, just keep working until the bitter end? For what—for her? What about me? When was he planning on telling me?

I felt like a melon that was being scooped out with a serrated blade.

"Everything is going to be fine," I said, to myself as much as to her. "You'll stay here. I'll go to New Hampshire."

Once my mother had calmed down enough to drive, I went home to be with my rabbit. But O.W. must have sensed that

I was unhinged, because he hid from me. I grabbed the rest of the fresh basil from the fridge and got down on the living room floor to bribe him for emotional support. His nose led him from the bathroom to my side. I stroked him with one hand while I called my father.

You've reached the confidential voice messaging system of Dr. Walter Lev. I'm sorry I'm not able— I hung up. I wasn't going to leave a voicemail about how the way he was handling his own cancer was hurting me personally. I wasn't my mother. In a text, I asked him to call me when he had a break between patients.

To avoid googling "pancreatic cancer," I watched Olivia's videos again. She was nearly unrecognizable. This was a completely different Olivia than the slightly awkward, shy people pleaser I knew. On-screen, Olivia was mesmerizing, chaotic, unselfconscious. She was having fun playing with her audience. She refused to be their object of pity. I watched the strobe light video, where she twerked to things you're not supposed to say to someone grieving, six times. *I can only imagine what you must be going through.* How could anyone watch this and not take Olivia's side? She'd gained a hundred thousand followers overnight. She was catching up to Jake's status as the star of the house.

Now that we could prove we had a bona fide orphan, we were one step closer to Sofia Scaccabarozzi choosing us. I went back to Craig's office to pitch him my idea. Until my dad told me otherwise, I was going to operate under the assumption that I still had time. At least enough time to produce the campaign, collect my commission, and fly home to help him through chemo or radiation or whatever the treatment was. My mother didn't know what was ahead—she hadn't even asked him. If we landed the Scaccabarozzi campaign, I could live on my commission for months in New Hampshire. I wouldn't have to spend hours a day checking job sites and panhandling on LinkedIn and writing custom cover letters for roles I was overqualified for. The money was time. I could drive my father to every appointment. I could cook for him and connect all my streaming memberships to his TV.

To begin filming, all I needed were the garments from House of Scaccabarozzi. They needed to be airmailed immediately.

Craig was still at his desk.

"Which twin are you?" he asked, squinting.

"The younger one," I said.

"The beautiful one."

I bit my lip and sat in one of the chairs facing his desk. "You charmed her. I think my mom has a little crush on you now."

"Did you tell her I was already taken?"

"Are you taken?"

Craig came to sit beside me.

"No," he said, "but there's someone I have my eye on."

"What's she like?"

He looked down at his hands, thinking.

"I've known her for a long time, but I also feel sometimes like I don't know her at all. She's a mystery to me."

"What do you want to know about her?"

Craig leaned in and put one hand on my thigh, pausing to see my reaction before he went any further. My whole body awakened under his touch, as if from a deep sleep. He swept my hair from my face so he could whisper in my ear. "Does she think of me the way I think of her?"

Silently, I nodded.

Before he asked the next question, he stroked my long hair.

"Does she like this?"

"Yes," I said.

Craig took his time gently kissing my forehead and my face.

"This?"

"Yes."

He pulled the collar of my blouse aside to reach my neck. When he finally kissed my mouth, I was enveloped by a plush darkness, like a gold coin in a black velvet pouch. A delirious haze obliterated my worries. My mind was an empty room. I ran my fingers through the waves in his hair, wanting to entangle myself in the knot of Craig.

After several minutes, I pulled away, breathless.

"The first time I came here, I thought you would kiss me."

"I didn't know that's what you wanted."

"I was awake all night, waiting for you to come into my bedroom." I felt shy, confessing this.

"Then you would have thought I brought you all the way across the country for this." He stood up and extended a hand so I would follow his head. Then he turned me around and pressed me against his desk until I was sitting and he was standing over me. I looked over his shoulder at the open door, to make sure no one was watching us.

"You would have doubted everything I said about your art," he said, tilting up my chin so he could kiss me again.

"You're right," I said. "You were very noble." With my finger, I traced the beautiful lines time had written around his mouth. I touched his soft lips. His huge hands were on my waist.

"We can go somewhere," he said.

"I want to. But we have to talk about work."

"Forget work." He buried his face in my neck.

"Remember when you said I was a mystery you tried to solve?"

"The investigation is still ongoing."

I smiled. "Let's play a game."

"I'll shut the door."

"A guessing game," I said, pulling on his jacket lapels.

"Go ahead."

"What do all the creators have in common? Guess."

"They have no memory of 9/11?"

I laughed, which made him smile in surprise. "True," I said. "But what else?"

"They were raised on screens," he said.

"I don't mean creators in general—I'm talking about Olivia, or Jake."

"They all live in the same house?"

"They all want to know what really happened to Becca."

At the sound of her name, he let go of my waist and backed away from me, as if I'd burned him.

"No," Craig said.

"I know she doesn't live here anymore," I said, rushing to explain. "But my idea for the House of Scaccabarozzi campaign is that all the creators dress up in the clothes and go through the house, trying to solve the mystery of what happened to her. If we send her a message, maybe she'll answer."

"Becca is no longer a part of this."

"What does that mean?"

"She wanted out."

"Why? Did the house do something to her? You told me not everyone is strong enough to—"

Craig abandoned me to go sit behind his desk again. Awkwardly, I hopped down.

"Let's focus on the creators we actually have."

"You may not be aware of this, but there are internet forums dedicated to Becca. Becca has a bigger fandom than anyone in the house. People say her tarot videos changed their lives. Including Olivia. Our orphan. Why did Becca go dark? Her fans want closure. This is a story we can tell around the house. It's a story we can tell *with* the house."

"No," Craig said. "Next idea?"

"Next idea?"

"How about a costume party?"

Where was the intrigue in *that*? I crossed my arms. "Why did you even invite me here? I thought it was because you trusted me. You said my ideas were brilliant."

"I do think you're brilliant," Craig said. "And I'm sure you can find another mystery to solve, Nancy Drew."

I refused to laugh. *Nancy Drew?* No wonder he needed me here to translate; he was from another century. Fuming, I took my vape from my pocket, but the battery was dead. I wanted to scream. I didn't have another idea for him. This was it. I couldn't believe he was rejecting me.

My phone started to vibrate in my pocket. It said: *Dad.*

"I'll be right back," I told Craig.

As soon as I was in the hallway, I answered the call.

"Is it stage three or stage four?"

"Hello, Dayna," my dad said. "Sorry I keep missing your calls. For some reason my phone doesn't ring."

"Is your phone on silent?"

"Which setting is that?"

"It's a switch on the left side of the— Dad, let's do the tech stuff later. Mom told me you have cancer?"

He cleared his throat. "I know this is upsetting for you to hear."

"Why did you call Mom before you told me?" I felt like I was a child again, competing with her for his attention and affection, wishing he would prove he loved me more.

"I'm sorry, Dayna. I was planning to tell you. I've never done this before."

"Is it stage three or stage four?"

"Stage three," he said. "They're going to operate."

"Well, that's good," I said, encouraged. I was pacing the living room like a dog. "Right? They can just take it out." As I said this, I realized how little I knew about the function of the pancreas.

"From my understanding, not the entire organ. They're going to remove parts of it, and my gallbladder."

I swallowed. "And then what?"

"And then chemotherapy. It's spread to my lymph nodes. But if I decide that at my age I don't want—"

I couldn't let him finish the thought. "When is the surgery?" I asked.

"November first."

It was eleven days away.

"I'll be there," I told my father.

There wasn't enough time to come up with another idea. There wasn't enough time for anything.

I leaned against the doorframe to Craig's office, my face in my hands. The adrenaline that had been coursing through me while I was on the phone was completely spent. I was all out of fight.

"What just happened?"

"My dad is really sick."

With my eyes closed, I felt him take me in his arms, and I melted into his chest. If my legs gave out, he would catch me. Craig was so much taller, broader than Luke, it felt like being sheltered by a giant tree in a redwood forest. The canopy so thick that the light looks like a miracle. Soft needles underfoot.

He kissed the top of my head. "I'm sorry," he said. "Do you need to leave?"

"I don't want to leave," I said. I didn't say, *I need this campaign. I need the money.*

"I understand if you have to go. He's your father."

I needed him to understand how my idea would help us both: It would showcase the house. It would make us a lot of money. Then he could restore the Deckler House.

"What can I do for you?"

I desperately needed to build a bridge through time, back to when he wanted me. "Do you know who I just thought of?"

"I have no idea," Craig said.

"I'll give you a hint. She's famous, but not to everyone. Only to people who know her."

"A riddle."

"She'll always be young." I stared into his dark eyes. "She's the reason we met," I added.

Craig inhaled. "Francesca Woodman."

"Do you remember what happened to her?"

"I believe she jumped off a building."

"Yes," I said. "And she grew a cult following for her photography because of her suicide. Everyone's always more interested in your work if you're dead."

Craig's expression darkened; he grabbed the tops of my arms and held me in place like a child who'd broken the rules. "You're making this very difficult for me. I should have known, from reading all those salacious articles."

"What articles?"

"The ones you wrote for the magazine. You're interested in celebrities once they're destroyed. You always have been. It lights you up. You think just because Becca had a following, these vultures deserve a bone from her body?"

I couldn't look at him. My eyes burned with angry tears. Five years ago, I would have been able to take feedback and move on to a new idea. But now I lived full-time in rejection land. I couldn't find a job in media. My boyfriend had decided he couldn't face forever with someone like me. Now Craig was another closed door to throw my weight against.

Before he could see me cry, I left his office.

At home, I texted Mollie, Do you have time to talk?

She replied right away with a photograph of the only table in her apartment, covered with ceramic tea mugs, a raw amethyst cathedral, fertility medications in tiny glass bottles, and an array of syringes and needles. She was manifesting through science. A second photograph followed, of acid-yellow dime-sized bruises on her stomach. Both images were familiar to me—I'd already seen them on her Instagram account. Was I just one of Mollie's followers now? Was that the extent of our relationship?

Ouch, I said.

Let's catch up soon!! It's been too long. She added six red hearts.

I gave her a thumbs-up, a fingers crossed, and a half dozen egg emojis.

You're just tired, I told myself. *You've had a long day.*

All I needed was a little dose of sympathy. Who needed Mollie? There were hundreds—if not thousands—of people out there waiting for a good story about someone else's nightmare. Luke had given them one.

Why couldn't I?

I opened the app and, for the first time, turned the camera on myself.

I looked like shit. When Olivia made herself up like a dirty little waif from a Dickens novel, it was sweet. But I was too old to wear hot mess. Frustrated, I swiped through the filters: Did I want to look like Kris Jenner? I did not. I tapped and now my cheeks were lightly dusted with freckles. I held my phone aloft, the way I'd seen Olivia do, and walked around the small guest house searching for the best lighting. I kneeled on the couch, facing the lamp on the side table, and held my phone slightly above my face so there was maximum delineation between my jawline and my neck. I should have put on more makeup.

"My dad has cancer," I said out loud, to my own reflection, and then I paused, embarrassed by the silence that met me on the other side of my confession. Until I posted it, I was still alone.

I realized that I didn't have to be on camera at all. I could make a carousel of photographs instead, like Olivia had done, and set it to music. The images would tell a story: a picture of Luke gently holding Owen Wilson, followed by a picture of me as a toddler, riding on my dad's shoulders. My mother, dancing in my father's arms at someone's wedding, her eyes glowing red as a demon's from the flash reflecting off her retinas. A photo of me and a co-worker working the red carpet at the *500 Days of Summer* premiere, at the Egyptian Theatre. A screenshot of a *Los Angeles Times* article about the Deckler House decaying.

I wrote captions for each one:

My boyfriend dumped me on Reddit
Then I found out my dad has cancer
So my mom wants me to find her a rich boyfriend
I'm too old to get a new job in my industry
I made out with my boss

I used to lose hours to staging my self-portraits, culling and editing the images in Photoshop, and carefully curating which ones I shared with an audience. That was art. This was content. There was no distance between my inner world and its presentation. I hadn't created anything of value. I had only said, *Look at me.* Even if the carousel told a true story, it was flat. True didn't make it interesting.

Before I posted something I would live to regret, I texted

my dad the photo of us together, when I was small enough to ride on his shoulders.

Then I opened my For You page. The first video it showed me was captioned, *This video found you for a reason.*

"Of course it did," I said aloud.

That was when I realized it was one of Becca's tarot videos—I recognized her hands. The date stamp was from July. She held up the Seven of Swords to the camera and then a new caption appeared on-screen: *You need to be practicing freedom. Just make sure to cover your tracks.*

I was glad there was no one there to see my reaction. I felt at once exhilarated by the message and deeply embarrassed by my susceptibility to the algorithm's influence.

I just need to practice freedom!

What were the odds that I would be sent such an old video of Becca's, with this message in particular? I got out my laptop and started working. Craig had been drawn to my photographs because I'd staged them to hold a mystery. I could do it again. I knew better than he did what would get the most engagement. He wasn't even on the platform. He never needed to find out about our search for Becca. If House of Scaccabarozzi liked my idea, I would come up with a second idea for Craig, like a matryoshka doll to hide another doll inside. Give him the opportunity to approve something I'd designed for his approval. Cover my tracks.

On the couch, I moved a pillow so Owen Wilson could sit beside me while I worked. He immediately started sniffing the upholstery: There were four dime-sized stains the color of spilled Coke above a larger stain, shaped like a small fist. When I put my own face down to the spots, I smelled nothing. Knowing how fastidious she was, Paula could have performed a magic housekeeping trick to get out the stain. Craig must have tried to clean it himself. Before he hid it behind a pillow.

"Stop," I told O.W., and moved him to the other side of the couch.

The deeper I got into the presentation, the less I thought of Craig. Work was anesthesia. I checked the chat window one more time, to make sure Craig had signed off for the night, before I emailed his assistant.

In Manila, it was already tomorrow.

Hi Annabelle, I wrote. Craig has so much on his plate right now with the renovation that he asked me to forward you this strategy deck I made for the House of Scaccabarozzi campaign. Please send to Sofia as soon as possible (no need to cc Craig). If they like it, let's expedite this—the sooner we can get the clothes, the sooner we can start shooting.

After graduating from art school, in the final months of her life, Francesca Woodman tried to figure out how she was going to make a living. She thought of becoming a fashion photographer like Deborah Turbeville, who posed her *Vogue* models in communal showers and crumbling interiors, like lithe, languorous prisoners. In my deck, I included Deborah's eerie sepia-tinted photo of a woman in a black veil floating down a curved staircase, and another of a model on the floor of Versailles, in a pile of dead leaves. On the cover, I put Francesca's black-and-white photograph of a young woman standing in the rubble of an old factory in Rome, reaching through a plaster wall to pull the hand of another woman, trapped on the other side.

On the platform, I followed a beautiful woman and her beautiful daughter. They always posted together, from the girl's lavender bedroom, wearing matching overalls, or matching pigtails, like sisters. They had the same long, thin nose and big, round anime eyes. They never spoke. They only dressed up and put on makeup and danced and lip-synced to songs that gave viewers clues to their situation: Like Rapunzel, they were captives. Why were all their videos filmed in the same room? Why was there an intercom on the wall, and why did they cover it with artificial flowers when people asked about it? Why was the only window in the bedroom up high—too high through which to escape? Why wouldn't they answer our questions?

We invented a visual code for the mother and daughter to communicate with us.

wear red if your in danger

wear Blue if you are kidnapped <3

post three black hearts if you can't call the cops

I texted Dayna a video they posted with three black hearts in the caption.

This is great, Dayna said.

Encouraged, I sent another video, where the mom wore a blue scarf in her hair and the daughter dressed as sparkly Minnie.

But nobody knows how to help them escape, I said.

I watched the dots flicker as Dayna composed her reply.

If they escape, the story is over, she said. It's all the unanswered questions that keep people watching.

Then she said, Where are you?

In my room

Perfect. I want you to go look in Becca's room for anything we can use in our campaign. A diary? A charm bracelet? Etc.

I put my phone face down on the bed so I could think. It was the middle of the afternoon. I desperately wanted to see Becca's room and search through what she left behind, but I also knew that it was Craig's room now. I'd been avoiding him ever since he got angry at Morgan for dressing me in Marion's clothes. What was I going to do, knock on his bedroom door, ask if I could have a look around? How would I know he wouldn't be there? How would I know he wouldn't walk in on me?

Olivia? Hello?

Maybe you should do it, I said. Craig likes you.

Craig can't know about this.

I don't even know where her room is, I said.

I'll distract him while you look. He'll never know. Be quick. Film it on your phone so I can see. Once we get the clothes from Italy, we might make more content in there. You got this. She sent me three flexed biceps emojis and the winking face with the tongue hanging out.

I took one of Becca's pills to settle my nerves. *I'll go downstairs and ask Morgan*, I thought. Morgan would know where Becca's room was. We could look together. I didn't have to do it alone.

On the staircase, I passed Paula carrying a basket of clean laundry. She was wearing black pants and a black short-sleeved blouse; her dark hair was pulled back in a tight, tiny bun. On the landing, I stood aside to give her room.

"Good afternoon," I said. I felt guilty already.

"Olivia. Are you occupied?"

"I'm not doing anything."

"Good," she said. "Come." She set her laundry basket on the landing and I followed her downstairs.

Instead of turning left toward the first-floor bedrooms and Craig's office, we turned right. Past the dining room and kitchen, at the very end of the hall, was a concrete wall, a dead end. But when Paula kept going, I saw there was another hallway that unraveled to the right—a mystery hiding in plain sight. Without any windows, this wing of the house was musty and forgotten. Somewhere, a faucet slowly dripped.

Paula turned her back to me to open a hall closet, and I took the opportunity to scan the dimly lit hallway. One door was ajar. I thought I could see a twin bed inside.

"It's going to rain," she said.

The closet was filled top to bottom with plastic buckets and metal tubs and bowls as big as cauldrons. There was even a baby bathtub. I followed her lead, grabbing as many as I could carry. Back in the main artery of the house, she taught me to look up and read the ceilings. When I saw a brown-and-gray water damage stain, I put a bucket underneath.

"When it rains, she cries," Paula explained.

That was when the lorazepam hit my system. Paula let me find the most obvious stains and my imagination turned them into dragon fire, eels, alien spacecraft, dancing phantoms, mitosis. I could do this all day. Meanwhile, she was putting bowls in odd corners and on top of furniture in the dining room, periodically stopping to touch the walls like she was taking their temperature, the way a mother would.

"The architect thought gutters were ugly. You can ask Craig all about it."

"I will," I said.

One stain at a time, I made my way down the long hallway. At the end, Dayna and Craig were talking outside his office. I couldn't hear their conversation, but she was laughing and touching his arm.

The baby bathtub slipped from my hands and hit the tile floor. They both turned to look at me.

Dayna's eyes went wide. "Olivia," she said.

"It's going to rain," I said. "I need to get more buckets."

"I think you should," she said. She glanced at Craig, but he was staring at the bathtub in the middle of the floor.

I floated, smooth as a spaceship, back to the room I suspected was Becca's. At least I knew where Craig was. Dayna would hold his attention.

I slipped inside and kept the door slightly ajar so I would hear if anyone approached. The room was not much bigger than my own upstairs. The furniture looked like a matching set someone had ordered off a website: a twin bed beneath the only window, one dresser, one bookcase, a desk and chair. *Teenage Girl's Bedroom, United States of America, c. 2021.* Daylight stuttered through the window, which was obscured by dry bushes and vines. I kneeled on the bed to turn on a yellow reading lamp that was mounted to the wall. The bed was neatly made. The room smelled sweet, like a girl: roses and vanilla, yellow cake, ripe pear.

Behind Becca's desk, I recognized the decorated wall from her videos. Seeing it in person was like stepping onto the set of a movie you'd only ever seen on your laptop. With

my phone, I filmed the wall for Dayna. The entire thing—
from desk to ceiling—was covered in postcards of old paintings of young women as nymphs and fairies, Polaroids of
palm trees, sketches of horses and angels and faces, and a
wall clock with the face of the moon.

Up close, I recognized the sketches. There were drawings of Piper looking down at her phone, her hair in her
face, and multiple versions of Jake in profile, as she tried to
get his jawline right. She had sketched all the creators in the
house.

The Eight of Swords card was right there, on her desk.
It was a drawing of a woman with long black hair, wearing
a long dress. Her eyes are covered with a blindfold and her
body is bound in rope. She's standing in what looks like a
slough, far away from the castle where she came from.
There are eight swords standing up in the ground, like a
treacherous fence.

"I became the Eight of Swords," Becca said, in the last
video she ever posted. I brought it up again on my phone.
The lighting was bad and the crop was so close. Most of her
videos were of her hands, turning over the cards for us. She
only showed her face in her last video, which she filmed late
at night. She kept repeating the date, August 8, and told us
that a mystical portal was opening. Usually, her videos were
about us, delivering the message we needed to hear. In this
one, she was trying to tell us something about herself.

The Eight of Swords must have been the last card she
ever pulled. I shivered and slipped the card in the back
pocket of my jeans.

When I took a step back from the desk to look once more
at the entire wall, I saw a photo booth strip of Becca and
Morgan, practically sitting on top of each other, making
glamorous faces. In one frame, Becca offered up her cheek
for a staged kiss from Morgan. There was a Polaroid of

them together in Morgan's car, wearing sunglasses. I remembered my own trip in Morgan's car to the thrift store, the way the sun and the breeze felt on my arm when I stuck it out the window. Impulsively, I peeled the photo booth strip from the wall, to bring to Morgan as an offering.

Far off to one side, there was a photo of Becca leaning over to blow out candles on a small chocolate birthday cake. She held back her long, dark hair so it didn't get on the cake. Her eyebrows were furrowed by the effort of making her wish. Someone had their arm around her shoulder, but their head was missing from the frame. I removed the pushpin from the photo so I could hold it closer.

It was a man's arm around her. I could tell by his dark suit. There was only one person in the house who wore dark suits.

I heard voices coming from the direction of the kitchen. My ears started ringing—I'd spent too long at the wall. I hadn't even searched the bookcase, her dresser, or her closet.

I put the photo in my pocket and slipped outside the bedroom. Instead of turning right, I kept following the dark hallway to a destination unknown.

In this neglected wing of the house, it was easy to stay in the shadows. I didn't risk turning on my phone's flashlight. I just kept walking, assuming I'd eventually reach a door to the outside. But without any windows, I quickly became disoriented. I pictured the house from a distance—the way it looked in drone photos I'd seen on the internet. It sat atop a tall, broad platform that made it look like a fortress. Was that where I was now? Inside the house's foundation? But I hadn't gone down any stairs.

Against the walls, there were large pieces of furniture draped in canvas drop cloths, dusty piles of floor tiles, stacks of framed posters. I crouched low behind one of these stacks, where I had a good line of sight on the door to Becca's bedroom, so I would know when Craig went in.

That was when I remembered I'd left the lamp above the bed turned on.

Maybe he wouldn't notice.

"Stupid," I whispered in the dark.

I remained completely still as Dayna followed Craig into the bedroom. I waited until they closed the door.

Then I peeked at one of the posters, which wasn't a poster at all, but a large framed photograph of a girl wearing a plaid skirt in a bathroom stall, standing on a black toilet seat in black Mary Janes like the ones I'd worn in my first orphanage video. In one hand, she gripped a black cord that led to something out of frame. Most of her head was cut off; her dark hair fell past her collarbones.

In the next photo, she was reclining in a wooden pew, her bare knees touching underneath the same plaid skirt. Again, no face. A bruised thigh against a white bedsheet. A mouth gagging on a bouquet of roses, in black and white. A girl's narrow nude back, one hand contorted behind her— braced for arrest—the other violently pulling her own dark hair. A girl kneeling in black tights, bare midriff, breasts unseen; she was holding a split pomegranate beside her hip.

As far as I could tell, every single photograph was of the same girl. The images were close to violent, but somehow controlled.

Who had taken these? And why were they hidden in a hallway, where no one could see them?

When I pulled out my phone to take pictures of the stack, I was distracted by a stream of missed messages.

Are you done? Dayna asked.

Olivia?

Hello?

We're coming

Hide

There were more messages from Morgan, who had apparently seen all my videos from the night before.

hey quick question do you want to go live with me about coming out as an orphan

we can answer people's questions together!!

Two missed calls from my aunt. One text: Call me Olivia

Coming, I texted Morgan.

On her vanity, I laid down what I'd pulled—the birthday photo, the Eight of Swords, the photo booth strip—like I was the tarot reader.

"That's Craig," I said. I was standing over her shoulder.

Morgan picked up the birthday photo and studied it. "I was there," she said. "We had her party here."

"He's very close to her."

Morgan looked again. "Where did you get these?"

"Dayna told me to sneak into Becca's room and look for something we could use."

"Use for what?" Morgan tilted her head.

"For the campaign. Dayna didn't tell you?"

"No."

I frowned, confused. Morgan knew more about fashion than any of us. She was currently wearing a black silk kimono over a tank top and green track pants, with a gold lamé turban. Worried I'd mispronounce the name of the designer, I pulled up the House of Scaccabarozzi website on my phone and showed Morgan.

Silently, she scrolled.

"We're going to make content looking for Becca, as soon as the clothes arrive from Italy."

"Dayna didn't tell me." She handed back my phone.

"Does she know you're here because of Becca, too?"

"I must not be part of the campaign." Morgan looked away from me and started arranging her makeup brushes. Once they were organized, she affixed the photo booth strip to her mirror with a piece of washi tape.

"I'm sure you are," I said. "She must have just been waiting for the right moment to tell you."

Morgan wouldn't look at me. I feared she might start crying.

I put a hand on her back. "We'll find her," I said. "Don't worry."

"I'm not a standard size, Olivia. That's why Dayna didn't tell me. The clothes aren't for me. The dresses are for you and Piper."

"Oh," I said. I tried to think of something kind and reassuring to say, so she would know how much I admired her creativity and daring. *Weird is beautiful?* That sounded like a T-shirt slogan. *I think you're very fetching?* No.

Before I could say the right thing, there was a soft tapping that sounded like it was coming from her closet. Morgan sprang from her seat at the vanity. The tapping grew louder.

Paula opened the door to Morgan's room without knocking. "It's starting," she said. She handed Morgan a plastic trash can and Morgan took it into the closet.

I expected Paula to say something about how I'd disappeared earlier, when I was supposed to be helping, but she just handed me my own trash can. "For your room," she said. "Hurry."

"Olivia Grace," my aunt said when I finally called her back, as if using my middle name would remind me I was still a child. I was lying on my stomach in bed, my shoes dangling off the edge of the covers. The rain had stopped dripping through a comet-shaped stain on the ceiling. Already I missed the sound of the rain on the roof. It reminded me of home.

"Hello," I said.

My twelve-year-old cousin Aiden had showed her my account. I'd appeared on his FYP. I wondered which video he'd seen—that would tell me what else Aiden was watching. What the algorithm believed he wanted more of.

"Was I crying?"

"When?"

"In the video," I said.

"You were dancing."

I didn't need her to say another word. My memory filled in what Aiden had seen: me in my crop top, short shorts, dancing alone in my room with the kind of abandon that was only possible if I believed no one I knew would ever see me.

"I thought you were moving to LA to be an *actress*," she said, like the word was a synonym for *fool*.

Now that I was sixteen hundred miles away, I was surprised by how little her disapproval affected me. If I disappointed her, who cared? She'd sat in my high school auditorium when I played Emily Webb in *Our Town*, but she wasn't my audience anymore. I didn't have to please her.

"I did," I said.

"Well, I don't see which part of this is 'acting.' This is your mom and dad. This is real." I pictured her drawing her long cardigan around herself and folding her arms; she was like an ugly old sofa, draped in soft throw blankets to hide the wear and tear of time. "What do you have to say for yourself?"

Was it even worth trying to explain to her that if I wanted to be an actress I had to build an audience first? I didn't have any famous family members who could help me cut to the front of the line. I had to prove I had something that strangers wanted to spend their attention on. And I was doing that. I was succeeding. If Aiden showed her my numbers, she would know.

"I think my mom and dad would be proud of me," I said.

She laughed. "You used to be a very smart girl."

You're actually smart, Peter had said.

Too smart to be here, they meant, dressing up a rabbit like Oliver Twist, or dancing alone in my room, or pressing so hard on my own insides that I cried, just for views and likes and follows. It was like I was becoming famous in a country where my aunt didn't speak the language. Everything had to be translated for her.

"I know what I'm doing," I said.

"Are you coming home for Thanksgiving?"

I hadn't thought about it. She might as well have asked, *Are you coming home for the anniversary of your parents' death?* Even if I'd wanted to, I couldn't afford to fly back. Not yet, anyway. I was still in Craig's debt on rent. Dayna promised I'd make money with the House of Scaccabarozzi campaign.

"I have other plans," I told my aunt.

She cleared her throat. "If it's the cost, we can help. We can buy your ticket. Aiden would like to see you."

I lay on my back and opened the camera roll on my phone. I could hardly remember the last Thanksgiving I'd had with my parents, almost two years before; at the time, I didn't know I needed to preserve it, like a flower pressed between glass.

In *Our Town*, Emily dies and begs the Stage Manager to let her go back and live one more day on earth. The other dead people in the graveyard try to talk her out of the idea; they know how much it will hurt her. But the Stage Manager says okay—which day? My twelfth birthday, Emily says.

When she travels back in time, she meets her mother again. Emily knows that in fourteen years, she'll be gone, but she also knows everything about the future that her mother can't possibly foresee. Emily thinks she can wring one last moment of happiness from the past, to take with her, but all she can see is how little anyone appreciates how good they have it.

I still knew my lines by heart: *I can't. I can't go on. It goes so fast. We don't have time to look at one another.*

In my camera roll, there were four different angles of the uncarved turkey. Six shots of rolled lefse on a blue-and-white plate. Close-up of my mom's hand lighting a candle in a glass holder shaped like an autumn leaf. Pretty photographs of the end of my life.

Maybe it was true what the adults said—that the platform wasn't the real world. But it was real enough. You could leave this world for that one without dying. The old people who were so mad that we were spending all our time on the platform weren't giving us a better alternative. Who would choose the real world—with all its suffering and humiliations—over a platform that excluded everyone who believed you were wasting your life? This *was* my life. Everyone on the platform had already bought into the platform. We were in on the joke. The joke was on them.

"Thanks," I told my aunt. "But I have to work."

As soon as I hung up, I cried efficient, bitter tears. I didn't see how I could go back home without some kind of achievement I could wield like a defense against her doubts.

I wanted to take another pill, but my supply was dwindling, and I decided I would limit myself to one a day. There might be a day when I really needed two. I had to be disciplined.

In the tiny upstairs bathroom, I dumped the trash can of rain into the sink. I pressed a cold, damp washcloth to my face until it looked less red and puffy. Then I went back downstairs.

His bedroom door was slightly open. Through a sliver of light, I watched him working at his desk. His phone was face down, like he was punishing it.

I watched Jake through Becca's eyes: He was solid, focused, driven. When he wasn't performing, he was sincere and direct. Here was someone a girl could count on. Morgan had hinted that they might have been a couple, but I couldn't see it. Becca was into nymphs and fairies; Jake had a separate monitor for his laptop. She was a girl and he was a man. But she could have had a crush.

"Jake?"

He swiveled his chair toward me. "Yeah?"

"I know you're busy," I said. "I just wanted to apologize."

"Come in." He gestured for me to sit on his bed.

"I'm sorry I ever let Sue Gambino into our house. It was a mistake. I'm not making excuses. I should have protected you from her."

He paused before responding.

"This might sound weird," he said, "but Becca warned me about Sue."

He didn't know what Morgan had planted in my head, about him and Becca. He didn't know she'd told me he was the last person to see her.

"When?" I asked.

"Right before she disappeared. She said I didn't have enough boundaries and that's how people were going to get inside the house. I didn't really understand what she meant. She told me to leave, before it was 'too late.'"

"How do you know she was warning you about Sue? What if it was about me? I got inside the house."

"You're a good person, Olivia. I forgive you."

I wasn't a good person. But I let him believe it if he wanted to.

"Do you have a five-year plan?" Jake asked. "It's okay if you don't. Most of the people I ask don't."

"I'm going to be an actress. That's why I moved to LA. Well, that, and to find Becca."

"Dayna told me we're going to look for her."

Dayna. There was another person who'd gotten inside the house.

"She told me the same thing," I said.

He leaned back in his chair and looked over my head at one of his movie posters, thinking. When he crossed his arms, I could see his muscles flexing under his T-shirt. I tried not to stare. I got the same swirly nervous feeling in the pit of my stomach that I'd once gotten looking at Peter.

"Was Becca your fan?"

"No, it wasn't like that."

"She didn't come to the house to meet you?"

Jake shook his head.

"Was she close to Craig?"

"When we were all together, they hardly ever talked to each other. Morgan talked to Craig way more. They didn't seem close at all. But now I'm thinking they could have spent time alone together. Before Dayna moved in, Craig lived in the guest house. He could have brought Becca there. Why?"

"I found a picture of them together at her birthday party. He has his arm around her. He's her boss, right?"

"Whose birthday party?"

"Becca's."

"Becca never had a birthday party. Not while I was here, anyway."

"Huh," I said. "That's not what Morgan said."

"Is Craig creeping on you? Did he ask you to come to his office or something? You can tell me."

I shook my head. "Not me," I said. "Dayna."

DAYNA

When I followed Craig into Becca's bedroom and Olivia wasn't in there, I melted with relief. I'd already spent thirty minutes in the hallway trying to distract him with every unbelievable detail in the long saga of the teenage thieves of the Hollywood Hills, which I'd covered back when I was at *EW,* but once we were alone, Craig pressed me against the closed door and began kissing me. Against my back, the door felt strangely warm, like a body. As he moved his mouth to my neck and started sliding his hands up under my shirt, I stole a glance at where he'd brought me. Every surface of Becca's room was decorated with ephemera. The wall behind her desk looked like a scrapbook. I recognized postcards of John William Waterhouse paintings and Maxfield Parrish illustrations of angelic dreamers—Craig ran his thumb over the sheer cup of my bra and I inhaled sharply.

The bed was small, the size of a girl. He discarded his jacket and I unbuttoned his shirt. When I started to shimmy out of my jeans, he stopped my hands. He wanted to undress me. He took his time, kissing each inch of newly revealed skin. It had been so long since I'd been touched by a man who wanted to explore what turned me on, instead of running a programming sequence. He left the light on, but I closed my eyes. I felt like I was abandoning my own body—not to him, but to the room, which was so warm it made my limbs heavy and weak. The bed was swallowing me. I welcomed it. I wanted to disappear. I wanted Craig to make me disappear.

I made a sound and he stopped what he was doing to cover my mouth with one hand.

"Be quiet." He looked at the door like he'd heard someone in the hallway.

"First time you've snuck a girl into your room?" I whispered.

Craig smiled his secret smile and put his hand back between my legs. I craned my neck to kiss the heads of his shoulders, his chest. When he entered me, I gasped, but I didn't want him to stop or ask if I was sure this was what I wanted. He already knew what I wanted. At last, it started to rain.

THE NEXT AFTERNOON, Craig was stretched out, reading an old hardcover on the sunken living room sofa; he was so tall, he took up four rust-colored cushions. I kneeled on the rug beside him.

"Hi," I said.

"Hi."

"I have something to tell you."

He put the book on his chest. "You can tell me anything." He brushed the hair from my face. I looked at his mouth. His beautiful mouth.

I'd prepared to hide my plans from him—but that was before we'd had sex. Now I wanted to tell him the truth: Sofia Scaccabarozzi loved my idea. We'd won the job with the idea he'd forbidden me from pursuing. Could I get him to admit that I knew better than he did? Wasn't that why I was here?

But I feared a second rejection, so I brought him exactly what he'd asked for: something we could film without controversy. House of Scaccabarozzi would get a two-for-one. Win-win.

"Last night I came up with a new idea," I told Craig. "Have you ever had a wedding?"

"This relationship is moving pretty fast."

I laughed. "Stop," I said.

"I love making you laugh."

"I mean *here*. Have you ever had a wedding at the house?"

He paused before he answered, calculating his reply. "It's the perfect setting for a wedding," Craig said. "They used it for Faye Dunaway and Richard Chamberlain's wedding in *The King's Widow*. Tom Selleck and Laura San Giacomo in *The House of Asterion*. You remember her."

"Laura? I don't think so."

"*Sex, Lies, and Videotape*?"

"Never saw it."

"You're too young." Craig smiled.

When was the last time anyone had told me I was too young for anything?

"And of course my father and Viola were married here."

"Remind me who Viola is?"

Craig frowned. "Paula's mother."

I'd killed our easy rapport. The way he looked at me indicated this was information I'd already been given. Craig must have told me the story of his parents years ago, in the privacy of a chat window. He assumed I'd held on to it. And

I had—only it was in deep storage. At first, all I could recover was the tint of tragedy. Something awful had happened in this house. What was it?

"Your mother died in this house."

"She took her own life. My father was a doctor. He was the one who'd prescribed her the medication."

"Medication for what?"

"For her nerves, after Viola moved in. She was a single mother, a model and an actress barely scraping by, and my father took pity on her, or at least that's how he framed it. He denied they were having an affair. Some of my last memories of my mother are of her pleading with him." He rested the back of his head on the arm of the couch and closed his eyes, pained.

"Of course she knew Viola was her replacement. She'd always had a powerful sixth sense. I think she saw the future and decided she'd rather not be here for it. I was the one who found her in the bathtub. I was thirteen."

Self-Portrait at 13. My old handle. That's why Craig had it memorized, even all these years after I'd made her disappear. The suicide explained his interest in Francesca Woodman, too. He'd been a good friend to me and my forgetting was a kind of abandonment.

"Craig, I'm so sorry," I said. I put my hand on his thigh. He covered my hand with his.

"You know she was an artist."

"I didn't know. Or I forgot."

"She was a talented painter. She studied with the American surrealists. But she stopped when she had me."

My imagination filled in the rest. "So she decorated her bedroom," I guessed. The room I'd stayed in twenty years ago. The one Morgan slept in now.

Craig nodded. "My mother never got enough attention

when she was living to be memorialized when she was gone. Marion Deckler. If you search her name, nothing comes up."

"We were married here, too, Craig." Paula was standing in the hallway, holding a bottle of wine in one hand and two crystal glasses in the other. I removed my hand from his leg. How long had she been watching us?

"My French husband and I," she added, for my benefit.

"I'll get the wedding album," Craig said.

He left us to go retrieve the album from his office, and Paula crossed the room to sit in a chair near the big picture window, at a deliberate distance from me. She poured herself a glass of red wine. It did not seem like her first.

"I'm sorry about your French husband," I told her. "I remember meeting him the first time I came here."

"For your little show. Yes, I remember."

I waited for her to pour me a glass of wine; when she didn't, I vaped.

"You must think we're strange people," she said.

"Not at all," I lied.

"Few can understand the burden and the responsibility," she said.

"Of what?"

"Of preserving a home like this. The trouble is money. After she married George, my mother went through his money like there would always be more of it. She spent it recklessly. She spent it all on me." She let out a dry, bitter laugh. "Private school. Riding lessons. Horse show ribbons and pearl necklaces and tennis bracelets and French classes. Like I was her own little Jackie Bouvier."

I pictured young Paula, cheeks flushed pink, wearing stirrup pants and a little helmet, straddling a pony. Impossible to picture her experiencing anything like joy.

"George died before he saw what the earthquake did to

this house. She was old-fashioned, my mother. When the house started falling down the hill, she saw that I was the most valuable asset she had. I had to marry well."

"Why couldn't Viola sell the house?"

Paula sighed. "It was all she had left. Craig felt the same way. I was their last hope: Marry Lucien. He would save us. Mother pressured me to produce an heir before Craig did."

"Why?"

"She thought if Lucien paid for the restoration, and I started a family, Craig would understand that the house was meant to be passed down in our bloodline, not his."

So much for that plan, I thought. Look at the Deckler House now. No husbands or wives, no pets or children. Just crumbling architecture, threadbare upholstery, aging specimens of the twentieth century. All our futures hinged on the productivity of a handful of college dropouts with a dream.

"After Lucien died, right there,"—she pointed at a spot on the carpet behind me—"I found out that he had been, how I shall I say this, *selective* in disclosing his state of affairs. I had not married into good fortune. I had married into quicksand. Debts. There was less than nothing. There was no one to save us."

I had no idea why she was confiding in me. Maybe it was the wine. I had my father's gift for listening; other people read my face as an invitation to tell all. Celebrities confessed in my presence. Olivia spilled her guts. Craig had, too—even before he met me in person.

"But what about Craig? Can't he save the house?"

She leaned in conspiratorially. "A long time ago, it was already too late for me," she said. "But it isn't too late for him."

What did she mean—it wasn't too late to save the house? To get married? Have a baby? Before I could ask, Craig returned from his office with a white leather photo album. On the cover, there was an eight-by-ten, framed inside an oval window, of a slight man with a goatee, unsmiling, with a young Paula in a wedding gown with a square neck and three-quarter lace sleeves. She was wearing a simple strand of pearls. She smiled innocently, glowing from the inside. Hope made her unrecognizable. While Craig and I sat beside each other on the couch to flip through the album, Paula got up to pour herself another glass of wine.

"You were a beautiful bride," I said.

This time, Paula poured a glass for me. I turned the thick pages, reliving the scene. There were a few dozen guests, seated on the terrace for the ceremony, and then indoors for lunch. I was searching for Craig. I flipped past a photo of the groom lifting the veil from the face of his bride. There she was again, seated at a table laid with tall candles and trails of red rose petals, eyes closed, tilting her face up for a kiss.

Finally I found Craig, slow-dancing in a black tuxedo, his hair as dark and thick as the first time I ever met him. Then, he was younger than I was now. The way he was looking at his dance partner was the way he looked at me. He was in love with her.

"Who's this?"

"That's Dawn," Paula said. She wasn't even looking at the album.

Dawn had long, straight hair almost to her waist, which made her look girlish. On her left hand, there was a diamond ring.

"You were engaged," I said.

"But never married," Craig said. He tried to turn the page, but I held it open.

"When I met you, were you engaged?"

"I'm trying to think."

"We met in 2001," I said.

"Then yes."

"You were engaged to Dawn but you were talking to me on the internet?"

"What's wrong with talking to you on the internet?"

"I just don't understand why you didn't tell me," I said. I didn't really want to get into it in front of Paula, but why did he make everything a riddle? What else was he hiding?

"Dawn is very religious," Paula said, as if that explained anything.

"She wasn't here," I said. "When you had my photography show. I didn't meet her."

"Dawn couldn't tolerate the house," Paula said, her tone laced with bitterness.

Craig didn't correct her, or offer any other explanation for the end of his engagement. I let him close the wedding album. There was an awkward silence.

"Well," I said, heroically changing the subject, "I think it's about time we had another wedding. It's such a romantic setting."

"Whose wedding?" Craig asked.

"Piper and Sean. All the clothes will be House of Scaccabarozzi. The first hype house wedding: Think of all the press. I talked to Mindy Bliss last night. She's going to collaborate with us."

"I knew you'd come up with something," he said.

I got an alert on my phone about the delivery from Milan and ran outside before the UPS guy could ring the bell. He was wearing shorts. He had a tattoo of a longboard on his calf.

"Can you help me carry these inside?" I asked him. There were a half dozen six-foot-tall garment boxes.

"No, ma'am, I cannot," he said. It was probably his last drop-off.

I had to laugh. "You're setting a boundary."

"Have a good one," he said.

After I signed for the packages, I went inside to find Sean and Jake. "Is it arms day or legs day?" I asked Sean.

"Legs," he said. "Why?"

"Follow me."

I supervised the men's work as they carried the first box up the dark, creepy staircase that led from the street-level entrance to the first floor of the house. I liked watching the synchronicity of their movements, the wide spread of their arms around each box, the strong grips of their broad hands, Jake's lats flexing as I followed him up the stairs. That I shouldn't be looking at them like this was part of the thrill of looking.

"Can I make a suggestion?" Sean asked, putting the box down. He blotted his forehead with the sleeve of his T-shirt.

"Please," Jake said.

"Instead of carrying these up the stairs, we go through the courtyard and around back, through the kitchen door. Where do you want these?" He looked at me.

I didn't have a good answer. They wouldn't fit in my guest house. I couldn't store them in any of the common rooms we used for shooting. There was the long hallway off the kitchen, where Olivia had played hide-and-seek, but that led to Craig's bedroom, and I didn't want to have to go near his room every time we needed a wardrobe change. If we kept them outside on the terrace, the raccoons could end up in couture.

"Just split them up for now," I said. "Two in your room, two in Jake's, two in Morgan's."

"We can put them all in my room," Jake said. His bedroom wasn't the largest, but it was clean and organized, which made it seem palatial.

"Thank you," I said, relieved. Impulsively, I squeezed his shoulder.

By the time they finished carrying all the boxes, darkness had fallen. Exhilarated, they high-fived. Then Jake turned to me, said, "Down low." I laughed and met his gesture. Instead of pulling away, he clutched my hand in his.

It felt weird to tip them, but also weird not to.

"I should buy you guys dinner," I said.

Sean said thanks, but Annabelle had connected him with a meal kit service that salvaged the vegetables that were too ugly and deformed to be sold in stores, and tonight he and Piper had to shoot an ad for it that didn't look like an ad.

Jake and I were left alone, standing at the threshold to his bedroom.

"What are you doing right now?" he asked.

"Standing outside your room," I said. "What are *you* doing right now?"

"Should we, uh, see what's inside the boxes?" His nervousness to invite me in triggered my own nerves. I'd been in his room before. But there was a new charge between us.

Jake shut the bedroom door behind us and turned on his white noise machine. Either to prevent us from hearing the sounds of the house or to prevent the others from hearing us. He turned on a single lamp that cast a soft light.

"May I offer you a beverage?" His mini fridge was stocked with cans and bottles from sponsors.

"I'll take whatever is the opposite of an energy drink," I said.

The boxes from Italy completely blocked his desk and chair. There was nowhere to sit but the bed or the floor. I slipped off my shoes and sat on top of the covers, legs parallel to the pillows, back against the wall.

He handed me a sparkling CBD tonic and got to work opening the first box, cleanly slicing through the packing tape and shipping labels and the plastic pocket of customs documents with an X-ACTO knife. He was calm, focused.

"I don't know how you got Craig to go for it," he said, his back to me.

"I didn't," I admitted.

"But we got the clothes."

"I told Craig we would do the campaign around a wedding."

"Whose wedding?"

"Piper and Sean," I said.

He turned to face me and gave me a tiny, amused golf clap.

I raised my canned beverage. "Thanks," I said, laughing.

The first box was filled with menswear. Jake took a dark jacket from the box, held it in front of his chest, and turned to face me, his mirror.

It was a navy tuxedo jacket with black velvet trim.

"Are there pants?" I asked.

He found them. The pants were even better. They were brocade.

"There's a vest, too," he said. "I think I should try it on." He was looking right at me. We were playing a game now.

I swallowed, but didn't break eye contact. "Only if you want to," I said.

Without turning away from me, Jake removed his jeans and casually tossed them onto the bed, beside my legs. He was wearing black boxer briefs. His legs were tan from the California sun and strong like a soccer player's. I had the instinct to cover my eyes with one hand, like a child. *You're both professionals*, I told myself. *This is a fitting.* Jake took off his shirt. He was ripped. I sipped my drink.

"How much could I get on the dark web for a picture of you in your underwear?" I asked.

Jake laughed as he pulled on the pants. "More if I was holding Owen Wilson."

"Be right back," I said. I didn't move from his bed.

Still shirtless, he started removing the jacket from its plastic bag. "So, I guess we aren't looking for Becca anymore?"

"No, we are. We will. But Craig doesn't need to know that."

Jake froze and raised his eyebrows.

"Wait," I said. "Don't put on the jacket. Or a shirt. Just the vest."

He followed my instructions, and when he was done, I took out my phone. He put one hand in a pocket and posed. I told myself I would take a few pictures I could email to Annabelle tonight so she could let Sofia know the boxes had safely arrived. My eyes traveled from the Jake on my small screen to the Jake standing before me. He was irrefutably hot. If I said that out loud, would I lose the game? Or win?

When I was done shooting him, Jake picked the knife back up and opened the second box. I got up from the bed to join him. Before I could see what I was looking at, I had to rip off the plastic garment bags. We made a pile on the floor. Then I reached inside and stroked the silk and cashmere, the silver zippers and heavy sequins, the marabou trim.

I pulled out a stretchy burgundy velvet tube dress so I could see it better in the light. It had thin satin strings that tied around the neck in a halter.

"This is what I would wear. This is what I *would have* worn. When I was your age."

"Try it on," Jake said.

I laughed.

"It would look good on you."

I blinked. "Try it on right now?"

"I'll turn around if you're shy," he said.

Before I could process what was happening, I turned around. So did Jake. I took off my pants first. Then my shirt. The soft lining skimmed my body as I pulled the dress up my bare legs, along my thighs and hips. It fit perfectly. Before I could tie the strings at the neck, I realized I would have to take my bra off. I looked over my shoulder to make sure Jake was still turned away, and unclasped my bra and removed it, folded it into a polite pile on the edge of his dresser. I reached in and lifted my breasts so they sat high on the shelf built into the lining and spilled out over the top of the dress. I felt like a cross between '90s Courteney Cox and a Rubens painting of cleavage.

When I reached up to tie the strings, I felt Jake standing right behind me.

"Let me help," he said quietly. His hands were in my hair, moving it out of the way.

"You can just tie it in a bow," I said, my pulse racing. "It doesn't have to be—" Before I could finish, his lips were on my neck. He kissed my bare shoulder. My entire body jolted awake, anticipating where his mouth would go next. But then Jake stepped back to carefully tie the strings of my dress. I turned to face him without looking in his eyes. I didn't know what to say. I tilted my face up toward Jake's and he met me in the space between what we each thought we were allowed to want. He had one hand on my face and the other around the small of my back, pressing my body toward his. He moved so fast, it was like a pop song on the platform, sped up to double time. There was nothing hesitant about the way Jake kissed me. He kissed me like I was a risk he was willing to take. As we kissed, I unbuttoned his vest so I could run my hands over his smooth, warm skin.

When he pulled away to look at my face, I marveled at his.

"That guy didn't deserve you," Jake said.

Craig? I didn't want to be thinking about Craig. He had his secrets. Wasn't I allowed mine?

"Which guy?" I asked.

"The guy who wrote the Reddit post."

I smiled, relieved. "You googled me?"

"No," Jake said. He had both arms around my waist, like we were a couple of kids at a dance. "I couldn't google you. I didn't know your last name. I googled 'Owen Wilson rabbit.' It was the first result."

I buried my face in his chest; he smelled like fresh lime, lemongrass. "It's not the way I expected to go viral."

"What did you expect?"

"Oh, I don't know that I ever expected to go viral. Of course I wanted attention for my work. The right kind of attention. Respect from my peers. To get paid to do something I was good at. I think that's what we all want."

"What were you good at?" Jake asked, touching my face so I would look at him again.

"I was good at photography, but that was a long time ago." I stopped myself before I could say anything more about time. Before I stumbled into an awkward joke about the years between us.

"What are you good at now?"

Jake sat back and held his hands out to me. I kneeled in front of him on the bed. He ran his hands down my bare arms. He had beautiful hands, the kind of hands you'd want to watch play a cello, not tap a glass screen. I straddled his lap. He moved his hands to the tops of my thighs. We made out with our clothes on. I felt the edges of my body dissolving, like I was reenacting the girl I used to be, in black and white, limbs blurred by long exposure. I only existed where he touched me. The rest of me was ghostly; the walls showed through my skin.

"Stop," Jake said. He'd gotten a notification on his watch.

"Stop?"

"I have to stream."

"Skip it," I said. The room was too bright. I wanted to go back under.

"I can't. I have to give them at least twenty minutes." His phone was already in his hand. Before he even opened the app, his mind was already inside it, running through the motions like a program.

"Do you want me to leave you alone?"

"No," Jake said, buttoning up his vest. I couldn't help but stare at his mouth. His lips were flushed, swollen. "Stay." He leaned forward to kiss me and then feinted left, kissed my neck.

Reluctantly, I got off his lap and sat at the edge of his bed to watch. He expertly screwed his phone into his standing ring light and arranged himself against a stack of crisp white pillows, one arm behind his head, his biceps flexing like a wink. I opened the app on my own phone, and because I was following Jake, the live video stream came right up on my FYP. I was one of thirty-six women watching. Before I could blink, there were 112. Then 393. I smiled at him and gave him a cheesy thumbs-up.

"If you're going to stay, you can't distract me," he said.

"Who? Me?" I mouthed.

"Good evening and welcome to the Jake Cho cinema club," Jake said, "where my name is Jake Cho and we talk about movies I've streamed recently that you probably saw when you were . . . I won't finish that thought. I don't want to call anybody out."

who are you talking to?? @happinessisachoice asked.

whose there with you Jake?

will you show us your rabbit again pls

For the first time, I found myself typing in the tiny wishing well at the bottom of the screen.

as much as I love the rabbit, I'd rather look at you, I wrote. On the platform, I was no one. I had let the platform auto-generate my username, a string of random digits, like a ticket in a lottery I didn't even want to play.

But Jake knew it was me. When my comment flashed before his eyes, he touched the corners of his mouth, to prevent the smile from spreading.

Jake don't tell us you have a girlfriend @thefutureMrsCho said.

wait what did I miss!!!! @tipsey.mommie asked.

"I deny all rumors. I do not—repeat—do not have a girlfriend."

As soon as he said this, Jake was showered with dozens of roses, six love balloons, fireworks, one tree house, and an autumn candle. Playing along, he wrapped his arms around himself and made a puppy face at the camera. "I feel so loved, fam. Thank you for taking such good care of me," he said.

More roses.

I posed for him like he was my camera. I reached behind my neck and undid the straps that he'd tied for me. That got his attention. Slowly, I pulled the top down, down, down. I said nothing. Jake tried to keep the banter going with his audience, but he was distracted, blushing. He lost his train of thought on Rebecca De Mornay. He swallowed. Before he could reach for me, ruin the stream, sabotage his dreams, I pulled up my top, grabbed my clothes, and snuck out of his room.

When I opened my laptop, Craig was waiting for me in the chat window.

Dayna? Sent forty-five minutes earlier.

Here, I typed. **Sorry!**

I was just talking to Annabelle about the House of S. campaign

I felt sick. What had she told him? Did he know I'd gone behind his back and asked her to pass the strategy deck on to Sofia without including him?

I told her about the wedding but then she asked how orphans fit in.

Dayna?

I'm thinking, I typed. Olivia's search for Becca was entirely driven by the loss of her parents; being an orphan was her motivation. But I couldn't tell him that. I couldn't even mention Becca's name.

Annabelle came up with a few ideas, Craig continued. Orphan as flower girl but instead of petals she's throwing tears, orphan tries to catch the bride's bouquet but trips and falls in the pool, or the married couple adopts her.

How are Piper and Sean going to adopt Olivia? They're the same age! I'm sorry, but these are all bad. They're just stunts. They aren't stories.

Just trying to help, Craig said.

Sitting there in my burgundy dress, I was losing track of what was real and what was performance. Why couldn't I just say *great idea, thanks,* and then continue moving forward, exactly as I'd planned? Why did I feel like I had to defend my position by proving my ideas were superior? I didn't trust Annabelle. How old was she? She was getting too involved. Her job was to send emails.

Jake will propose to Olivia, I told Craig.

I didn't even know they were an item.

They're not. But she's an actress. I know she can pull it off. Jake can "fall in love" with her because of her tragic past. Happens all the time on The Bachelor.

I would find a way to explain it to Jake. We just had to film it so Craig would see; I would come up with a reason later for why we couldn't actually post the video.

Why have one wedding when you can have two, Craig said.

Then he said, Do you want to come over?

I sucked in my breath. What did I want? To keep Craig

and Jake in separate chambers, each with a private entrance,
so I would never have to choose one door over another? Or
to hide myself in the heart of a labyrinth, waiting to see who
would find me first?

Not tonight, I said.

IN THE LIVING room, we made a showroom. The morning
sun was a cold, bright beam on a dress form and an old iron
garment rack that Morgan had found in her bedroom.
There was an ancient brown steamer trunk Sean had helped
her carry. I asked him and Jake to bring the black lacquer
screen, inlaid with a mother of pearl cherry blossom design,
from the dining room so Piper could change behind it. Then
I followed Jake into his bedroom, where he opened the remaining boxes so I could bring the clothes to Morgan. I
tried to stay out of Jake's way, but every time I stepped back,
Jake found a reason to stand closer, brush my arm with his,
or touch the small of my back.

Nothing happened, I told myself.

Everything happened.

I felt wired on a deficit of sleep. I needed a reason to keep
my hands busy, keep moving.

Like a warehouse robot, I loaded my arms with garments and transported them to Morgan, who freed them
from their plastic bags. She hung the dresses and jackets
and vests on the rack; she piled the blouses and pants on the
trunk.

I went back to Jake for more. He closed his bedroom
door and backed me up against it. No one could see us. Before he kissed me, he read my face for a signal that I wanted
to keep playing.

"You're not helping," I said.

"How could I be more helpful?" he asked.

When he bent down to kiss me, a rush of heat flooded my body.

"When can I see you again?"

"You're seeing me right now."

"You know what I mean," Jake said.

"Soon," I said.

"I can come to your house," he said. "We'll be alone."

"There's something I need you to do for me."

Before I could tell him about the proposal to Olivia, Morgan called me from the other room.

She had attached her phone to a tripod and was recording herself dressing the headless female torso. She fastened a diaphanous pink tulle skirt around its waist and added a brown shearling vest with large embroidered flowers, and a silver choker around its neck.

"I think they sent a lookbook," I told Morgan.

"I don't need it," she said. She was in her element.

If Morgan was the stylist and the director of this shoot, then I was the animal handler. O.W. was in his travel carrier. When the room was ready, I texted the group. Olivia came downstairs from her bedroom to watch. Jake stood right behind me like a shadow. Sean led Piper over by the hand. She was wearing a beige sweatsuit that could have fit six Pipers inside.

"Is Owen Wilson here?" she asked me.

I nodded.

Piper exchanged a happy look with Sean; he squeezed her hand. Then she disappeared behind the lacquer changing screen.

We started filming a "get ready with me." Piper became Morgan's mute mannequin. Her blank canvas. There was nothing that didn't look good on Piper: cropped culottes, a brown corduroy vest worn over a bra and nothing else, a long-sleeved denim minidress that zipped up the front. Every time an outfit looked complete to my eyes, Morgan stepped forward and added another piece that completely transformed the look: a skirt pulled up over Piper's flat chest like a dress; a men's button-up tied at the waist like a skirt. Under Morgan's gaze, Piper became interesting.

"Do we like this?" Piper asked as she stepped out wearing the burgundy dress I'd worn the night before. I'd returned it this morning.

"Yes," Jake said behind me.

"Not my favorite," I told Piper. It looked incredible on her.

"Why?" she asked. She looked down at herself.

"Wait," Olivia said. She crossed the room and handed Piper a card. Piper looked down at it. Olivia said something I couldn't hear. Then they both disappeared behind the screen.

When Piper emerged, she was wearing the same dress, but its long string ties made an X across her chest, a kind of lattice in front of a tarot card. Piper was now wearing the Eight of Swords like an amulet.

"That's the last shot," I told Morgan. "End on that." The clue was so subtle, I thought we could get away with it. I doubted Craig would watch more than thirty seconds of Piper dressing up. Any Becca superfans who watched to the end of the video would get the reference, and they would want more.

"Where's Sean?" Piper asked. Worry flashed across her face.

"He'll be right back," Jake told her.

"Let's do the rabbit video," I said.

I told Piper to change; if Craig came out to watch, I didn't want him to see the tarot card.

When she came out, she was braless in an ice-blue silk slip with thin straps and lace trim.

"I think that's a nightgown," I said.

"It can be whatever you want it to be, Dayna," Piper said, in a tone that let me know I was showing my advanced age.

"Nymphet," Morgan said approvingly. Standing behind Piper, she efficiently parted her black hair into two long pigtails that fell over her bare shoulders. Then she searched the trunk until she found a pair of white socks with lace cuffs. She slipped Piper's feet inside red heels that were two sizes too big.

"Maybe she should wear a sweater over the nightgown," I said, nervous now that Sean was about to propose on camera to a sexy baby. We hadn't told Morgan about the proposal.

Piper faced me, arms open like an angel. "I'm ready," she said.

"Okay."

I unzipped O.W.'s carrier, and we all waited for him to decide to venture forth. He wasn't a dog. By nature, he was prey. "Try sitting on the couch," I told Piper, handing her a couple of pieces of Swiss chard from my belt bag.

"Snack time," I told O.W. I pointed at Piper. He hopped to sniff my finger. But he wouldn't cross the carpet. It was open territory. There was nowhere to hide.

"He doesn't like me?" Piper asked.

"It's not you," I said. I grabbed the soft vest off the dress form and made a little nest for him on the couch. Then I gently picked him up and carried him over in my arms. I felt him tremble and twitch, in the agony of not knowing whether he wanted to be put down or held close. "Piper is our friend," I said into his fur. "We like Piper."

"All I wanted was to do, like, one stupid thing with the rabbit," she said, becoming agitated. "Why doesn't anything ever work out for me?"

"Let's try not to catastrophize," I said calmly. I put Owen Wilson down on the vest, but I didn't leave his side. Piper held out the Swiss chard like she was already prepared for his rejection. He gave me one last look and then hopped toward the leaves. I crawled away, off frame, just in time for Piper to look right at Morgan's camera and let out a perfect gasp of delight.

Now Piper was more than just another young, pretty woman on the internet. She was a young, pretty woman feeding a rabbit.

Everyone had their phones out. Piper posed like the rabbit was her tiny, handsome boyfriend. She leaned coyly in and coyly away. Tucked her legs beneath her and stretched them out long. Teased the treat above Owen Wilson's head, to make him beg. The blue nightgown floated like a flimsy bell over the NSFW parts.

When Sean approached her in a three-piece suit and a lot of hair gel, she didn't break her concentration.

"Piper," he said, getting down on one knee. Piper put both hands over her mouth and froze. The Swiss chard fell to her lap and Owen Wilson climbed in.

I held my breath. Jake was filming this. I couldn't squeeze his hand.

Sean began to read from the text he had revised for the occasion.

"Last summer, when I slid into your DMs just to say how are you doing, I didn't actually think you would respond to me. But you did. I could never have predicted that I would get to wake up every morning next to you, and all our blessings and stuff. I promise to spend the rest of my life convincing you that you are enough. Piper Bliss, will you—"

Piper removed the hands from her mouth. "Yes," she said, grabbing the lapels of Sean's jacket. "Yes."

When I looked at Olivia, we were both crying.

OLIVIA

We stood on the terrace in the morning sun, over-dressed and exposed, a couple of phonies. Jake was sweating in a floral tuxedo. I was shivering in a peach disco dress and silver high-heeled sandals that were two sizes too big. As long as I didn't try to walk, it was fine. I was wearing too much makeup for daytime, but I'd had to cover a pimple on my upper lip with concealer and once I'd done that, I just kept going. Why couldn't we have shot this at night? What was the hurry? Dayna wanted to shoot during the day so Craig could observe.

"Hi," I said to Jake. We were facing each other, but not touching. I ran my tongue over my teeth, afraid of lipstick stains. It felt like the nervous start of an improvised scene, before you know what your scene partner is going to pull on you for cheap laughs. I was never the quickest with jokes, but I could be flexible. I could follow his lead. Would we be astronauts in space? Detectives on a case? Would he pretend to deliver my baby and announce it was a monster?

"This is awkward," he said quietly. He ran one hand

through his hair. Oh no. He didn't know what to do either. He expected me to start the scene.

Dayna had sworn to us that no one would ever see this video except Craig. We had to make fake content to keep him from finding out which trail we were really following. But pretending felt awful. What had happened to me? Had I lost my ability to act? Once I'd put my real life on-screen, I could no longer pretend to be someone else. Everything I performed was now lit up with the glow of the real.

"It's because the awkwardness is real," I said.

"What are you saying," Jake whispered.

"I'm saying we're really two people pretending to get engaged."

"The engagement is fake," Jake said. He looked into my eyes. His concern was real. "Right?"

"But the pretending is real."

Jake turned away from me, shielding his eyes with one hand, to look at Dayna for direction. The adults were standing on the other side of the pool, near the sliding doors to the kitchen.

"It looks very staged, the two of them just standing there," Craig said, loud enough for us to hear.

"Give me a minute, Craig," Dayna said.

"It was better yesterday. The rabbit added something."

"We can't do *two* proposals with a rabbit."

"Maybe Jake could be doing something and Olivia could walk over," he said.

"Doing what?" Dayna asked. "Cleaning the pool?"

"That would be a good hook, actually," Jake said. "Let's try it." He went to get the pole.

Dayna filmed Jake with one hand, and with the other, gestured at me to stay out of the frame. I shuffled off into the shadows. The fact that Dayna was filming should have clued Craig in. We never let her film us. We always filmed one another.

As Jake scooped leaves and petals from the pool in his dress clothes, in broad daylight, it looked like the morning after a party at the Gatsby mansion, a millionaire fishing for his Rolex.

Living truthfully under imaginary circumstances: That was the definition of acting. Off camera, I took off the strappy sandals and held them in one hand. I flipped my hair over and clipped it on top of my head in a messy twist. I rubbed my eyes with my knuckles to smear my mascara. I blurred my lipstick outside the lines. If Dayna wasn't going to let us shoot in our evening wear in the evening, then let's say the scene started the morning after the party. We'd been up all night.

"Can I take off the jacket?" Jake asked.

"Slowly," Dayna said.

"Not yet," I said.

Barefoot, I walked the wet ledge of the pool until I was at Jake's side. "Pretend we had a fight last night," I whispered in his ear, "and now we're going to make up."

I took the pole from his hands so he could remove his jacket. Then I threw the pole in the water without breaking eye contact with Jake. I threw my shoes in the pool. I took off my earrings and threw them in, too. I could do whatever I wanted. It was the kind of performance art that happens once and never again. No one would ever see the video. The more I acted upset, the more I upset myself. What were we—Dayna's puppets? Why hadn't Jake or I pushed back, told her it was a waste of time to make content we couldn't even use? Before I could jump in the pool myself, Jake grabbed my arms to stop me. Once he felt how cold my skin was, he took off his jacket and put it around me.

"That looks good," Dayna yelled. "Like you're in love." I wished she would shut up. She wasn't directing this one. I was.

I put my arms around Jake's waist and pulled him toward me until our bodies were touching.

"I don't know what to say," he whispered. Jake knew how to perform when it was just him and his camera, but he didn't know how to act with another person. He'd never learned.

"Pretend I'm someone else," I whispered back.

He looked at my face. That's when I knew he understood what acting was. He closed his eyes and kissed me then; I dissolved into his make-believe. For Jake, I could be the girl he really wanted. With my eyes closed, we could be anywhere but here. He kissed me for a long time; maybe so Dayna wouldn't make us do it again. If acting meant taking true feelings from life and bringing them to the performance, could you also take the performance with you, a souvenir? Before he pulled away, he kissed my forehead.

Then Jake got down on one knee, right in the pool water. There would be no second take. This had to be it. From his pocket, he pulled out a velvet ring box. Inside was a cocktail ring from Morgan's room. After I pantomimed *yes*, Jake put it on my ring finger. I knew we weren't going to kiss again. When I remembered this was supposed to be sponsored content, an ad for the clothes, I took a few steps away from the pool and spun in circles so the skirt of my dress bloomed like a peach cloud.

"Good work," Dayna said. She put her phone away in her pocket and took out her vape.

"Will this cause controversy in Jake's community?" Craig asked. He sounded excited.

"It's Olivia's fantasy," Dayna suggested. "It's a dream sequence."

"Like *Oklahoma!*," I added.

Dayna ignored me. "She'll stand in for all the women who wish Jake would propose to them," she told Craig. "It will take me some time to edit. It could take all day. Do you want to help?"

Craig raised his eyebrows. "Where should we do it?"

"My place?"

I tried to catch Jake's eye, to say, *See? Was I wrong to pick up something between them, something extracurricular?* But Jake wasn't looking at me. He was looking at her.

Before Dayna left us, she gave me the same direct stare she'd given me in the hallway when I was putting out the buckets to catch the rain. The stare said, *Now.* While she distracted Craig, we could go make something real.

"Follow me," I told Jake.

"I always wondered why her bedroom was so far away from ours," Jake said.

"Maybe she needed extra privacy. To channel messages or whatever." We were standing in Becca's doorway.

"But it's also the smallest."

"My room is small," I said.

"Yeah, but you just got here. Becca was here before I was."

"Did she ever invite you to her room?"

Jake shook his head. "We usually hung out in Morgan's room because it was bigger."

Now that I was wearing House of Scaccabarozzi, I had Jake film me sitting at Becca's desk while he panned the wall behind me. I was still wearing Jake's jacket around my shoulders. Then I went over to the dresser and picked up the small, childish tokens she had left behind in a ceramic tray. One at a time, I held them in my palm for the camera: a stack of friendship bracelets; a coin purse in the shape of a panda; a card of plastic barrettes. Jake filmed the book-shelves that I hadn't had time to explore the last time I was here.

"Look," he said, taking down a Bible with a blue leather cover. He handed me his phone so he could hold the book with both hands.

"Some of this is highlighted."

"Read one," I said.

"Uh, 'When thou art come into the land which the Lord thy God giveth thee, thou shalt not learn to do after the abominations of those nations. There shall not be found among you any one that, uh, maketh? Maketh his son or his daughter to pass through the fire, or that useth divination, or an observer of times, or an enchanter, or a witch,'" Jake said. "Deuteronomy."

I turned the camera on myself. "Thou shalt not be a fortune-teller," I paraphrased.

"I knew it," Jake said. "I knew she was from a cult. Wait." One of the pages was flagged with a sticky note.

"Is that her handwriting?"

Jake skimmed the page. "This is the part where Jesus is born and there are three wise men, right?"

"Right," I said.

Jake held up Becca's note. In tiny handwriting, it said, *The Magi were astrologers! They saw the signs in the stars!*

"Maybe she wanted to prove there's nothing wrong with looking for signs," I said.

"We're putting this in the video." Jake smiled for the first time that day.

"There's something else I want to show you," I said.

In the dark hallway off her bedroom, I turned on my phone's flashlight so I could see where I was stepping, bare-foot. The floor tiles were cracked, or missing. I was afraid I'd cut myself on glass or a rock. Sometimes the floor came up like a wave, like something strong was trying to grow underneath.

"Where are we?" Jake whispered.

"I think it's where they store stuff," I said.

After a minute or two, we arrived at the stack of framed photographs: the girl in her Mary Janes in the bathroom stall; the pale bruised leg; her naked back, one hand pulling her long, dark hair; mouth filled with roses; split pomegranate.

"Wait, go back," Jake said. He wanted to look at the one of her back. I held the flashlight so he could study the photo in detail.

"Who is this?" he asked.

"Look at the hair," I said.

A flash of recognition crossed his face. He knew exactly who this was. He had come to the same conclusion I had.

"It's Becca, right?" I said. "That's Becca's hair. You knew her."

The more I turned over the images in my mind, the more certain I became. She was Becca's age. Her face was missing from all of them—just like she never showed her face in videos on the platform. Only her hands. Except for the final video, but the lighting was so bad in that one.

"I'm not sure," Jake said.

"You're not sure?"

"What if it's not Becca? What if it's someone else?"

"You're the one who just told me she came from a cult. Maybe she was innocent, or naïve, when she got here. Like all she knew was how to read tarot cards but that was forbidden where she came from. So she ran away, but the house corrupted her. What if the house made her do things she would never have done back home?" I didn't tell Jake about how the house possessed me, too. The way the temperature went up in my room when I manically posted. The lights flickered. I was afraid he'd tell me he didn't feel the same thing.

"I don't know, Olivia."

"Why else would all these pictures be hidden in this hallway, right outside her room? We have to film it."

Jake hesitated for a moment and then raised his phone. I held the flashlight under my face like I was telling a ghost story.

"What did you find, Olivia?" Jake asked. He was a bad actor. His reluctance made his voice flat.

"I found these huge photographs of Becca hidden in the house."

I couldn't see Jake's reaction in the dark.

"Who took them?"

The second he asked, I knew.

"Craig Deckler," I said.

"And who is Craig Deckler?"

"He owns the house where Becca lived before she disappeared. He owns the house where we all live."

"Pick it up," Jake said. I gave him my phone so my hands were free to hold the photo of her back and her long, dark hair. With one hand, he aimed the flashlight like a spotlight; with the other, he filmed. Portrait of a girl with a portrait of a girl.

"Maybe we should run it by Dayna before you post it," Jake said.

We were sitting on his floor, our backs against his bed, editing the footage together. "Why? This is what she wanted," I said. "Clues. We found them."

"What if Craig sees it?"

I felt a flicker of defiance. Craig and Dayna expected us to be as obedient as schoolchildren, following instructions on a standardized test. But nothing about this was standardized. The only way to win the algorithm's favor was to be a freak.

"Did you know she was taking medication?"

"What kind of medication?"

"I found these pill bottles with her name on them in Craig's office. I looked them up online. They're antipsychotics."

"Whoa," Jake said.

"I have them in my room. If he comes after us for this video, we'll confront him. You can film me confronting him. Why did he take away her medication? We'll expose him." I could already see myself acting out the scene in my imagination. I'd back Craig against a wall: *Wait, I can explain everything.*

Jake nodded, serious. He wasn't looking at me. Then he impulsively got up to do push-ups.

"I don't care if he sees the video," I said, "as long as she does."

Give us a sign, I wrote in the caption. Hashtag rabbithole. Hashtag eightofswords. Hashtag houseofscaccabarozziwinter22collection.

I hit post.

Upstairs in my room, I unzipped my dress, threw it on the chair, and sat on my bed in my underwear. My skin felt greasy. I opened the platform, thinking if I got a little bit of attention or validation, that would motivate me to shower. But it was too soon. My new video had only been viewed a few hundred times. The algorithm hadn't yet learned who needed to see it.

One of my notifications was unusual. I saw that @user888273912 had stitched one of the videos I'd made about my parents. I almost didn't click it. It could have been someone laughing at me. It could have been someone older than me, telling me to get over it. Or worse—it could have been someone saying they didn't believe I was telling the truth.

I clicked.

First I had to endure several seconds of my own sweaty face, recounting the car accident. Then a stranger's face filled the screen. He was only a few years older than me, wearing a trucker hat. He had sleepy brown eyes, ringed in dark circles, and smooth, olive skin. He could've been a student at UND, the morning after pulling an all-nighter. He was sitting in the driver's seat of a car or a truck, drinking coffee from a paper cup.

"Hey, Olivia," he started. "I didn't know any other way to get ahold of you. Anybody else that sees this, I'm not here to get attention or go viral or anything. I just came on here to say I'm sorry to Olivia. I was driving that night. It was an accident. A horrible accident. For the rest of my life I'll be thinking about that day, wishing there was something I could do different." Then his hand reached out toward me to stop the recording.

I was too frozen to touch the screen. The video played again from the beginning. There was my face. There was his. His voice was flat, but not insincere. I didn't even know his name.

I know what happened to Olivia's parents, he'd written in the comments last week.

Prove it, I'd said.

I went numb with disbelief. What were the odds that this truck driver in North Dakota was scrolling the platform one night before he went to sleep and there I was, recounting his nightmare? Haunting him through his phone? Did it feel like his guts were in a blender, the way I'd felt when Becca's message came across my For You page, like he'd stumbled into destiny?

I wanted to DM my mom in the afterlife. I wanted to send the video to my cousin Aiden and ask him to show it to my aunt—but would she be able to grasp how significant it was that the platform had known to deliver my story to him? Becca would have understood. If her DMs were open, I would have sent it to her. I couldn't share it with Dayna; she would want me to make content around it. But he said he only wanted my attention.

I decided to send it to Piper. This couldn't have been the weirdest thing she'd ever seen on the internet.

deceased, she said two minutes later.

I know, I said.

like WHATTTTT

I'm trying to think of what I should say to him, I said.

To that, she gave a thumbs-up.

That was when Dayna entered my room without knocking and found me topless.

"I'm changing!" I screamed, before I could think. Horrified, I pictured myself from her point of view: my naked boobs, my stomach hanging over the top of my underwear, holding my phone like a nasty little gremlin with a magic orb.

Instead of leaving, Dayna turned and shut the door.

"I'm sorry," she said, still facing the door. "You can finish changing. I won't look. I have to talk to you."

"I'm kind of in the middle of something?"

"It can't wait."

Quickly, I threw on jeans and a T-shirt. And then a sweater on top of the T-shirt. And socks and a beanie.

"Okay," I said.

"Again, I apologize. I didn't see anything."

She would only say that if she *had* seen something; I felt my face turn red. I grabbed a makeup remover wipe and started rubbing.

"Olivia, what is this?" Dayna asked, holding up her phone. The video I'd made with Jake was paused on her screen.

I was confused.

"You told us to go shoot content about Becca. This morning."

Dayna sucked her vape. She was trying to make a concerned face, but her smooth forehead resisted the effort.

"Tell me everything you know," she said.

"Everything I know about what?"

"What are you holding in the video?"

"Is this a trick question?"

"How many photographs are there? How many did you find?"

"I don't know," I said. "Ten? Twelve? They're in frames, in a stack—"

She let out a low moan and crumpled to the floor. "I don't understand what's happening," she said.

"What's wrong? What does it mean?"

"This whole time, I thought Craig sold them." Dayna sounded incredulous, bitter. "He told me he sold them. But he didn't sell any of them. He just kept them for himself? All of them?"

"Sold what—pictures of Becca? To who?"

Dayna shoved her phone at me again. "These aren't pictures of Becca. They're pictures of me. In this video, you're holding a photo of me." She kept saying the same thing over and over, until I understood that the girl with dark hair that Craig was hiding was Dayna, not Becca. How could I have known that? Even Jake saw what I saw.

"Craig asked you to, like, pose for him?"

"They're self-portraits. I took them. With an actual camera."

"When?"

"When I was young," Dayna said. "When I was your age. Craig brought me here—to Los Angeles."

I tried to imagine Dayna sitting in Craig's office, answering interview questions that would lead him to tell her what made her special. To make her content stand out.

"I didn't know there were hype houses back then," I said.

She sputtered a laugh. "He put on a show of my photography. Here at the house. It was a kind of fundraiser. He told me that he sold my work to . . . collectors. For a lot of money. Or what seemed to me at the time like a lot of money. Christ, I feel stupid. Of course there weren't any collectors."

I wasn't sure what she wanted me to do.

"Do you want me to take the video down?" I asked. "I think you're one of the only people who has seen it."

I pulled up the video on my own phone. The view count was now over 80,000. Becca's fans were flooding the comments with rabbit emojis.

"Leave it up," Dayna said. "I'm going to send him the link myself."

After she left, I watched it again. *I found these huge photographs of Becca hidden in the house.* I had been so confident. I'd made yet another mistake and now that mistake was going viral. I dry swallowed one of Becca's pills, even though consuming something that had once belonged to her brought me no closer to finding her.

They're photographs of Dayna, I texted Jake. **I feel so stupid.**

He didn't respond.

In my notifications tab, I saw the truck driver's video again, and I felt flattened. Incapable of responding to him, I closed my eyes and let the medication knock me out.

When I woke up, I didn't know if I'd been asleep for minutes or hours. My phone was still in my hand.

There was a new notification. Becca Chambers had tagged me in a video. It was the first video she'd posted in three months.

I checked that it was really her account and not a copycat account with the same photo and bio. She was filming against a background I didn't recognize, but it was definitely her account. I watched her pale hands shuffle the cards, which were black with a gilded sun and moon and stars. Her nails were short and unpainted. She chose a card at random and held it close to the camera: in the center, the Knight of Swords rode a unicorn. Becca propped up the card inside a bowl.

You're getting closer @littleorphanOlivia, it said in the caption. Hashtag rabbithole. She was playing along with us. I forgot to breathe. Immediately, I searched the significance of the Knight of Swords: big opportunity, assertive, direct, seize the moment, daring, brave, soldier.

It was only on my fourth watch that I realized the bowl was yellow.

DAYNA

"He's your Sue Gambino," Jake said. Owen Wilson was in his arms. We were standing in front of the blank wall in the guest house. There were several aluminum hooks mounted to the wall, holding nothing.

"You think he's obsessed with me."

"Obviously he's obsessed with you."

I swirled the wine in my glass as the memories flashed on a slide projector carousel: the drive up the hill, Craig squeezing my shoulders, posing in the pink bedroom, cold wine on the terrace, the city below us like a blanket of stars. The beginning of my life. The bedroom photos I edited and never posted. That last black shadow.

"I quit something I was good at," I said, "because of him. I can't believe I quit because of him." Once I said it out loud, I realized that as angry as I was at Craig, I was even more furious at my younger self for giving up. I wanted to shake her. I may have had the talent, all those years ago, but I lacked the nerve.

O.W. sensed my distress and started to twitch; Jake gently put him down on the rug. I poured us both more wine and we sat on the couch.

"What did Craig do to you?"

"It's not what you're thinking," I said. Already, the story was spinning out of control. It was easy to imagine all the ways successful older men preyed on younger women with big dreams. Maybe Jake thought I'd been assaulted and I'd come back here to reenact my trauma. But Craig had never even come to my room that night, when I wanted him to. Craig had been engaged. Why hadn't he told me he was engaged?

"It's complicated," I said.

"You can tell me."

"He invited me here when I was your age, to exhibit my photography. There were twelve prints and he told me he sold them all to collectors."

Jake looked again at the blank wall.

"Oh shit," he said.

"After that, I became extremely self-conscious. I thought that all these people were watching me, expecting me to do amazing work or something. I thought the bar was so high. I couldn't do it. I couldn't be the center of so much attention. I ended up getting a job writing about the kind of people who seek attention. That felt more comfortable. But I never knew that he . . ." I covered my face with my hand.

"Olivia thought she screwed up. But she didn't. You're a clue."

"What do you mean?" I looked at him.

"Becca didn't respond to the video of Piper and the tarot card. She responded to the video of *your photographs*. That's when she told Olivia, *you're getting closer*. Craig has a type. You're it. And Becca looks just like you."

"Why, because we both have dark hair?"

"And sad eyes. Maybe Craig invited Becca here because

of her content, but he made her stop posting, too. But now she's back. Because of you."

"I don't have sad eyes."

Jake took my face between his hands and studied it. I held my breath until he finally kissed me. His warm hands slid around my waist, under my sweater, slowly traveling higher. My skin felt like it was sparkling. I reclined back against the arm of the couch, gave him space to move on top of me. I laced my fingers through his belt loops and pulled. He slid one hand under my back to unclasp my bra. I peeked at the blinds, to double-check they were shut. No one could see us. No one could see us.

"Does this place have a bed?" he whispered.

That was when his phone started vibrating on the coffee table.

"It's Olivia," he said. "I don't have to answer it."

"Go ahead," I said.

We both sat up and adjusted our clothing as if she could see us from her bedroom window. He put the call on speaker.

"You're not answering your texts!" Olivia blurted, breathless.

"Sorry," Jake said. "What's up?"

"Those aren't her hands," she said.

"What?" I asked.

"Is Dayna there?"

"Hi," I said. "What do you mean, those aren't her hands?"

"It's Becca's real account, but in the new video—they're not Becca's hands."

I looked at Jake. "Wait," he told Olivia, "we're gonna look right now."

I picked up my own phone. There were several missed calls and texts from Craig that I dodged in order to rewatch the video.

"She doesn't have long nails in this one," I said.

"It's more than the nails. Look at the fingers," Olivia said. "Read the comments. I'm not the only one who noticed."

There were so many comments. "This is amazing," I said.

"If these aren't Becca's hands, whose hands are they?" Jake asked.

"That's what I'm trying to figure out."

"Good," I said. "Maybe there are some theories in fan forums. Let us know what you find."

"Maybe we should do it together," Olivia said.

Jake looked at me. *I can't*, I mouthed.

"You're good at this stuff," Jake told her. "You know all the forums."

I nodded.

"Okay," she said, dejected.

"Goodnight, Olivia," I said. "We'll talk first thing in the morning."

Jake stood up from the couch. "Carpe diem?" He extended one hand.

I took him to bed.

EVERYTHING WAS GOING so well. House of Scaccabarozzi quickly sold out of the peach dress Olivia wore in the viral video; in the comments, people were asking where they could buy posters of my self-portraits, as if they were official merchandise. I told Annabelle to set up an online storefront. On my hard drive, I still had the digital files from twenty years ago. Why should Craig be the only one who had them? They could be decorating the walls of teenage girls' bedrooms all over the country. I could be a rediscovered artist.

You can't avoid me forever, Craig texted.

Once I found all the old photos on my hard drive, I opened our chat window and sent him the ones he'd never seen, of me in Marion's bed with the shadow at the door. I was regressing. I was being deliberately inscrutable, to punish him for lying to me.

He didn't respond.

I emailed Annabelle and told her to add the diptych to the store.

Sean's proposal to Piper had been viewed seven million times. There was even a comment on that video from Soraya, Piper's ex–best friend from her last hype house, that said happy for u, which had garnered over three thousand likes and triggered a wave of response videos from the Piper fandom, who were thrilled at the friends' reunion, and the anti-Piper fandom, who interpreted the comment as scathing sarcasm.

Most importantly, Becca was back. She was, miraculously, a part of the campaign. Olivia reported that some fans thought her account had been hacked, and that explained the unfamiliar hands, while others insisted that an autoimmune disorder could explain both her absence and a change in the color and texture of her hands.

"It's not just the color of her skin, though," Olivia told me. "It's the size of her hands. Even the wrists are bigger."

Other sleuths were trying to decode the connection between the Eight of Swords card that Piper wore strapped to her dress and the Knight of Swords in Becca's comeback video. What was in between the Eight of Swords and the Knight of Swords?

Nine of Swords: You're weeping in bed, obsessed with worry. Nightmares.

Ten of Swords: You've been stabbed in the back.

Page of Swords: You're clever. You know how to turn a conflict into an opportunity.

On a podcast, when asked what she'd been watching lately, Chrissy Teigen said, "Is anyone else following this hype house drama like it's *Blair Witch Project* 2.0?" We turned the audio clip into a meme. Morgan lip-synced Chrissy's words in a "get ready with me" video; Sean filmed Piper holding a flashlight under her face in the dark, pretending to cry, in a parody that showed off her new engagement ring.

Now the press was paying attention.

My former colleague Meg Frank reached out to interview me about the campaign for *Rolling Stone.*

"Dayna," she said. "Long time."

"Thanks for reaching out," I said.

Once I gave her permission to record, Meg said, "Over the past several months, a few hype houses have dissolved or disbanded. Some of these creators are really young and they say their managers have taken advantage of them."

"I'm sorry," I said, "what's the angle of this piece?"

Meg paused. Then she said, "Do you remember Brittany Murphy?"

"Of course I remember Brittany Murphy."

"We covered it."

We had both been working at *EW* when she died. The whole city was shocked. The media fed on the story for weeks. The coroner said she died of pneumonia and severe anemia; they found pain meds and three different benzos in her bloodstream. There were two dozen empty pill bottles found at the scene. Meg and I competed for scoops about the controlling husband, how he'd whittled away at Brittany, and what he was doing now in the house in the Hollywood Hills with Brittany's mother. Was he drugging her, too? Were they sleeping together? Meg would show up at the house and wait for the husband to come out; I didn't know what she planned to say to him that would get him to talk to her instead of any of the other reporters trying the same tactic. I snooped online, searching for sources who could tell me about their relationship. When she returned from her field trips and found me still hunched over my computer monitor, she would perform exasperation at my laziness.

Five months later, the husband was dead, too. That story had both our bylines.

"Beautiful young women move to Hollywood, hoping to get discovered, but sometimes they get discovered by dangerous charlatans," Meg said. "It's an old story."

"Yeah," I said, "but it's not the only story. Have you reached out to Jake or Olivia, to ask them how they've benefited from being a part of the Deckler House?"

"I'm happy to talk to them. My question is how you and Mr. Deckler take care of your creators, and protect them."

"They're not my children," I said. "They're all adults. They're professionals. I help them manage opportunities as they come in, and we work collaboratively on the content. I give them a say in what we create and what gets shared with the public."

"Have you witnessed any behavior of Mr. Deckler's that would lead you to believe he caused Becca to run away from the house, or worse?"

"Or worse?"

"Do you think Mr. Deckler harmed Becca in any way?"

"You're fishing, Meg. This isn't Me Too Mad Libs. I don't know if I ever told you this, but Craig gave me my first opportunity in LA. He showed my photographs at the Deckler House. It launched my career. I would not have come back here if I didn't trust him." I was not going to let her ruin my work by publishing rumors and allegations. If she tried to take down Craig, I would suffer the consequences. Fail or succeed, the campaign was mine.

"Congratulations," she said, flat.

"I'll send you some of the photographs, in case you want to use them in your story. A couple of them were taken at the house."

Meg cleared her throat. "Some of Becca's fans are angry at the hoax."

"Angry where?"

"Like on Reddit," she said.

Meg was using Reddit for journalism. Amazing trajectory.

"Ah," I said. "Well, it's not a hoax."

"Can you elaborate?"

"It's not like we staged her disappearance. House of Scaccabarozzi came to us with a unique opportunity, and I said, let's see where this goes. Becca's decision to start posting content again was organic."

"You mean you're not in contact with her?"

"That's correct," I said.

"So you have no idea how your own campaign will end?"

I laughed. "I guess not," I said. "I guess I'm violating social media manager best practices."

Meg didn't think this was funny. "Okay. Last question. About the ethics of true crime content. Can the victim consent? What about the family and friends of the victim, who have to be reminded of their loved one's death or disappearance or assault?"

This was the journalist who'd stood outside Brittany Murphy's house, salivating for a quote from the creepy con artist who drugged his wife?

"There isn't a crime here, Meg, and you know that. This isn't *Serial.* This is a mystery you can shop. The future of media is retail. There. I gave you your pull quote. Now if you'll excuse me, I have forty-eight hours to finish planning Piper and Sean's wedding."

I just had to make it through the next couple of days. All

the wedding details could be coordinated with Paula; I would talk to Morgan about décor. But if all the creators were in the wedding, who would watch?

Who do you know who could be seat-fillers on short notice? I texted the group.

Then I called Mollie. She answered on the first ring.

"How did you know?" she asked.

"Know what?"

"One of my embryos is normal," she said. "I just found out. You're the first person I've told."

"That's wonderful," I said. "Wow. What does that mean?"

"It means they can implant it. How did you know?"

"I was just thinking about you," I said.

"How *are* you?"

"I'm good!"

"You're seeing someone."

I laughed. "How is it possible that I can say six words to you and you know everything I'm not telling you?"

"I'm an intuitive Libra."

"Listen, I have a favor to ask you," I said. "It requires driving to the east side."

I was genuinely happy for Mollie. She was so close to getting what she wanted. She'd steered her destiny in the direction she wanted to go. She would be one of those moms who loved getting her fingers messy in paint and cutting sandwiches into fun shapes. And at the same time, a childish part of me felt left behind. There was no beginning to look forward to. Ahead, all I could see were endings.

I booked a red-eye from LAX the night of the wedding. I called my dad to tell him I would be home soon.

"I spoke to a journalist today," I said.

We were in my bed. It was well past midnight, hours after his bedtime livestream.

"She asked me how I take care of my creators."

Jake laughed. "Did you tell her you provide certain services?"

"Yes. I'm a service provider." I turned to rest my cheek against his smooth chest. "Please rate and review."

"Four and a half stars."

"Is that all?"

"You'll have to earn the other half," he said. He traced a line with his finger down my torso, until he was between my legs once more.

"Again?" I laughed.

"Again," he said.

I wanted his touch to wipe my mind clean of thoughts, but I was too preoccupied with how our story would end. Jake was another dazzling charm on my bracelet. I'd never committed to anything in my life that outlasted its sparkle. I only risked intimacy with the ephemeral—fame, youth, the internet. We were already finished the second we began.

"Stop," I said. "I lied to you. About my age."

"You're thirty-nine."

"I told you I was thirty-two."

"I saw your age when I found the Reddit post."

I squeezed my eyes shut. "I'm sorry," I said. "I shouldn't have lied."

"You look so sad," Jake said.

"You deserve a girlfriend," I told him. "A real girlfriend. Someone your age that you can be seen with in public."

"You don't think I would go out in public with you?"

"Come on, Jake," I said. I stared into his eyes. "We have an expiration date. That's the only reason this works."

He kissed me. I held his face in my hand.

"I want to take care of you," Jake said quietly.

"Okay," I said. "Just tonight."

I lay on my stomach and he entered me from behind, my

face pressed into the pillows, one of his hands on my breast. When I felt completely smothered, I came.

THE NEXT MORNING, I saw that Meg had used the black-and-white photo of me on Marion's bed in the article; she embedded Olivia's and Becca's videos. Immediately, I sent an email.

> Hi Sofia (and Annabelle!),
>
> See below for a few links of the great press the campaign is getting—beyond even my own high expectations!
>
> Click here for Becca's most recent video
>
> Can Dayna Lev Resurrect the Deckler House from the Dead—And Solve an Online Mystery Along the Way? (*Rolling Stone*)
>
> Cheers,
Dayna

> Dear Dayna,
>
> We are so enthusiastic at the pleasant response you have been receiving. I could not read the article without a subscription but I share in this celebration with you.
>
> Please excuse me for being direct, but in our contract, you have agreed for ALL the creators in the house to demonstrate the collection. In Becca's video you kindly sent us, it is difficult to view what she is

wearing. Please can you guarantee in next video that
she is wearing House of Scaccabarozzi? We defer to
Becca on styling the look because we know it will be
authentic and there will be a wonderful demand! Is
any of this not clear?

grazie mille,
Sofia

If we couldn't get Becca in a House of Scaccabarozzi outfit, could they say we hadn't fulfilled our end of the contract? Did that mean we wouldn't get paid? For all the work
we'd already done? Even though they were already making
sales because of our content? Which was all my idea? There
was no one I could ask. This was my fucking job. I'd fucked
this up entirely by myself. I'd self-fucked. My hands shook
as I sucked my vape.

Sofia,

Of course I understand! I will talk to Becca about it.
Sometimes the creators can be pretty opinionated
about what they wear but I will try haha

Dayna

There was one person who knew where Becca actually
was, and that was Craig.

No more secrets. He had to tell me where she was. Then
I could figure out how to get clothes to her. She didn't even
have to come back to the house! She could stay on her compound in the middle of red America. How much would it
cost to overnight couture to Alaska?

Craig answered on the first ring.

"Dayna," he said, relieved.

"Where are you?"

"In my room."

"Stay there," I said. "I'm coming right now."

I brushed my teeth and dabbed concealer under my eyes. I curled my lashes and stroked them with mascara. "I do not have sad eyes," I said to my reflection, forcing a smile.

"I am not here to blow up your life," I said, still smiling like a possessed child in a horror film.

O.W. didn't want me to go. He stayed on the bath mat near my feet as I got ready. My little shadow.

I entered the house through the sliding doors off the terrace, hoping no one would see me go to Craig's room. But Morgan was in the kitchen, eating cereal alone in the dark.

"You scared the shit out of me," I said.

"I need to talk to you about something." Her lower lip trembled. Please, God. No.

"Can it wait?"

"I guess," she said. "I guess I can always go last."

I looked at the ceiling so I wouldn't roll my eyes. "Give me a few minutes. I just have to talk to Craig first, okay? It's important."

"Whatever." She hunched over her cereal bowl.

I'd never seen Morgan so aloof and self-pitying. Had one of the other girls been mean to her? Was she jealous of how well Olivia's video had performed? Did I have a sandwich board around my neck that said "psychiatric help five cents"?

Now I'd forgotten what I'd planned to say to Craig the second I entered his room. Something direct, but also alluring. Not too cutting or confrontational. I would acknowledge that I'd been avoiding him but also intimate that I wanted to continue working with him. There was a little problem, but we could fix it *together*.

I remembered what Jake had said: *You're a clue.* Was I?

There's something that comes over me when I'm inside this house, I'd tell Craig. *Do you know if Becca felt it, too?*

I took a deep breath. His door was open. As soon as I entered, Craig shut the door behind me, blocking my exit with his body.

"I am not going to let this happen again," he said.

"Let what happen?"

"I'm not going to let you avoid me for another twenty years."

The anger rushed to my head, instant and familiar. I was stuck in traffic on the 101, reading Luke's post. I was sixteen. I was twelve. I was a girl waiting to reach the age when men would take her anger as seriously as their own.

"You lied to me," I said.

"I was only trying to help you."

"Help me? You told me you sold them, but you kept them all for yourself! How does that help me in any way? I could have been an artist."

"I didn't want to break your heart," Craig said.

He moved away from the door and led me over to the bed. We sat on the edge.

"I didn't want you to think you'd come all this way to show your photographs and no one was interested in them. I didn't want you to be disappointed."

I didn't know what to say. I looked around the room, at all Becca's girlish trinkets, her fairy postcards and angel sketches. The distance between my life and Becca's was thousands of days. I used to think I was so mature for my age; after all, I'd flown all the way to LA without telling my parents. Maybe Becca felt the same way. But from Craig's perspective, I was just like Becca: a girl whose feelings needed protecting.

"I thought you'd sold my photos to complete strangers. I thought all these people were following me, and I couldn't stand the pressure. I didn't know what to post next. I quit photography."

Craig took my face between his hands and kissed my forehead. I closed my eyes.

"You could have told me," he said.

"I was young. I was embarrassed. I didn't know how to handle it." The narcotic effect of the house was dissolving my anger. My limbs felt loose in their joints. My face felt flushed.

Slowly, I kissed Craig, like it was the first time. He ran his fingers through my hair. If Jake was stamped with an expiration date, then Craig was nonperishable. He was history. He was a block of carved concrete; he belonged to the house. The house wanted me to belong to it, too.

I broke our kiss. "No more secrets, okay?"

"Okay," he said.

"I know you know where Becca is."

He clenched his jaw, said nothing.

"And I need you to tell me, because if you don't, we're going to lose the whole campaign. That means no money for the renovation, no money for me. All this work for nothing? I would be *so disappointed*." I thought this might make him laugh—smile at least—but Craig withdrew from me and put his face in his hands. He didn't seem angry at me— he seemed tormented. I rubbed his back.

"Becca is playing along with us, but we have to ship the clothes to her so she can wear them in her videos," I said quietly, like I was soothing an upset child. "I just need her address. I'll handle everything. She won't even have to know that you gave it to me."

"Dayna, you don't understand."

"But I want to understand. Help me."

Finally, he sat up to look at me.

"She went back to live with her mother."

I lit up. "That's great! Where?"

"Dawn lives in Fresno."

Becca was in *Fresno*?

"Wait," I said. "Dawn-your-fiancée?"

Craig looked at the rug. "That was a long time ago."

I grabbed his hand. We were so close to the edge of revelation, I was terrified that I would say something that would shut him down. "You can tell me," I said.

"No, I'm breaking a promise I made. This could be very bad for Becca. She was not well when she left. She was having visions and hearing messages. I tried to get her help, but she refused to take medication. Thought everyone was talking about her. She said, *Dad, they're sending me messages.* And after what happened to my mother—"

"What the actual fuck, Craig," I said, standing up. The ground shifted under my feet and I stumbled, causing a vase of dried roses on Becca's desk to fall forward with a crash.

"Now you see why I couldn't tell you."

"No! I don't see!"

"I had to promise Becca that no one was talking about her. I had to protect her. I told you not to make those videos."

"You had a child? With Dawn?"

"Yes."

"Becca grew up here? In this house?"

"No. Dawn believed the house was possessed with a demonic energy. She didn't think it was safe and they left when Becca was two. She only let me have her in the summers."

I almost asked, *Why didn't you follow them?* But I knew the answer without asking. Dawn chose her daughter and Craig chose his house. He was committed to the house.

"You're doing all this for her," I said. "You want to leave the house to Becca. She's the heir."

Craig nodded. "It's for her future. It's all I have to leave her."

I sat back down beside him. "Would you like to see her? How she's doing?"

"More than anything."

"Drive with me. We'll go together." Fresno was only a few hours away.

"Maybe I should call and let her know we're coming."

"It's better if we just show up. How is Dawn going to refuse to let you see your daughter if you're there at her door?"

I told him to meet me outside in fifteen minutes. All I had to do was pull the clothes from the boxes in Jake's room and grab my purse from the guest house. Would Becca want to come to Piper's wedding? She'd already shown us she was willing to play along. Maybe I could even persuade her to drive back with us.

When I got home, Owen Wilson wasn't there to greet me and follow me optimistically to the refrigerator. I called his name and waited for his little nose to pop out from under the couch. Nothing. I checked all his favorite napping spots; I looked behind the bathroom door. My chest clenched with panic. I climbed the narrow stairs to the loft where I slept— there was no way he could hop up here on his own, but I had to know—and no Owen.

Where was his travel carrier?

I sucked my vape. I sucked it again. Someone had been in my house. There were no other signs of intrusion or theft, except for the missing carrier—and my missing son. I never locked the door—the whole property was gated. The only people who could get inside my house were the same people I worked with every day. I'd been naïve to trust them.

Did someone take Owen Wilson? I asked the group chat.

No! Olivia texted right away, with the wide-eye emoji.
take???????? Piper asked.
I'll help you look, Jake said. Don't worry we'll find him.

That wouldn't work. Wherever he was right now, he was probably terrified. I couldn't have a search party look for him—to O.W., that would look like a pack of coyotes hunting him instead of just one.

An email came up on my phone from Annabelle. The subject line read, "My turn."

When I opened it, it was a photo of Owen Wilson. It looked like he was in Morgan's bedroom. I could see her tripod ring light. She was recording something with him.

I stared at the photo, waiting for my brain to catch up with my eyes. How could Morgan send a photo from Annabelle's email address? Her turn for what? *I need to talk to you about something.* And I had told her it had to wait! I had aged a hundred years since coming to this house and now I was ancient, decrepit, a moldering skeleton, staggering through a crypt of my false assumptions. Did Annabelle even exist?

What the duck Morgan, I replied.
FUCK
WHAT THE FUCK

Morgan was already crying when she opened the door to my room. I was in bed, stoned on pills, struggling to keep my eyes open on the Reddit thread I was reading.

"I need your help," she said.

"Okay," I said.

"Owen Wilson is missing," she said.

"I know."

She wiped her nose on her kimono sleeve. "I kidnapped him. But then I lost him. And now he's missing."

"Holy buckets," I said. "Why would you do that?"

She squinted her tiny eyes. "Dayna has her favorites. Don't pretend like you don't know you're one of them. Jake got to livestream with him and Piper and Sean got to do their proposal video and you got to dress him up as an orphan. What about me? What about me and Owen Wilson? Don't we deserve a storyline? I wanted to dress him up as a rabbit. It would be meta."

I was too high to understand the vision. "Did you ask Dayna if you could film with him?"

"Dayna never has any time for me. She's always with Jake. Or Craig. Craig or Jake. My room is right next to Jake's. They aren't *that* quiet."

I forgot to blink as my imagination filled in the details. It was one kind of horror to envision Craig preying on Becca and another kind of horror to picture Dayna and Jake. Touching. Kissing. Topless. If Craig was the one who told us what was forbidden, Dayna was the one who issued commands. What did Jake see in Dayna? What didn't he see in *me?*

"Don't be naïve, Olivia."

"Where did you last see Owen Wilson?"

"In my room," she said. "I turned around for one second. . . . I don't know where he went." She covered her face with her hands and resumed sobbing. She had long fingers, and short, clean nails. I knew those hands.

I got out of bed so fast, the blood rushed to my head.

"I'm not naïve," I said.

How had Morgan done it? How had she posted the video to Becca's account from her phone? Did she know Becca's password? Unless she had Becca's phone. But how could Becca exist without her phone? To exist without a phone, you'd have to be dead. When I'd said, *I'm here because of Becca*, Morgan said, *So am I.* Morgan had to know where Becca was. The question was, *what had she done to her?*

Dayna was downstairs, yelling Morgan's name. Morgan just stood there in my room, like a bronze statue. Like if she stood still, this would all go away.

The adrenaline was overcoming the pills in my system. I reached up and grabbed her by the shoulders, turned her around, and pushed her out the door. "We have to find him," I said. "I'll help you. If we find him, you won't be in trouble. Everything will be okay."

As we went downstairs, Morgan held on to my arm, loudly whispering in my ear, "We can tell Dayna it was your idea. You thought Owen Wilson should be in the campaign. Because it's called Rabbit Hole, right? You found, like, a new clue for the rabbit to sniff. A hair scrunchie or a pair of underwear. I didn't even know that you hadn't already gotten Dayna's permission. I just helped you get him from her—"

I jerked my arm away and stumbled on the next step. "No way," I said. "I had nothing to do with this."

"Be careful, Olivia. You seem a little . . . unsteady."

I broke away from her and ran down the remaining steps. Everyone was standing at the bottom of the staircase, drawn out of their rooms by Dayna's yelling.

"What's going on?" Jake asked. He was shirtless.

"Dayna never gave me a turn," Morgan yelled from the stairs.

"A turn at *what*?" Dayna yelled back.

"Making a video with O.W.!" Her mouth was wet from crying; her braces dripped.

"I'm sorry, okay?" Dayna said. "You're right. That was an oversight. Of course you deserve a turn."

But I could tell she was frustrated with Morgan. Her tone wasn't soothing at all.

"You give all your attention to Olivia and Jake," Morgan continued. "You're obsessed with them. Do you think we don't know they're your favorites? I'm just the stylist. 'Can you style Piper?' 'Would you mind doing all the décor for the wedding?' You don't even care about *my* content."

Dayna gritted her teeth. "Of course I care about your content," she said.

With one hand, Sean was eating a piece of jerky, and with the other, he was filming them.

"Sean, please," Dayna said.

"You never know. You might want it later. Evidence."

"I'd be happy to let you make content with Owen Wilson," Dayna told Morgan, "as soon as he's had a chance to recover from this stressful situation. Just tell me where he is."

"I don't know where he is," Morgan said. "I lost him."

Craig found us all standing in the hallway. "I was waiting outside for you," he said to Dayna. "What happened?"

"Morgan murdered my son," Dayna said, and burst into tears. "She's a killer." Craig wrapped her in his arms as she cried into his chest. He gave Morgan a dark look.

Jake looked wild. He held his hair off his forehead with both hands like it would help him think. "We don't know that he's dead," he said. "Morgan? Is he dead?"

"I'm supposed to be getting married tomorrow," Piper said.

"Babe," Sean said, "come on."

Dayna slid from Craig's arms and collapsed on the tile floor. "I never should have come here. This house is cursed." Both Craig and Jake hovered above her, trying to console her.

"I work so hard and no one cares," Morgan said. "No one appreciates everything I do to make this place a success."

I felt like I was in a bad play, one of those French ones where everyone turns into a rhinoceros and all the walls are mirrors and someone throws a party but the guests are invisible and the chairs onstage stay empty.

I was walking backwards, slowly, so I would notice if anyone saw me disappear from the scene. I remembered what Dayna had told me about Owen Wilson: He wouldn't head toward an open space like the hallway or the living room, where there were predators. He would go huddle in some dark corner where he wouldn't be perceived. I thought he was probably still inside Morgan's bedroom and she hadn't looked long enough. She didn't know where to look.

The second I slipped inside her bedroom, I shut the door so O.W. and I were trapped in here together. It was also quieter with the door shut. I knew he wouldn't come out if he could hear everyone screaming at one another. He might be in even more distress now, if he heard Dayna crying. I didn't call his name.

I scanned the room, looking for what Morgan might have missed. First I got down on my hands and knees and looked under the bed with my phone's flashlight. Nothing but dust and socks. There was his travel carrier, but he hadn't hopped back inside it. Next to her vanity, there was a stack of cardboard boxes from all the brands that sent her makeup and clothes. I carefully looked inside the empty boxes. No Owen. Taped to the vanity mirror was the photo booth strip I'd found of Becca and Morgan. And there, right there on the vanity, impossible to miss, was the yellow bowl. Becca's favorite bowl. *No one appreciates everything I do to make this place a success.* Becca had never responded to my video. It was Morgan all along. Morgan was scamming us. But why?

The house knows, I thought.

I put my hand on the pink wallpaper, squeezed my eyes shut, and whispered, "Help me help me help me."

When I opened my eyes, I saw the door to the closet was open. I ran inside and closed the door behind me. It was pitch-dark; I had no idea where the light switch was. I got down on my knees with my flashlight and looked for Owen behind the pants and shoe racks of pumps and flats, boots and slippers. This was exactly the place he would hide. I would find him for Dayna. He couldn't be dead. He was just a baby. He was an orphan. Until I found him, he was a hundred percent still alive. I didn't realize I was crying until I tasted the tears.

The closet went on and on, a claustrophobic hallway, a

secret passageway, a dark black mouth. Whoever had designed this house was obsessed with confining its inhabitants in narrow corridors and low-ceilinged rooms. I kept waiting for the expansive release that always followed the contraction. I had to go slowly so I wouldn't miss Owen's little body. I listened for subtle movement. Silk and wool brushed my hands and cheeks as I crawled deeper. It smelled like leather and jasmine perfume. There were decades of clothes crammed from floor to ceiling. I was tunneling through history.

At the end, instead of hitting a wall, I arrived at a blue door. I stood up, my heart in my throat. I wiped my tears from my face.

The polite thing to do was knock, so that's what I did.

When the girl opened the door, she was holding him in her arms. His nose twitched with life. Lit up by my flashlight, her face was milk-pale and stoic. Her hair hung in long, dark curtains. She looked so familiar. She looked just like Marion. If it hadn't been for the adrenaline coursing through my blood, I might have thought the blue door was the threshold of death and I was meeting Marion and Owen Wilson on the other side.

"Becca?"

"I've been waiting for you," she said. "You're just in time."

BECCA

I recognized her immediately as my Queen of Cups.

"My queen," I said. I set the rabbit down on the floor and he hopped under the crib. The queen shut the door to the nursery behind her; poor thing, she looked as scared as her bunny.

"Please, sit down." All I had to do was gesture to the rocking chair and it grew eight feet high to become her throne, inlaid with shells and sea glass. Sand under my fingernails, sun in my eyes.

"I'm not sure if you know this," she said, "but a lot of people are looking for you?"

"I had a lot of work to do. And I couldn't do it with everyone jamming the channel."

I arranged my watercolors on the drafting table Morgan had set up in the corner. In the little bathroom, I filled a jam jar with water for my brushes.

The Queen of Cups was looking at all the cards I'd hung. The old wallpaper, with its woodland creatures and fairy-tale characters, was sweet, but I'd covered it up with string, where I clipped the finished paintings, organized by suit, with wooden clothespins.

Her robe would be peach, with soft blue waves lapping at her hem. Her cup and crown would both be gold.

"You've been painting us?"

I took down the Four of Pentacles to show her Morgan in a puffer coat, hunched over a gold coin, hoarding more gold coins under her feet. The Four of Pentacles wears the crown of a king, but no one regards her as one.

"Has Morgan been keeping you, like a prisoner or something?"

I shook my head and smiled.

"Sometimes she lets me out at night to creep around," I said.

"But why can't you stay out there? With us?"

"A prophet has no honor in his own house," I said.

Her eyes grew wide and she sat up tall in her throne, ready to listen.

IN HIGH SCHOOL, I found a subreddit for the Deckler House. There, it was rumored that a baby had been born in the house in the early 2000s, but no one knew what happened to it; a few people thought it had been murdered in a ritual sacrifice because the house was designed to look like a Mayan temple. *No I just live with my mom now,* I wanted to post. But I was afraid they would search for us, and I wanted to protect my mom from even knowing the forum existed. She wanted me to have a relationship with my dad, but she didn't want me to have a relationship with his house. She suspected that the two years I'd spent there as a baby explained my strange infection. She always regretted not leaving with me sooner.

We are all given spiritual gifts, but I learned at a young age to hide mine. Fear flashed on her face when I told my mom what I could see: injured pets, lost jobs, impending death. I was always finding white feathers. She prayed for whatever was inside me to leave me in peace, unharmed. But the praying didn't change what I was able to see; it only separated me from her. I couldn't be who she wanted me to be, so I learned what to keep secret. I went to church every Sunday and youth group every Wednesday. At the food pantry, I volunteered to help paint a community mural.

At night and on weekends, when I said I was doing homework, I read the forum. That was where I found @annabellesghost.

As one of the forum's moderators, she posted scans from old newspapers, photographs of my grandparents I'd never seen before, and images of several unsigned paintings that another user had discovered in a Nevada thrift store, believing they might be Marion's. Annabelle's own theory for the house's curse traced back to its architect, who left his wife for another woman and built an estate in Wisconsin where they could hide from everyone who thought their relationship was a scandal, but then a mentally ill servant lit the house on fire and murdered her with a hatchet while the architect was away. He also murdered her two children. *George Deckler also cheated on his wife. It led to her death by suicide,* she wrote. *Coincidence? Or destiny?*

My father never wanted to talk about my grandmother's death. Here was someone who wanted to talk about it all the time. When @annabellesghost said she was doing her senior project on the Deckler House, I realized we were the same age. I sent her a direct message.

I live there, I said.

You LIVE there??

In the summers. With my dad.

YOUR the baby?

Shhhh don't tell, I said. Where do you live?

I can see your house from my window, she said. Do you think I could interview your dad?

Her name was Morgan Bokelberg; her avatar was a character in *House on Haunted Hill.* I told my mom I wanted to go to LA for Memorial Day weekend and I invited Morgan over.

Because of her chosen avatar, I expected Wednesday Addams, but Morgan got out of her old Subaru wearing shorts and a T-shirt and started taking pictures before we'd even said hello. She arrived as a tourist to our lives.

My dad showed her the wall in his office of framed photographs of actresses he had posed with years ago, before I was born, when the house was still used as a movie set. She interviewed him: "I read somewhere that frat boys did initiation rites here after *House on Haunted Hill* came out. Were they arrested? Do you have their mug shots? I heard they were covered in pig's blood."

"They finally left us alone after my dad started sitting out in our driveway every night, with his dog and a shotgun."

"No way," Morgan said.

Morgan was surprised that I didn't have a bigger bedroom, but I liked my little room at the back, off the kitchen. I had it exactly the way I wanted it, with a daybed, a single window, and plain white walls I could decorate with my drawings. All my tarot decks were at my dad's house—he was the one who bought them for me, because my mom didn't allow them at her house. He never made me feel ashamed for wanting to use the cards to make sense and order of my premonitions.

Morgan was shocked I didn't stay in my grandmother's bedroom.

"That's where I would sleep," she said, "if I lived here."

"We can sleep in there tonight if you want," I said.

"Oh my God, I love you."

I blushed and looked away from her. I moved through the world shrouded in a heavy cloud; I'd never met anyone who wanted to climb inside the cloud with me.

That night, we were under the covers of the canopy bed when Morgan showed me the platform for the first time. It was one in the morning. I was looking over her shoulder at her phone and I said, "Show me again." Two white girls were dancing to a song they knew the words to. The video was long, like a full-length mirror, instead of wide, like a window. It had been viewed twelve hundred times. At the end, they laughed and stopped the recording by reaching a finger toward us like they were God and we were Adam reaching back.

The very next day, Morgan started making content. She got up close and personal with the stained-glass windows in the living room and the glass mosaic above the fireplace and the patterned blocks that wrapped the exterior. She gleefully ransacked my grandmother's closet, dressed me up in a short dress and a hat covered in daisies, and filmed me from behind, walking the terrace and then stopping to look down at the holes in the south side of the house, gaping like caves carved out of the hill. She put all the clips together and added voice-over with facts and dates about the design and construction. When my dad saw them, he thought they were amazing; he couldn't believe he hadn't thought to make videos of the house before.

"You've made the house come back to life," he told Morgan. "Do you think the videos could help us raise awareness and bring in donations for the restoration?"

"A thousand percent," she said. Before she hit post, she added text on-screen asking viewers to donate.

But no one watched these videos. Donations did not pour in.

This was no problem for Morgan. She just needed to find her niche. Or help me find mine.

"Have you ever done tarot readings?"

"Only for myself," I admitted. I didn't tell her I'd never had any friends to practice on.

"Do me," she said. She stared hard at my deck. "I'm thinking of my question. I'm not going to tell you what it is. I want to see if it really works."

"You don't have to tell me your question," I said.

I did a mini Celtic Cross reading for Morgan. In the first position, I drew the Six of Wands.

"This means success is in reach," I told her. "You'll achieve recognition."

"For my videos about the house?"

"That's too specific. I'm not sure. This next card is the complicating factor." I drew the Five of Wands and laid it horizontally across the Six. "Oh, there's going to be competition and disharmony. Other people are going to bother you with their demands. You may have a rival who gets in the way of your achievement."

Morgan nodded, solemn.

"And the last card gives us guidance on how to approach the situation. The Magician is one of the Major Arcana cards, so this is a powerful guide. It means you'll use your talents to do what needs to be done."

Morgan was the only person I invited to my birthday dinner; my mom would never have come if I asked. I was wearing my favorite purple dress. Even Morgan had dressed up—the clothes in Marion's closet weren't her size, but Morgan had been inspired to go thrifting and get creative by mixing items from different decades and pairing casual with evening wear.

For the occasion, Paula set the dining room table with silver candelabras that had belonged to my great aunt Gypsy and red candlesticks that dripped wax onto a silver tray. I stared at my reflection in a vase of white lilies. For a second, it looked like there was a shadowy figure hovering behind me, but when I turned around there was no one there.

"Your aunt and I have something to tell you." My dad smiled sadly.

Morgan looked like she wished she were recording this.

"This will be our last celebration in the house."

"What?" I asked. "Why?"

He and Paula exchanged a look.

"We can't afford to keep her, Becca," she said.

"We tried," my dad said. "We tried for years. For you."

"But where will you go?"

"You don't need to worry about us," he said.

"Wait," Morgan said, "Becca will inherit the house? When you're dead?"

"She's the heir," Paula said.

My dad shook his head. "But we can't afford the restoration. Paula and I have no choice but to sell. We've tried everything else."

For a few minutes, no one spoke. Morgan carefully refilled everyone's water glasses from a crystal pitcher. I stared at my fettuccine Alfredo, but I was too emotional to take a bite. It was as if my dad had told me he was going to die. I knew the house was his life; without it, his life was over.

"What if we put the house to work?" Morgan asked. "Instead of me making videos about the house so strangers will donate, the house itself earns revenue."

"How so?" he asked.

"We invite other creators—I mean in addition to me and Becca—to move in. We all create content together."

"What do you mean?" I asked.

"Think of it like a film set," she said, explaining it to me and my dad in a way we would understand. "Becca and I are the actors, but we live on set, and we aren't playing characters. We're being ourselves, but we're still making content that people want to watch. And we could have auditions."

"Like reality TV?" He frowned.

Paula silently finished what was left in her wineglass and blotted her mouth with a linen napkin.

Morgan continued pitching my dad. He was the decision-maker. "We'll do it really professional. You'll be our talent manager. I can be your virtual assistant, so when brands email us they think you have, like, a whole staff," she said.

"Tonight is supposed to be about Becca," Paula said. I thought for a second that she was going to squeeze my hand, but she was only clearing my plate.

I stared straight ahead at one of the flickering red candles, forbidding myself to hope for anything. I would be stoic. This might be the last meal I ever ate in this house. This might be Morgan's last raid inside our treasure chest.

"It's not the worst idea, Paula," he said, sitting back in his chair, arms crossed. "Remember when I wanted to buy Bitcoin and you told me not to? Imagine if I'd bought Bitcoin when you told me not to."

I looked at my aunt. All my life she had worn the same face, a kind of mask of beautiful, gloomy endurance, as if she had grown up in a Soviet country, in the winter, without any brand-name clothes, speaking a language she never taught me, so there was no way to truly communicate with her, instead of right here, in California, playing tennis and riding horses, fortunate enough to spend a fortune, but not clever enough to earn it back once it was gone.

"Don't start, Craig," she said.

When Paula turned away to carry our plates to the kitchen, Morgan leaned in toward my dad.

"My parents will pay you rent," she said. "If you let me move in. Just until I start earning income from brands. I swear to God it can work."

"What about college?" He looked at me. I'd been planning to go to a community college near my mom's house in the fall.

Morgan answered for me.

"Becca and I both want to take a gap year. Think how good a hype house will look on our application essays next year. It's like a start-up. What's everyone else doing during their gap year? Folding T-shirts at the Galleria? Picking up coffee orders? Right? Becca?"

I looked down at the napkin in my lap to stop the room from spinning. I was the one who had brought Morgan into our house. She wanted to look in every cabinet, open every door. But if they said no to the hype house, it would confirm what I feared: that the adults in the room were even more powerless than I was. No one else was coming to save us.

When Paula came back, she was carrying a chocolate cake. Everyone sang the song; Morgan was off-key yet enthusiastic. My dad put his arm around my shoulders. Morgan pulled out her Fuji instant camera and snapped pictures of me holding my hair back, blowing out the candles in one big breath.

"Eighteen," he said. "Hard to believe." His eyes looked wet. He kissed my cheek.

"What did you wish for?" Paula asked.

"I think it could be fun," I said quietly. "To try the hype

house. More people would know about the Deckler House. People all over the world. I wished that you would tell Morgan yes." I stared at the dining table. I didn't want to see anyone's expression.

"We've tried everything else, Paula," Dad said.

"If it's my inheritance, then let me and Morgan try to keep it," I said. Morgan squeezed my hand under the table.

Paula looked at my dad. "Your call," she said finally. "If it's a disaster, you have to clean up the mess."

He and Morgan both grinned at the same time.

"Just one last thing," Morgan said. "I think it will look unprofessional if people know that Becca is your daughter."

"Becca *is* my daughter," my dad said.

"Totally get that," Morgan said. "But we don't want it to look like nepotism. To the public."

"What do you want us to do?" he asked.

"Treat me and Becca the same. Don't give her any special treatment. Pretend she just moved in."

My aunt actually laughed. "I'm not that good of an actress," she said.

"I believe it's never too late to learn new skills," Morgan said.

Three to five times a day: That's how often Morgan required us to post. Piper and Sean had each other for support; Jake had his fan club. While Morgan played dress-up on camera in her bedroom, I created my tarot videos. Take what resonates and leave the rest. A message from your ex. A secret they've been waiting to tell you. A dream they had about you last night. What to know if you find a feather on the ground. The one you've been thinking about is thinking about you, too. They want to be more than friends. This video found you for a reason. You did not stumble across this message by accident. Someone is obsessed with you. Share this with a friend to claim. People from your past are talking about you. If you feel called to stay for this reading, stay. Someone is not telling you the truth. Someone regrets what they did to you. A message for those struggling right now. You asked for a sign and this is it. You feel different lately. You're about to come into a divine blessing. Do not ignore. There is something you should be aware of. They're still not over you. Follow to claim.

It required so much more energy and focus than all the readings I'd done in private, for myself, during summer vacations. Each time I created a video, I felt the vibration of my deck and subtle forces directing me toward meaning. Every card draw was like a blood prick.

My commenters were on their knees, lapping it up. They knew I wasn't faking. I wouldn't know how to fake it.

I've tried to scroll past the readings but then I'm like . . . wait this girl's frl

wow this resonated with what is happening in my life and my mind. I claim!

he moved on but i know he's my soulmate

crying at the club rn

I claim with pure intentions

I claim with light and gratitude

thank you angel it's been a lonely healing

is my son with me can you tell did he cross over

June turned into July. The more readings I did in a day, the more I felt hollowed out, bloodless, like an empty chalice. There were some nights when I didn't even have energy to eat dinner. Once, Piper asked if I could give her a reading and I started crying from exhaustion. Morgan tucked me into bed with an aromatherapy eye pillow. Although I was careful to never show my face on camera, and my username was only my first name, my recurring nightmare was my mom seeing one of my videos and recognizing my hands.

"Don't worry," Morgan said, and ordered press-on nails from Amazon. Even my hands could wear a disguise.

One summer night, Morgan flew into my bedroom without knocking.

"You won't believe what I found in my closet." She was holding an old shoebox. Inside was a cache of small paintings and photographs. The latest discovery of Annabelle's Ghost.

"They're tarot cards," I said. The paintings were based on Pamela Colman Smith's illustrations, but the colors were darker and more sophisticated, the faces more realistic and detailed.

"Do you recognize this one?"

"That's the High Priestess," I said.

"It looks just like you. Isn't this the dress you wore to your birthday party?"

I looked closer. Usually the High Priestess wears blue, but this one was draped in purple. She had my dark, wavy hair. Around her neck, a cross. She was holding the Hebrew Bible in her lap. The High Priestess is the daughter of the stars, the guardian of untold mysteries, the most holy of all the cards. A black stone column on her left was marked with the letter B; on her right, a white column was marked C.

"Before Christ?" I guessed. Usually the letters on this card were B and J, for Boaz and Jachin, the pillars of Solomon's Temple.

"Becca Chambers," Morgan said. "Marion predicted your existence. She saw the future. I think every one of these cards is someone who lived in the house. There's a letter in here, too."

I seized the box from her hands and sat on my bed.

"'You did not stumble across this message by accident,'" I read aloud. The letter was written in small cursive handwriting on a sheet of monogrammed stationery. "'I have hidden my work until the time came to reveal it. I trust that my legacy will be completed by the destined party.'" There was no "love" or "sincerely" or "warm wishes," only the sign-off "Marion Jean Sullivan (Deckler)." I counted twenty-two paintings: she'd only gotten through the Major Arcana. On the Tower card, my grandfather George and his second wife, Viola, were plummeting from a window, headfirst toward the ground, fear written on their faces. As the Hanged Man, Marion had painted herself upside down, bound with rope to a painter's easel.

"She's also the Fool," I said. The Fool is so young and innocent that she believes she's at the beginning of a great adventure. The card shimmered in my hand, like it was gilded.

"Look," I told Morgan, "if you read the Major Arcana in order, it tells a story. The Fool must be my grandmother before she met my grandfather. She's at the beach, smiling. The next card is the Magician. Wait, I think this is my dad." Instead of a cape, she'd painted him in a three-piece suit.

"Show me," Morgan said.

"But she never met my dad."

Morgan laughed. "She gave birth to him!"

"I mean she never . . . saw him grow up." I frowned. "The third card is the High Priestess. That's me. The story is a family tree: the Fool, the Magician, and the High Priestess. My grandmother, my dad, and me."

"Who's after you?"

"The Empress. She's fertility and abundance; there are rabbits at her feet. Or she could represent material reward. I don't recognize this woman. Do you? From any of your research?"

"Is it Viola?"

"Definitely not. She's on the Tower card—see?"

"Or Paula."

"I think Paula is the Hermit," I said, flipping ahead. The Empress didn't look like my mother either.

"Let's ask your dad," Morgan said.

"Not yet." I was still processing the discovery for myself. *There is something you should be aware of. You asked for a sign and this is it. You feel different lately. You're about to come into a divine blessing. Do not ignore.* I was never cursed. I was born the High Priestess. I could see beyond the veil. How could my glimpses be evil? Were they not heaven-sent?

"What are you going to do?"

My mom had tried to rid me of my intuition; my dad had hidden Marion from me. If I finished her deck, they would see. I would show them how wrong they each had been to obstruct the path to my throne.

I claim with gratitude and light.

"I'm the destined party," I said. "I'm going to finish Marion's deck."

Once I claimed my assignment, the channel opened between me and my grandmother. She showed me where to look and how to see. Her influence was like adding a filter to a video—it gave everything extra shimmer. Watching Morgan put a bra on top of a shirt, or wear a dog collar as a choker, or hot glue stuffed animal heads to her slippers, I saw the childish Page of Wands. Piper cleaning up her spilled coffee at breakfast was the regret of the Five of Cups, and when Sean, her Page of Cups, brought her a new one, there was a fish sticking its head out of the mug. Piper didn't even notice!

"What," she said, glaring at me.

"Nothing," I said.

I watched Jake sorting through all his fan mail and pictured all his followers swarming together, naked, in a mass of flesh, until they formed a huge beast that he could ride like a horse—they screamed, they loved it—as the Knight of Pentacles. They were writhing, trying to throw him, but he tamed them, pulling on the bridle, kicking their flanks. Jake was all pentacles: grind, grind, grind.

My assignment was fifty-six cards. Five plus six is eleven, and if you add one and one, that's two. Two's a partnership. My dad once told me that Marion had gone to art school in Chicago before she married George. I wanted the person in the Deckler House forum who was an expert on Marion Deckler's art to see the finished deck and not be able to tell which of us had painted the Major Arcana, and which of us had painted the Minor.

But before I could begin painting, I had to develop my skill. I started by sketching everyone in the house and collecting my symbols: castles and thrones, cups and bowls, walls and blindfolds, angels and trumpets, swords and pillars. The first card I sketched was the Two of Cups, my grandmother and I toasting our chalices, bordered with the pattern I copied from the concrete blocks that wrapped around our house.

It wasn't easy to keep up with my posting schedule at the same time. Usually, I pulled cards and simply passed along the message they revealed to me in a video, like I worked for the postal service. *Take what resonates and leave the rest.* But a slow invasion was beginning, across the barrier that separated my life in the house from my life on the platform. I had so many followers, with so many problems. Somehow they picked up that my channel to the other side was wide-open.

That's how they were able to get in.

The first time there was a violation, I was reading a comment from one of my followers. She'd asked if her husband would ever change his mind and want her back, and he appeared to me instantly, vividly, buzz haircut and belly straining his polo shirt, holding tight to his staff, as the Nine of Wands. *He's never coming back to you*, I thought. *He's going to avoid you until the end of time.* I took my hair down and scratched my scalp so hard one of my press-ons popped off, trying to rid the image from my brain. Her husband didn't belong in my house. He wasn't allowed to be my Nine of Wands. I never wanted to see him again, so I deleted the woman's comment and then I blocked her.

The invasion multiplied. Reading their desperate comments, I was flooded with children in cancer wards, cheating spouses, parents lost to dementia, an overwhelming number of daughters and sisters and nieces who were all victims of unsolved crimes. Two mothers found each other in my comments section, wondering if their adult children knew each other in Kensington, where heroin was cheap. *Becca's videos are the only thing that gives me hope he'll come home.* Angel wings emoji. It would have been cruel to delete their comments. I saw their children as hunched figures, bundled in layers of hoodies and beanies and fingerless gloves, in the snow, in front of a boarded-up church, as the Five of Pentacles. Beneath their hoodies, I knew their arms were infected with sores. I began nervously pulling out my eyebrows. I kept losing nails and Morgan kept pressing them back on. In a nightmare, I saw a giant Wheel of Fortune obstructing the front window of a semitrailer, hurtling down an icy road toward me in my car. *He can't see where he's going*, I thought. When the truck hit me, I shocked awake.

It wasn't enough to avoid the comments sections of my posts. Every time I opened the platform, messages from Marion appeared on my For You page: *5 signs they're serious about you 6 signs your Spirit Team is trying to get ahold of you @mystic56 the importance of paying attention to little signs @lightworker1111 this is your sign to go all in and make art.*

I think I need to take a break from posting, I texted Morgan.

What? No! You can't!

I put my head down on my arms and groaned.

Why not, I said.

You're the heir! All of us are trying so hard to save the house for YOU

By August, I'd stopped sleeping. It didn't feel safe to shut my eyes. When I did, I saw my grandmother in the bathtub, like I was my dad, discovering her. Naked and dead. Another recurring scene was my mom screaming for my dad because I'd fallen in the pool and I was floating face down. How had I gotten to the pool? I could hardly even walk. Who had put me in the pool? It was a miracle I survived. I hadn't been to church or prayed in months. I turned on my bedside lamp and tried reading the Bible. Maybe my mom had been right from the beginning: My family suffered from a dark condition. It skipped my dad but spread in me like mold. Maybe the darkness only cursed the Deckler women.

I picked up my phone.

Vape? I texted Jake.

He had offered in the past, but I'd never taken him up on it. Now I thought pot might help me sleep.

Jake met me on the terrace, wearing basketball shorts and a hoodie that said JUVENIS. I'd forgotten to put on shoes or socks. There was a sliver of moon, but no stars.

"Let's go over here," I said, indicating a spot away from the house, under the pine trees, where as a girl I used to pretend I was a princess.

We sat cross-legged on a mat of dry pine needles. The

only light came from Jake's vape pen when he inhaled. He passed it to me.

"You don't have to hold it in," he said. "That's in movies."

"Oh," I said.

I closed my eyes and waited for the wave of pleasure. I wanted to feel silky, like satin ribbon, unspooled.

"I don't feel anything," I told Jake. "How long does it take?"

"Is this your first time?"

"No," I lied. I inhaled longer the second time. My hair felt hot and heavy against the back of my neck. As I pulled it into a bun, I felt like I was watching myself at a distance, my hands becoming Marion's hands. My hair was her hair. Her hands were mine. The hair became a rope so long it traveled the length of my body, wrapped around one of my ankles, strung me upside down. I shivered.

"Do you know what I'm thinking?" I asked.

"No, what?"

"I mean, can you see inside my head?"

Jake laughed. "Dude, you're the psychic one. Not me."

I sat up straight. My legs were on the ground, not up a tree. "If you had to choose," I said, "would you rather have a hundred million followers, if it came with a terrible curse, or lose all your followers, and literally no one knows you exist, but you're happy? And at peace?"

"Gain a hundred million followers."

I shook my head. "No," I said.

Jake laughed again. "You asked me what *I* would rather have. I'd rather have the followers because—"

"I'm not joking. I said it comes with a *curse.*"

"Whatever the curse is, if I had that many followers, I'd be making so much income, I could pay for anything that would bring me happiness and peace."

"The curse is not something that you can buy your way out of. It's outside of, like, capitalism."

"What do you mean, 'curse'? What's the curse?"

And that's when I saw the vision of what would happen to Jake if he stayed in this house. His fame was going to lead to destruction and pain. The writhing beast he rode would come to destroy us. He never should have come here.

"Becca?"

I shut my eyes and shook my head in the dark.

"You aren't going to tell me?"

Jake inched closer to me. Now our legs were touching. I didn't know I was shivering until he put his left arm around me and squeezed my shoulder.

"We have something in common," I finally said. "Our boundaries aren't strong enough. There are holes in the foundation. And that's how other people get inside our house. The best thing you could do is leave right now. Before it's too late."

He was silent for a minute, thinking, his arm wrapped so warm around me. The longer he took to answer, the more I thought he was taking my warning to heart.

Then Jake pulled me closer and kissed the top of my head. "You're a weird girl, Becca," he said. "But don't worry. I still like you."

When he kissed my hair, the sensation ricocheted through my body. *Again*, I thought. *More.* I turned up my face and kissed Jake, tentatively at first, and through his surprise, until he started to kiss me back. It was slower and more intense than I expected. I held his face with both my hands so I could be sure this was real. As long as we were touching, I existed.

Suddenly, Jake let go of my shoulder and pulled away from me. He put up the hood of his sweatshirt; I could no longer see his face.

"What did I do?"

"You didn't do anything," he said. "I'm sorry. I'm too stoned. I can't."

"We can take a break," I said.

"No." Jake stood up. "What you said is really freaking me out. I thought this was going to be a chill thing. . . . It's not chill."

"I don't understand what's happening."

"Don't take this the wrong way, but you're really young. All your life experience is from, like, reading tarot cards, and being online. Someday you'll go to college and realize there's a whole world out there."

I couldn't look at him. Everyone wanted my prophecy except the people who actually knew me.

"Come on, don't be mad," he said. "Let's go inside."

"Leave me alone," I said.

When he finally accepted that I wasn't going to follow him, I lay in the bed of pine needles, incredibly high. I touched my lips with my fingers and it felt like someone else's hand.

Marion had painted herself as the Fool and the Hanged Man, but I'd neglected to draw myself. That was why everyone was sneaking inside my fortress. I'd erected no boundaries. I had to draw an outline of where I ended and everyone else began.

"Who am I?" I asked out loud.

Instantly, I pictured the knife block in the kitchen. A knife was a dagger and a dagger was a sword and a sword was a thought. In bed, anguished, reading Job, I was the Nine of Swords. *For the thing which I greatly feared is come upon me, and that which I was afraid of is come unto me. I was not in safety, neither had I rest, neither was I quiet; yet trouble came.* The swords were the upsetting images that rode my brain waves, but they were also weapons. I remembered Morgan saying I had to keep posting and imagined the surprise on her face when I snuck into her bed and disemboweled her with a dagger.

"Stop it," I said out loud.

I had no control over what Marion wanted me to see. One violent image led to another until I was at church in Fresno, on the pulpit, holding my mom's hair back with one hand and a knife to her throat with the other.

I leapt up and ran across the driveway to my dad's house. I didn't even know what time it was when I knocked on his door.

"Becca? What's wrong, sweetheart?"

I started crying immediately, but no tears came to my eyes. "I think I'm going to hurt someone. Did I hurt someone?"

"Who? Come in." He helped me over to the couch. One of my feet was bleeding; I was tracking blood across his floor. My dad went to run a washcloth under the faucet so he could clean me up, but I couldn't feel anything.

"What happened?" he asked.

I started from the beginning and explained that I was the destined party and Marion was showing me how to see now that the channel had opened, but my followers were ruining everything, jamming the channel with their problems, and we were all in danger if we didn't close the borders.

"Everyone thinks I should draw their cards, right? *Pick me pick me.* But I'm supposed to draw the people who live in the house. That's what she wants me to do. Like you— you're the Magician. Did you know that?"

"I did not know that. Who's the Magician?"

"The card that comes after the Fool. Your mom was the Fool. She wanted to be an artist, not a wife. She had a baby magician, right? But I was the magic. I should have died in the pool, but I lived. She's the one who died in the pool. You found her. You know. She loved me so much that she gave her life so I could live. She made me the High Priestess, but now she wants me to use my sword and I don't know if I can." I started crying again. The Magician hugged me and I hid my face in his cloak.

"I think it might be time to sleep, and we can talk about this more in the morning."

I shook my head. "Not safe to sleep. Sleeping makes it much worse."

"How about this: You can sleep upstairs in the loft and I'll stay here on the couch, to make sure nothing happens."

"You have your magic wand?"

He nodded. "I have my magic wand."

Someone who can help you. That's where we were going. *Yes,* I thought. I was elated. My portfolio had stunned the committee. Finally someone had recognized my gift. I was the youngest person they'd ever admitted. I belonged with the most advanced painters. You wouldn't know that magicians drive cars because it's not something you see every day, but they do.

"You don't have any rabbits, do you?" I asked.

"Not that I . . . know of," he said.

"The Empress has some. But so does a magician," I said. "That's what I'm trying to figure out."

Every billboard we passed on Sunset Boulevard had a message for me: Injured? Consider this a sign. Losing faith? For your consideration: stranger things.

"Becca, what are you—"

I'd unbuckled my seatbelt so I could take off my sweatshirt and tie it as a blindfold over my eyes. "I don't want to see the signs," I said.

When we got there, my dad asked if I wanted him to go in with me.

"It's okay, Dad," I said. "I know what to say."

I smiled at the dean and followed him into his office.

He asked a lot of questions about my gifts and wrote down everything that I said. I explained the collaborative nature of my work and how I received my visions through the channel. I only became frustrated when I talked about the platform. He'd never used it before and didn't believe how many followers I had until I took out my phone to show him my account.

"My daughters will be very impressed that I met you."

I started to pull my sweatshirt over my face. "Please don't tell me about them," I said, "or I'll start to see their cards, and I don't want to see their cards."

"Becca, I'm going to talk to your dad and prescribe some medication that will help you with sleep and the other issues you've been having."

"Is it a requirement of art school?"

"The medication?" He looked up from his notepad. "Would you like to go to art school?"

"I would love to," I said. "Thank you so much."

The timing could not have been better. It was August 8, the date of the Lion's Gate Portal opening, an auspicious date for manifesting. Tonight, the stars would align. I was going to have to tell Morgan I was leaving. When a door to a mystical portal in the universe opened, you had to step across the threshold. Who knew when the door would be open again?

In my bedroom, I packed up my clothes and my art supplies and Marion's deck. That was when I had a moment of hesitation: Would Marion and I still be able to work together if I left the house? But if I stayed here, I would have to keep posting on the platform. That's what had put the swords in my hands. I used to think I was inside the platform, but now the platform was inside of me.

I brought my bags with me, to say goodbye to Morgan.

"Where have you been? Is your phone off?"

"I've been accepted to the academy." I showed her the bag from the pharmacy.

She read the labels. "You can't take these, Becca."

"I already did." The Magician had watched me take my first dose after he drove me home.

"It's a trick. It's what they did to Marion. Remember? When she was finally able to see what he was doing to her, George gave your grandmother drugs? This is what they do to women who are visionaries. They give them pills. She never should have taken them. Your dad found her. She never finished her deck."

My teeth started chattering. It was what they did to the little slave girl, too. Her fortune-telling made money for her owners, but Paul didn't like what she was saying and he cast the Spirit from her. When she lost her gift, she was of no value to her owners. Morgan was the only one who wasn't trying to rid me of what I could see.

"I'm his little slave girl," I said.

"I don't know what that is, but I think you're experiencing burnout, which is extremely common," Morgan said. "Let me show you something."

She held my hand and led me deep inside Marion's closet, all the way to the back, where there was a blue door. The door to the portal. It was here inside the house. On the other side was a dim nursery.

"I was a baby here," I said. I didn't remember. I knew.

Morgan nodded. "I think it was your dad's nursery, and then yours. What if we made this your art studio?"

"You said I had to keep posting."

"Forget I ever said that," Morgan said. "You're too sensitive. It's too much for you. Your gifts are meant for greater things. What's important is that you finish Marion's deck.

That's how you'll save this house. I'll bring you everything you need. You can rest."

She kept talking, but I stopped listening. A blue peace settled over me in the nursery. It was as dark and quiet as sleep. It was so dark because I was blindfolded, my body bound in rope. Three swords to my left and five swords to my right, plunged into the soft, wet ground. Behind me, a castle, unreachable. Each sword represented a different way through the maze.

"But my dad thinks I'm going to art school," I said.

"Don't worry. I'll tell him you went home to Fresno because you didn't want to post anymore. I'll tell him you quit. And that you don't need these." She took the pharmacy bag from my hands.

My final video did not look like any of the other Lion's Gate Portal videos; I recorded it in my bedroom. There were dark circles under my eyes. My hair hung loose around my face.

"You did not stumble across this message by accident. If you're seeing this, it's meant for you. Today is the eighth day of the eighth month. I was not in safety, yet trouble came. I became the Eight of Swords. I thought I was going to a place where they would untie me, set me free. But I understand now. There is a lot of strength in the number eight. With swords, I can cut the ropes myself. After the portal opens tonight, I'll be gone."

"WHAT DID YOU do after you posted it?" the queen asked.

"I gave Morgan my phone so I wouldn't have to read another comment."

Now that I had my Queen of Cups, the deck was complete. I'd painted fifty-six cards.

"I feel guilty," she said. "I was one of your followers. I was one of the people who thought you had a message just for me. That's actually why I came here—to your house."

"I know who you are," I said. I showed her the Wheel of Fortune card—the one I'd once seen in a dream. It was meant for her.

"You blame yourself for what happened, but it was the hand of fate turning the wheel," I said. "You weren't steering. It's hard for them to see you hurt this much, Olivia."

Her eyes shimmered with unspilled tears.

"I can't forgive myself."

"You're a queen. Forgive someone else, then."

"And what if I do?"

"Blessed are the merciful, for they shall obtain mercy," I said. "That's what they've been trying to give you. But you won't accept it. So the channel stays closed. It's like you pushed a bunch of furniture against the door and they can't open it to reach you."

"Okay," she said. She wiped her eyes with the back of one hand and picked up her phone to type a message. "I can't believe I'm doing this. He made me a video apologizing. I'm leaving a comment: *I forgive you.*"

The crown appeared on her head.

"Now I wish I had something to give you. I can take you to meet the Empress? This is her rabbit."

DAYNA

While the tarot cards were still hanging in the nursery, I went with Jake to film the room exactly how it had been when she'd hidden there. *Here's her old baby crib. Here's the little cot where she slept. Here are her watercolor brushes. Here's the powder room where she took her sponge baths.*

"You'll be able to drip content for weeks," I told Jake.

More remarkable than the fact that Morgan had been hiding Becca inside the house where she'd been born were the cards themselves. Because Becca was self-taught, she lacked basic skills like proportion and scale, and how to draw hands, but it gave her paintings a hallucinatory quality, like her figures were melting. One of the cards was a painting of Olivia, a queen on a throne, collecting her tears in a gold goblet. Each tear was the size of her nose.

All the swords were self-portraits. In the Two of Swords, Becca had painted herself reclining on a Freudian divan, blindfolded, with two swords crossed over her chest, while a male therapist in a chair looked at his cell phone. In the

Six of Swords, Becca was a tiny passenger in the seat of a car, staring out the window at the looming billboards on the Sunset Strip; one of the billboards showed an orange pill bottle, surrounded by six swords. On the left side of the Ten of Swords was Craig, his face creased with anguish, reluctantly throwing five swords at Becca, who was facing a ring light, filming a tarot video, her face pale and haunted. Her mother was in profile on the right side, angrily wielding the other five swords.

When I looked at Becca's watercolors, I remembered what it felt like to be a teenager, when every experience was an emotional twelve on a ten-point scale. That's how talented she was. By withdrawing from us, she'd been able to create something more real and true than anything that existed on the platform.

More people needed to see these cards. She could have a real career as a painter. The story of Becca was one I would have loved to cover if I were still a journalist. This was more than just the discovery of a missing influencer—it was the discovery of a new young artist.

Come to Piper and Sean's wedding, I texted Meg Frank. And I'll get you an exclusive interview with Becca Chambers.

There were so many angles that Meg could take: An inspiring story about a young woman who traded her ring light for a paintbrush. A feel-good intergenerational story about a content creator who taught herself to paint in order to collaborate through the beyond with her grandmother, a forgotten female artist of the mid-twentieth century. A story about architecture as the mother of all art forms, and how the masterpiece of the Deckler House influenced multiple generations of female artists and helped the house survive the pains inflicted by time.

Once the story came out, Craig could turn the nursery into a spartan artist residency: Relinquish your smartphone to an onsite teenager and confine yourself to a dark room where you'll be isolated with your own imagination for weeks. Basic meals provided. Call it "The Chambers." Or he could make Marion's bedroom a tourist attraction. Hang her paintings on the walls, alongside the photos I took in her canopy bed decades later, haunted by a specter. Let gawkers think it was her ghost. Let them inside her closet to touch the last dress she wore. Line right up to see where the Anne Frank of Hollywood was hiding. Take home Becca's tarot deck from the gift shop. *The Deckler Deck.*

When we were finished filming, Jake pulled me against his chest. "Don't go," he said.

I shut my eyes. "You know I have to," I said.

Owen Wilson and I slept in Jake's room—not that we got any sleep. There were so many wedding details to finish and finalize. Jake drew a map of where he would set up the cameras during the ceremony, for the livestream, and created the playlist. Morgan was directing all the visuals and I neutralized her by lavishing her with attention and praise: Her handmade crepe paper flowers were incredible. *Such an original choice*, I said, again and again. In bed, I held up my phone to show Jake the ring bearer outfit she'd made for O.W.

"She is not a good person," Jake said, refusing to look. "She lied to all of us—she even pretended she missed Becca as much as we did. That's *sick*. Why is she still here?"

He'd wanted Craig to send Morgan home, but all Craig could focus on right now was Becca's well-being.

"I understand why you're upset," I said. "But we need her for the wedding. It's the final deliverable."

"Just a few hours ago, you were literally crying on the floor, calling her a killer. And now you forgive her?"

I cringed. "I don't forgive her. I just need her. House of Scaccabarozzi has to see all of you tomorrow. The show must go on. What do you want me to do, Jake?"

"There should be consequences," he said darkly, but refused to elaborate.

Frustrated by our stalemate, I lay back in bed and put on his polka-dotted sleep mask. For weeks, Morgan had devoted herself to being Becca's keeper, like the witch in Rapunzel. Pity the witch: She was so insecure that she had to lock Rapunzel in a tower to prevent her from loving anyone else. But maybe I was giving Morgan too much credit. Maybe they were both Rapunzel, conspiring in the tower together, building a shared universe with its own moral code—like the teen murderesses in *Heavenly Creatures* or the asylum sisters in *Girl, Interrupted*. Keeping Becca's secret was what had made Morgan special. Maybe that's why I wasn't angrier at her. When Becca no longer needed her, who was Morgan?

After midnight, my phone rang. It was my dad.

"I've decided not to proceed with the surgery. And I'm telling you directly so you don't have to hear it from your mother."

"What? Wait—why?"

"It's not how I want to spend my time. But I would still love to see you."

"Okay. I'll be there soon," I said. I tried to say little so he wouldn't hear me crying.

Jake kissed my bare shoulder. "Everything is going to be okay," he said.

"I know," I said. We were all lying to one another. Stabbed to death with swords, bleeding out, telling everyone, *I'm fine.*

THE NEXT MORNING, all the girls were getting ready in Morgan's bedroom, where every flat surface was strewn with clothes and bath towels and lip gloss tubes and boxes of tampons and flip-flops and paperbacks and water bottles and scented candles. On a bench, Becca was silently staring out the window while Paula styled her hair. Mindy Bliss was choosing between two pairs of heels by asking her followers to vote in a poll in her Instagram stories. Olivia was creating content.

"Dayna, you look pretty," she said, backing up until she had my whole body in frame. Her eyes sparkled. "Who are you wearing?"

I laughed. "House of Scaccabarozzi," I said, and posed in my burgundy dress.

Then she panned to Morgan, who was working on Piper's hair and makeup at the vanity. After Olivia found Becca, Piper had begun treating Morgan with cold suspicion, like a domestic staff member on probation. She never asked me or Craig to kick Morgan out of the house, but she withdrew all her warmth and trust. I recognized this Piper as the jaundiced young woman I'd met when I moved in.

To win back her affection, Morgan was exercising rare restraint on hair and makeup. Piper looked grown-up and sophisticated in a silk dress with her hair in a French twist. Morgan pulled wispy pieces around her face. She glued tiny extensions to Piper's lash line. Mindy looked up from her phone to watch her daughter. In the vanity mirror, Piper pressed her glossy lips together and then fake smiled to check her teeth.

"You look absolutely stunning," Mindy said.

"I'm shaking," Piper said.

They locked eyes with each other in the mirror, like twins separated by a time travel plot. Mindy spent a lot of time and money trying to look her daughter's age. In her reflection, Piper was staring at her future.

Piper burst into tears.

"Shit," Morgan said.

"Oh, Pip," Mindy said. She asked Morgan for Q-tips.

Olivia put her phone down and started fanning Piper's face with her hands.

"I don't know if I can do this," Piper said. "Everyone's going to be watching me."

I felt nauseous. If Piper refused to walk down the aisle, what was I going to do? Wed Jake and Olivia? But that wouldn't work—we'd never posted their engagement video. The surprise would cause too much confusion. Jake's fandom would collapse. Could I make the whole livestream about Becca?

"This is your job, honey," Mindy said. She had her hands on Piper's shoulders and Piper stared straight ahead, stiff, a son about to go to war. "Dayna had to work really hard to get you a big sponsor, after everything that happened at your last house. Not all girls are so lucky. And I have sponsors for my mother-of-the-bride content, too. Part of becoming an adult is doing things even when we don't want to do them."

"It's not legally binding," I added. "It's just for the internet. We just need the wedding on camera. You and Sean can break up tomorrow and we'll still get paid."

"But I don't want to break up with Sean tomorrow. I want to *be* with Sean. *I love Sean.*" Piper was crying again.

Morgan offered a Q-tip. Piper shook her head. Everyone was frozen, afraid to touch or comfort her.

I was about to dispatch Olivia to find Sean so he could exert his sedative effect on the bride when Becca surprised Piper, embracing her from behind, taking an intoxicating whiff of her hair spray and mumbling some private joke that made them both crack up. Becca linked her arms around Piper's shoulders, a human friendship bracelet, and Piper softened, the tension of the moment broken. Morgan was left out of their chain.

"Where's your phone?" I whispered to Olivia.

She resumed recording just as Becca opened her box of cards and started shuffling through them.

Do you think I should take her to the hospital? Craig had texted me last night from the floor of Becca's bedroom, where he was keeping vigilant watch while she slept. At first, I thought he meant there was something physically wrong with her, like a vitamin D deficiency, but then I realized he was using the word *hospital* for *psych ward*. He insisted that this wasn't his daughter, and that I didn't understand because I'd never known her.

We need her for the wedding, I thought. *She has to wear the clothes.*

I couldn't say that. A hospital would be a very scary place to be right now, I'd replied. It might make things even worse. Let's see how she is in the morning?

Interacting with Piper, Becca appeared like a completely normal teenage girl: obsessive, intense, sensitive. Maybe Craig didn't understand her because he'd watched her grow up from such a distance.

"Is this me and Sean?" Piper asked Becca.

Becca nodded. "It's the Ten of Cups."

"Mom, look. It's our wedding. There's a rainbow. And two little kids."

"See?" I said. "It's fated."

"Tarot," Mindy said. "Cute." She took out her phone and made Piper pose, smiling, with her fairy-tale ending.

The weather was perfectly cool and dry. Hundreds of cream-colored crepe paper flowers were fastened with emerald satin ribbons to the guest chairs and around the giant brass hoop where I would officiate. On the terrace, Paula and Olivia had set up a little table, draped in an antique lace tablecloth and set with silver candelabras and red candlesticks, where Becca could do readings for guests. Craig had found an old red carpet from a long-ago movie premiere and we repurposed it as a wedding aisle that ran the length of the pool. While we were doing our hair and makeup, Sean and Jake were cleaning the debris from the water, making it camera-ready. The raccoons would stay away until tonight, when they would feast on whatever we left behind.

I stationed Olivia with me on the terrace, near the kitchen door, to greet guests and direct them where to sit. I wanted to personally escort Meg Frank to Becca's table.

Jake strode toward us in his navy-blue tux. His hair was parted on the side and smoothed in place with gel; he looked sharp, like a model in a glasses ad.

"Olivia," he said, as if I were a ghost. As if he didn't remember my dress.

"Yes?"

"I have something to ask you."

But before he could proceed, Mr. and Mrs. Cho stepped through the sliding door. Jake had finally told them about his secret dream of becoming a filmmaker and assured them they didn't need to worry about his future because he was already getting work as a wedding videographer.

"Your son is very talented," I said, shaking Mr. Cho's hand.

"Thank you for giving him the opportunity," Mrs. Cho said.

"Jake has a lot of fans around here," I said, trying to catch his eye, but he wouldn't look at me. I'd embarrassed him. From the inner pocket of my black binder, I took out my vape pen and watched Jake show his parents how he had set up multiple cameras and iPhones on tripods; one to livestream the whole ceremony; two more for close-ups of Piper and Sean. He pointed at the sky, predicting the path the sun would travel. It was the end of October; golden hour came early.

"What do you think he wanted to ask me?"

"Maybe he needs your help tying his bow tie."

She nodded, serious. "I can look on YouTube."

My mother arrived, wearing a dress with a jeweled collar. "Don't you just love weddings," she said, squeezing my hands. Her eyebrow pencil application was uneven, so it looked like she was making a wry joke.

"It's my first wedding," Olivia said.

"Weddings and funerals," my mother said. "That's what brings people together. But Dayna never wanted one. She's a modern woman."

I cleared my throat. "You remember Olivia," I said.

"Of course," she said. She was looking over Olivia's shoulder, searching for someone more influential in the crowd. Craig? I waved Sean over.

"Do I look skinny in this?" he asked Olivia.

"You look huge," she told him. Sean grinned and stood tall, inflated with fresh confidence.

"This is the groom," I said. "He'll show you to your seat."

"How do you do, ma'am?"

My mother was thrilled. She clung to Sean's arm. Her head barely cleared his elbow.

Mr. and Mrs. Bokelberg were immediately recognizable by their height. As soon as they were in their seats, Morgan's mom raised her phone and took a series of selfies with her husband, trying to get Morgan's paper floral arrangements in the frame.

When Meg stepped through the sliding door, I stopped vaping and smiled. She had a photographer with her. Both were dressed for journalism, in jeans and button-downs.

Meg had at least thrown on a dark blazer, which was speck-led with dog hair.

"Dayna Lev," she said.

"Long time."

"You look very . . . Honestly, you look very sexy in that dress."

I laughed. "Is that going in the article?"

"I'm sorry, I don't know why I said that. This house is a trip," Meg said. Her photographer, a lanky bald man in his sixties, took a few test shots to check the light. Then he wanted me to pose in front of the pool, with different varia-tions of my arms crossed and on my hips, like I was the czar of Gen Z. In a couple shots, I held my vape pen like a fat cigar.

"Got it," the photographer said.

"I didn't know I was going to be such a big part of your story," I told Meg. On our way to Becca's table, I paused to take a flute of prosecco from the tray Paula was carrying, to settle my stomach.

Meg declined the wine. "You've created one of the most talked-about campaigns of the year. I know of at least one agency that's trying to copy your success by collaborating with a true crime podcast to sell jeans. It's like what you told me: The future of media is retail. Or was it 'the future of retail is media'?"

"Jeans?"

"Yeah, like you can buy the same cut and wash that the victim was wearing when she was strangled to death. I can't remember her name, but they embroidered it on the back pocket. So she's not forgotten."

I frowned. Did she really think I would be impressed by something so distasteful? Or was she trying to provoke me into defending my work? Being around Meg made me feel like I was twenty-six years old again, pathetically trying to prove her assumptions about me were wrong.

"But that's not the same at all. Our campaign actually found Becca. That's what made it so successful."

"Take the imitation as a compliment," Meg said. Then she sat across from Becca at the table.

"Becca, meet Meg Frank. I used to work with her. Meg is a big fan of your work."

"Oh no," Becca said.

Meg and I both laughed, but Becca looked frightened. The photographer snapped her photo and she flinched and covered her eyes with her forearm.

"Maybe we can shoot her later," I whispered, "after she's more comfortable?"

Meg set out her digital recorder and a notebook. "So how does this work? Should I ask a question? 'Will my story about you go viral?'"

Like a lonesome child, Becca seemed more comfortable playing with her cards than talking to us. She randomly shuffled them face down on the lace tablecloth and drew three. She turned over the first two so they faced Meg, with one card crossing another.

"There's a professional triumph, but it's opposed by the Tower card. There's going to be a crash or a downfall. Or maybe the downfall becomes the triumph."

Then she turned over the third card.

"Your guide is the Empress. She's carrying the future of the house."

"All the cards are paintings of people who have come through the Deckler House," I explained. "I have a pet rabbit, so I'm the Empress."

"It really does look like you," Meg said. Her photographer quickly shot the tarot spread.

"My grandmother painted that one," Becca said. "We work together through the channel."

Meg checked her notes. "Marion Deckler? What do you mean by 'channel'?"

"She direct messaged me. It said: *You're about to come into a divine blessing.* And it was her gift for seeing. Now I have it. She loved me so much that she had to die to give it to me. I painted fifty-six cards and five plus six is eleven. Angel numbers. My numbers were one of the first things they noticed on my application to the academy. Some of the best numbers they'd ever seen. But George drugged Marion and Marion wasn't going to let Craig drug me. She said, *you're not taking these.*"

"Craig Deckler tried to drug you?"

My mouth was dry. I thought of her painting of the billboard with the pill bottle. Craig had said, *I tried to get her help, but she refused to take medication.*

"I don't know anything about Craig giving Becca drugs," I said.

"What kind of drugs were they?"

Becca looked over her shoulder. "I gave them to Morgan. Morgan knows."

This was going very badly. We should have practiced. I hadn't been thinking. Back when I was at *EW,* I was always in Meg's seat, the one doing the interviews at the press junkets and on the red carpet. I'd never been the publicist rehearsing with the talent, giving them canned lines to dodge questions they didn't want to answer. It had been my job to get the subject to reveal something they weren't allowed to say. And I'd been good at it.

Deflect! I thought. I looked at Meg. "Marion Deckler's work has been largely forgotten. She studied under the American surrealists, but she died before her work could get the attention it deserved."

"How did she die?"

"In the pool," Becca answered. "My mom found her face down. And she was just a baby. No one knows how she got to the pool."

"Like many artists, Becca has an extraordinary imagination," I told Meg. I stared at her pen, as if I could will it to write down the words I was saying. "Marion Deckler drowned in the bathtub. It was a suicide. Craig found her when he was thirteen. Maybe you can interview him later? Or I'm sure I can find him right now—"

I gulped my remaining prosecco and scanned the crowd, desperate for Craig to come help. There was my friend Mollie, chatting with Olivia. Mindy Bliss caught my eye and pointed to her Apple Watch, and then in the general direction of Piper, making the universal symbol for *crazy* at her temple. A tiny woman in a lavender fur coat and oversized sunglasses squealed and waved at me. I had no idea who she was.

"Surprise! Dayna!" she called. She was rolling a leopard-print suitcase behind her. "I came straight from LAX."

"Sofia?"

She pushed her sunglasses off her face and kissed both my cheeks. She smelled incredible, like pistachio and vanilla. Relieved to have the mortifying interview interrupted, I introduced Sofia to Meg. But Sofia didn't want to discuss the campaign or look at Becca's paintings—first, she needed to see Becca in her dress.

"Stand up, please, for me! I want to see!" Without waiting for Becca to answer her command, Sofia pulled her up from the table with both hands and kissed her, too. Then she got out her phone. Meg's photographer started shooting simultaneously. Becca stood there awkwardly, holding a tarot card in each hand, eyes downcast like a Renaissance painting of the Madonna. One of the spaghetti straps of her silk dress was falling down her shoulder but she made no move to correct it.

"*Che bella che sei!* Dayna, you did it, brava! We have a proud history of tarot in Italy. And the orphan is here, too?"

From Jake's Bluetooth speaker, a string quartet cover of "Wildest Dreams" began playing. It was my cue to get the bridal party ready to start the ceremony.

"Well," I said, smiling at Meg, "I hope you got something you can use! I have a seat saved for you up front."

Meg held up her notepad. "I haven't even started on my questions."

"Later," I said. "I promise! We're just trying to time the ceremony with the light. For the cameras. Jake Cho is directing. You can ask him all about it. He's an artist, too."

I dragged Becca with me, but she wouldn't put down her box.

"Do you want me to keep that somewhere safe for you?"

"I'm going back to my room," she said.

"Piper is getting married," I said. "Remember? You're a bridesmaid? The Ten of Cups?" I grabbed two more glasses of prosecco and handed one to Becca. I still couldn't find Craig anywhere.

Olivia was beaming by the kitchen door; she looked like she was in love.

"Jake wants me to be in his first movie," she told me.

"Wow," I said, surprised he hadn't mentioned anything to me.

"It's about star-crossed lovers from different hype houses. He wants me to play Juliet. I asked if he was sure he didn't want someone more famous and he said, *I want you, Olivia.*"

"Of course he wants you," I said, putting on a brave smile. Jake was doing exactly what I hoped he would do. He was moving on. So why did I feel sick?

"Excuse me for just a second." I walked around the corner of the house, where I hoped no one could see me, and efficiently threw up in a stone urn of dead plants. Was I officially too old to day drink? When I stood back up, I had a headache.

The second song, "Golden Hour," had already started. I ran my tongue over my teeth and checked that Morgan, Becca, Olivia, Sean, and Jake were all in place at one end of the red carpet. Morgan gave me a thumbs-up and I walked around the pool to the brass hoop where I was officiating the ceremony. Owen Wilson was safe inside his fenced-in habitat, a fluffy princeling in a silk cummerbund. The guests took their seats.

Down the aisle, they walked in twos and threes: Becca and Morgan, Olivia and Jake, Sean with his mom and grandmother. Sean stopped at one of the cameras to make a goofy face and peace sign.

Everyone stood for Piper. Between her parents, she was tense; it looked like she was walking *them*. She had changed out of her heels into a pair of Chuck Taylors; the silk train of her gown was so long that her mom kept stepping on it. Mindy wouldn't look at Piper's dad; she let her eyes skim the small audience, trying to absorb some of the warmth and admiration directed at Piper.

Wowee, Sean mouthed at her, and she smiled, flashing a crooked tooth. This part was real: Sean hadn't seen her in this dress until now. As soon as her parents left her at what stood for an altar, Piper gripped his hands.

"Thanks, everyone, for being here. I know this may seem like an unusual wedding. Or maybe not, if you're from LA," I joked.

From her seat, Mindy had her phone raised with one hand, like a girl at a concert, while her other hand pressed a tissue to her cheek.

I opened my black binder and started reading.

"When I first moved to the Deckler House, I wasn't sure what I was doing here. *What do they need me for?* I thought. I felt irrelevant. It had been a long time since I felt like I was what someone else needed. I've always felt needed from working, but feeling needed is also at the root of love."

"Yes, ma'am," Sean said.

Everyone laughed. There was Craig, seated in the back, but he wouldn't meet my eyes; he was staring at Becca, to my right, who was still clutching her box, silently mouthing something to herself with her eyes closed.

"Sean and Piper: People will tell you that you're too young to know what you want. That what you're doing online isn't real. That *this* isn't real. But, Sean, I've seen the way you love Piper for who she is, because that's what she needs, and, Piper, I've seen you let Sean love you, even when you find it hard to believe you're worth it."

Piper was looking down at her sneakers; she sniffled.

As the sun sank below the horizon, the sky streamed stripes the color of sherbet, violet, indigo. Little fairy lights, strung through the cracks in the exterior of the house, blinked on. *Dayna never wanted a wedding. She's a modern woman.* It was true that I'd never been one of those little girls who dreamed of being a bride, but now I had the image of myself in white, not with any groom, but dancing with my father. The dance we would never have. Because I'd never stopped feeling like a young woman with something to prove, I hadn't noticed the years go by. I'd skated on the surface of time, afraid to learn how thin the ice was.

"Do I get to kiss her now?" Sean asked.

"Wait!"

Jake ran behind one of the cameras to make sure he had the shot. All the guests took out their phones and aimed them at the happy couple.

"All good," Jake said, locking eyes with me.

"You may now kiss the bride," I said.

After the ceremony, Sofia Scaccabarozzi wanted a photo with Olivia, the orphan. Then she had a question for Craig about the architecture. Then she wanted her tarot cards read. She was like Veruca Salt at the chocolate factory: As the client, she was entitled to anything she asked for. For how many more hours would we have to entertain her? It was nearly dark outside, and growing colder. My red-eye departed in four hours.

"More prosecco?" I asked.

"Becca told me that Morgan has her phone," Sofia said.

"I think it's one of the phones Jake was using for the livestream."

"I have a beautiful idea." She clapped her hands together. "While Becca is still wearing House of Scaccabarozzi, she can do a reading for her fans. Not for me! After all, they have been waiting the longest to see her, no?"

I was powerless to say no to this woman. She was so charming, and she smelled so good, but more than anything, she controlled when we would be paid for this extravaganza.

Right there on the terrace, Sofia unzipped her leopard-print suitcase, and it was completely filled with leather pouches of jewelry she'd brought from Milan.

"May I?" Morgan asked.

The two of them set to work adorning Becca with a rhinestone forehead necklace, layers of silver chains, a rope lariat with a huge sapphire cross, a bracelet cuff inlaid with diamond-studded evil eyes, and stacks of rings. Paula lit the red candlesticks on the table. Morgan propped up Becca's phone, logged in to her account, and started the Live. Becca didn't touch the phone at all; it looked as if she'd never interacted with one before.

Standing behind the fortune teller, Meg and I could observe the whole thing from Becca's point of view. I watched as dozens, and then hundreds, of her fans joined. At first, their comments were expressions of amazement and gratitude. Heart and crystal ball emojis filled the screen. And then the questions poured in: *does David love me anymore why is she avoiding me can you help me reach my daughter how do I move on without him what do I need to do in order to heal from this will AJ come back should I quit my job or wait until I find a new one?* Becca slowly shuffled the cards on the table. Without asking, Sofia adjusted the phone stand so all the jewelry was visible.

"Where is she?" someone yelled. I turned toward the house and there was Craig, arguing with a woman.

As I quickly walked over to them, I knew. I knew it had to be Dawn Chambers. She had unusually long hair for a woman in her fifties, and was dressed casually, in a hoodie and jeans. Craig must have called her, but not in time for her to make it for the wedding. He had needed the wedding to happen, for the sake of the house, as much as I had.

"But I've been texting with her," Dawn was saying, "at college."

"She wasn't at college," Craig said patiently.

"She *told me* she was at college. She sent me her course list and her schedule."

"You weren't texting with Becca," I said. "You were texting with her friend Morgan."

Dawn looked at me. "Who are you? His girlfriend?"

"No," Craig said before I could answer.

"I didn't know where Becca was either," I said.

"*I knew* where she was! At college!" Dawn was incapable of moving on from this belief that Morgan had implanted inside her. "I want to speak with Morgan. I want to see my daughter."

"She's giving a tarot reading right now," I said.

Dawn's face flushed. "She's not allowed to play with tarot cards. It's dangerous."

"Dawn, I called you so we could figure this out together. What Becca needs," Craig said.

Dawn ignored him and strode ahead of us, toward the table. But Becca was no longer seated there. Where had she gone? No one was at the table. They were all swarming in excitement around some focal point on the ground, pointing and whispering. The photographer's camera flashed against the twilight. Flash! Flash! Flash!

"I think once you see her tarot cards, you'll understand—they're art," I said, trying to keep up. "Your daughter has a real talent. She could have a career as a painter."

As we got closer, I saw that Becca was on her hands and knees, crawling toward the pool, naked as an animal except for a pair of underwear. She had managed to cover her head with the dress like an execution hood. Every time the camera flashed, all the diamonds on her fingers and wrists sparkled. Sofia was recording all this—a scene out of Fellini—on her phone, too. While Morgan just stood there, motionless as a mannequin, Olivia scrambled into action, blowing out the candles so she could remove the lace tablecloth and cover Becca with it. Jake was crouched, at Becca's level, quietly trying to reason with her, as he physically obstructed her path to the pool. She kept shaking her shrouded head. I couldn't hear what either of them were saying.

With a pang of horror, I thought, *I made this.*

Dawn fell upon her daughter and Becca screamed, "I'm burning up! They're inside me now!" She shoved Dawn away and resumed her attempts to reach the pool, groping for the edge with her hands.

"What happened?" Craig asked Olivia.

"All she did was look at the comments, like, once, and everyone got inside her head. She said she cleared the channel but now it's blocked again. I think she's upset with Morgan."

None of this was about Becca's art. No one even noticed the paintings, scattered and forgotten on the table. They were not part of the story at all. All anyone could see was what Becca could do for them: tell their fortunes, assuage their anxieties, model their clothes, fall apart in a spectacle to teach us a lesson about the price of fame that we would forget tomorrow. These photographs would tell the story of Becca that the public would remember forever.

Craig had been right about me: I was a vulture. I had given up on making art because I was afraid I didn't know how to get better, and instead built a career out of publicizing other artists' ruins. That was what I'd always been interested in. The bruised parts of the fruit. Famous young women who died too soon: The appetite for those tragedies was never sated. Rather than help anyone out of their darkness, the way my father did, I put the darkness on display. Once I learned the worst about a public figure, I held it up and said, *Look at this.* When I gave up being an artist, I also dodged the risk that someone would do the same to me someday.

"This is off the record," I said to Meg. "You can't write this. I'm sorry. Please stop. That's enough." I blocked the photographer's lens with my palm. He flicked me away, a gnat.

"I said *stop.*"

"I've almost got it," he said.

I grabbed the strap around his neck and pulled so hard that he fumbled his grip on the camera. Olivia ran over to help me wrestle the camera away from him.

"Get your fucking hands off me."

We were physically smaller than him, but he was so surprised by our attack that he was clumsy and defenseless. He covered his face with his hands as if we were coming next for his eyes. Once I successfully unclasped one of the neck straps from the body of the camera, I was able to rip all the gear away from him.

Jake sprang up to physically shield me as I deleted all the photos of Becca, one by one, watching the grotesque scene in reverse, from her crawling on the ground, to her fashioning a blindfold, to her stepping out of her silk dress while everyone looked on—there was Mindy Bliss with her phone up, recording—to the anguish on her face as she absorbed all the comments on her phone. He'd captured all of it.

When I finally looked up, the girl had reached the pool. Becca was floating on her back, arms outstretched in the dark water, safer apart from us than in our company.

"She should be hospitalized," I said to Craig. "I was wrong."

"Wrong about what?"

I felt a surge of emotion. A twelve on a ten-point scale. I'd been so insecure, so fixated on proving my relevance, that I made aging seem like a shameful disease. The faces of my generation froze at thirty. We were so afraid of disappearing. When Olivia or Becca or Jake or Piper or Sean or Morgan needed help, I'd taught them to think of their audience. As if the fact that someone wanted to watch you live your life was proof that you had a life worth living.

"So much," I said. He briefly squeezed my shoulder.

All this time, the livestream on Becca's phone kept running. Most of her fans had left when Becca exited the frame, but the ones who remained, hoping she would come back, got to watch columns of black smoke climb from the mansion as the Deckler House burned to death.

ARSON SUSPECT ARRESTED AFTER DEVASTATING FIRE SHOCKS LOS ANGELES

BY MEG FRANK

The Los Angeles Police Department has arrested a suspect in connection with the fire three weeks ago that destroyed the Deckler House, a 10,000-square-foot neo-Mayan hilltop mansion that had recently captured the public imagination in a viral fashion advertising campaign that doubled as a search for a missing tarot influencer named Becca Chambers.

The suspect, Sue Gambino, 54, a resident of Yorba Linda, is accused of starting the fire during a rare opportunity when all residents of the home were attending a much-anticipated wedding, between influencers Piper Bliss and Sean Knight, taking place outdoors on the property.

After the ceremony, Becca Chambers returned to happy fans with a livestreamed tarot reading, but the fortune-telling turned to tragedy when the livestream captured flames and smoke erupting from the mansion. One video clip of the fire, overlaid with the text "Eight of Swords," has been viewed 74 million times. A handful of influencers have been rebuked for putting flame emojis in the caption when sharing the viral video.

According to the LAPD, Gambino didn't need to enter the house to start the fire that consumed it. The property had previously sustained structural damage in a series of natural disasters, beginning in the mid-1990s. LAPD alleges that Gambino climbed inside a human-sized hole in the foundation, where she started the fire, which spread quickly from the dry overgrown brush that had been accumulating for decades.

Neighbors of the house on Blackwood Avenue have been complaining for years about the dilapidated state of the property and the homeowners' delay in restoring the home to its previous condition, when it was used as a set in films including *The House of Asterion* and *The King's Widow*. The homeowners, siblings Craig Deckler and Paula Delacroix, opened their home to influencers this summer, hoping to earn enough income to renovate the property, which has belonged to their family for nearly a hundred years.

"This is exactly what we were trying to prevent," Deckler said, when reached by phone. "We wanted to save our family home. It was supposed to be Becca's inheritance."

Becca Chambers is the daughter of Deckler and Dawn Chambers, a resident of Fresno, who declined to comment.

Sean Knight provided *Rolling Stone* with a video, never before shared with the public, of a recent confrontation at the home between Gambino and Jake Cho, a 22-year-old content creator with an obsessive fan base of middle-aged women. Gambino wanted to take a selfie with Cho, but Cho declined.

In the video, Gambino can be heard saying, "You're just an ungrateful brat!"

Knight replies, "If you can't control yourself, we're going to have to call law enforcement."

A young woman in a white dress, whom Knight identified as his fellow content creator Olivia Dahl, pushes Gambino into the swimming pool.

Asked whether he contacted the LAPD at that time, Knight said, "Craig told us not to," referring to Mr. Deckler.

A friend of Gambino's, who asked to remain anonymous, said that Gambino was upset when Cho blocked her on social media. Gambino's friend believes that Gambino has spent as much as $5,000 in "tips" during Cho's entertaining livestreams, including one in which he held a rabbit, according to screenshots the friend provided *Rolling Stone*.

In the days after the fire, the suspect created a new account that she used to send Cho a string of messages, in one last desperate attempt to win his attention, even going so far as to confess to arson.

Through a spokesperson, Cho told *Rolling Stone* he plans to retire from his career as a content creator.

Morgan Bokelberg, another resident of the hype house, has created a website to collect digital artifacts and memories of this legendary part of Hollywood history. Visitors can also donate to a crowdfunding campaign to help Deckler and Delacroix rebuild their lives. The siblings are living temporarily in a home belonging to Sofia Coppola, a director known for setting her films inside bedrooms, who is rumored to have taken a special interest in the Deckler House.

WE'D GIVEN MEG the unseen footage of Sue begging for a selfie with Jake in exchange for her promise to protect Becca's privacy. I'd also asked Sofia Scaccabarozzi not to share any of the images she took of Becca's breakdown, convincing her that it would hurt her brand's reputation if anyone thought she was exploiting a young woman's mental illness to sell diamonds. Luckily, Sofia was amenable. The livestream of the actual ceremony was more than enough: The entire collection sold out immediately on Net-a-Porter. LVMH was now trying to acquire the label.

Thankfully, Meg left out that Becca was now being treated inpatient at UCLA's neuropsychiatric hospital. One of their top adolescent psychiatrists had been a student of my father, and he called in a favor to get her admitted.

Rather than undergo surgery or endure chemotherapy, my dad wanted to spend what time he had left writing his memoirs and being with me. It would be a waste, he thought, to do all that to his body if it meant reducing the faculties of his mind.

We'd turned the first-floor office into his bedroom so he didn't have to go up and down stairs anymore.

After I read the piece in *Rolling Stone*, my phone rang. It was Craig.

"Hi," I said.

"I just wanted to tell you I made the wire transfer."

While we were still on the phone, I opened my banking app. There was a pending deposit for twice as much as I had been expecting. The number was unreal. I'd completely forgotten about the bonus incentives in the contract. I blinked at the astonishing figure, waiting to feel something like victory or pleasure. *A professional triumph, but there's going to be a crash or a downfall*, Becca had warned Meg. Even after I mentally allocated where the money would go—to credit card balances and the IRS and my pathetic retirement savings—there was still so much left.

"This is too much," I said.

"What am I going to do? Spend it on the house?"

"No," I said, "on Becca."

"Don't worry. There's plenty for Becca."

"Dayna?" my dad called from the living room.

"I'll call you later tonight," I promised Craig.

Downstairs, Dad was sitting in his favorite chair, wearing slippers, about a hundred pages into *The Power Broker.* Owen Wilson was dozing on the carpet near the couch.

"Do you know what day it is?"

I checked my phone. "November twenty-first."

"It's your birthday." He smiled and adjusted his glasses so he could really look at me, a gesture that was so familiar that, for a second, time stopped. I was a girl again. I had his full attention. The future did not exist.

"I guess I forgot."

"After a certain age, that happens."

"I'm forty," I said. "I can't believe I'm forty." When I was young, it had seemed like aging was something that only happened to other people. The ones who weren't careful. Who didn't put up a stronger defense.

"We'll certainly need a cake," he said.

I laughed. "Okay," I said. "Don't you boys get into any trouble while I'm gone."

Nothing I'd brought with me from Los Angeles was weather appropriate. I zipped up my father's old brown winter parka, which went all the way down to my ankles and smelled like aftershave and spearmint. From the coat closet, I also grabbed a wool scarf and a pair of mittens, even if that would make me appear overdressed to locals.

It wasn't yet five P.M., but already the sky was a heavy blue. A crust of snow crunched under my sneakers as I made my way out to the car.

Downtown, the streets were dark and glassy, reflecting the holiday lights strung in all the trees. City Hall stood at one end of the town square; at the other end, a white gazebo was lit up like a lantern. I didn't think the co-op would have what I was looking for, so I parked in the lot of the chain grocery store.

In a daze, I walked the aisles, stocking up on name-brand snacks without checking the prices first, like a millionaire. I picked out a chocolate cake and then went to the pharmacy department.

My phone dinged with a message from Jake. It was a selfie of him and Olivia, in his car, wearing huge puffy coats. Olivia had an adorable pink beanie with a furry pouf on top. A flat brown landscape was visible in the window behind her.

We're in the badlands, he wrote beneath the photo.

I closed the message without responding. How was I going to tell him? It was premature to worry. I didn't even know my results. Until I knew my results, there was no point in rehearsing what I would say. Maybe my period would finally come. Maybe I would start bleeding in line at the cash register.

"It's my birthday," I explained to the older woman in a brown smock who rang up my cake and my pregnancy test.

"Well,"—she smiled—"I hope you have a *very* happy birthday!"

Back at home, I left the cake in the kitchen and went upstairs to take the test. Before I blew out the candles, I needed to know what to wish for.

I set the test on the ledge of the bathtub and waited, gritting my teeth so they wouldn't chatter. I stared at the white plastic wand so intently that it took on a new shape, morphing into a woman's pale upturned hand. Incredulous, I blinked several times to clear the image, but it remained, faintly glowing. The hand was holding a perfect egg. It pulsed with strange light.

ACKNOWLEDGMENTS

In 2020, I attended a Zoom lecture on Daphne du Maurier's *Rebecca* by Emily Stone, who said that it's hard to write a contemporary gothic novel because you need a reason the heroine is confined inside the house. When she said that, I remembered Taylor Lorenz's *New York Times* piece, "Hype House and the Los Angeles TikTok Mansion Gold Rush," published that same year, and I knew I had the setting for my gothic novel. Emily, thank you for your loyal friendship and wise mentorship for all these years.

To research this novel, I became a content creator on TikTok. Callie Zola and Theodora Lesperance were my study abroad chaperones on the platform. Callie, your meticulous research into niche subcultures (and comment sections) made my novel so much richer, and Theodora, your gravitational pull toward the strangest corners of the internet has been a gift to my life.

Thank you for talking to me about books, the internet, and the war between millennials and Gen Z: Dakota Bossard, Hailey Colborn, Juliet Ealy, Celine Keely, Josh Lora, Eleanor Stern, and Stacey Yu.

My friends Kat Rosenfield and Julia Strayer read multiple drafts of every chapter in this book, for more than three years, and helped me keep the faith when I lost it. May every writer be as blessed as I have been, to write in the company of smart women who grant you permission to get weird.

Erin Hosier, you have transformed my career and I'm so lucky to have you in my corner when I'm up against the ropes. You somehow manage to make book publishing look cool. Betsy Lerner, thank you for mentoring me in countless ways. I look up to both of you.

I won the lottery when Jesse Shuman acquired this novel for Ballantine. Jesse, you saw what I was trying to do and helped me close the gap between my intentions and my execution. You are such a gifted, incisive editor and I deeply appreciate the trust you placed in me to pull this off, even after I derailed myself with bizarre plot detours. I can't help but feel this book was *meant for you.* Thank you to everyone at Ballantine who took such good care of my book (and of me): Pam Alders, Cara DuBois (now I finally understand what a section break is), Elizabeth Eno, Jennifer Hershey, Kim Hovey, Lucy Kim (for the perfect cover), Jennifer Sale, Emma Thomasch, Ali Wagner, Kara Welsh, and Chelsea Woodward.

Thank you to my genius marketing strategist, Lexi Merritt, who believes, as I do, that the internet can be magic, and who helped me invent and build the digital universe of this novel. Destiny led me to Jennifer May Reiland, the fantastically talented painter who made Becca's tarot cards real. I'm in awe of your work.

Thank you to these friends, clients, and colleagues who supported me as I tried to solve the puzzle of this book: Rebecca Ackermann, Melanie Anagnos, Ingrid Aybar (my first tarot teacher), Phoebe Maltz Bovy, Claire Dunnington, Angelica Frey, Emily Helck at the Lost Bookshop (who generously gave me a writing retreat), Lynne Greene, Jolene Handy, Elizabeth Held, Ali Kriegsman, Penny Lane, Gaelynn Lea, Liz Matthews, Annabel Monaghan, Gila Pfeffer, Julia

Phillips, Sarah Lyn Rogers, Stacey Rubin, Alizah Salario, Julie Sarkissian, Jessica Saunders, Casey Scieszka and Steven Weinberg (for the incredible residency at the Spruceton Inn), Sharon Shula (who gave me my first tarot deck), Adam Smith, Danielle Starkey (for our Irvin Yalom conversations), Julie Sternberg, Nicole Thornbrough, Sarah Vogel and Beth Schatz Kaylor (for sharing North Dakota with me), Mackenzie Brady Watson, Jo Waugh, and Amelia Wilson.

Thank you to my dad, who first introduced me to the work of Frank Lloyd Wright, and to my mom, my expert on both the Bible and psychosis. Hattie, thank you for giving me insight into group therapy facilitation; I also appreciate the distinct flavors of encouragement you and Yang gave me when I felt like giving up. (Yang, I'll never forget you telling me I had to "eat glass.")

Of all the people I've ever met on the internet, Brian, you're my favorite.

IF YOU'RE SEEING THIS, IT'S MEANT FOR YOU

LEIGH STEIN

A Book Club Guide

A LETTER FROM
THE AUTHOR

Dear Reader,

In 2009, I put on a black leotard from American Apparel, fashioned a skirt from a purple cardigan, covered my head with a black scarf fastened with a gold butterfly brooch, and went as Little Edie to a Halloween party in Williamsburg, a scene I can best describe as proto-*Girls*.

Edith "Little Edie" Bouvier Beale, first cousin to Jackie Kennedy, lived with her mother, Edith "Big Edie" Ewing Bouvier Beale, in a decaying Hamptons estate called Grey Gardens. In January 1972, *New York* magazine made Little Edie their cover girl. The accompanying profile by Gail Sheehy begins: "This is a tale of wealth and rebellion in one American Gothic family. It begins and ends at the juncture of Lily Pond Lane—the new Gold Coast—and West End Road, which is a dead end. There, in total seclusion, live two women, twelve cats, and occasional raccoons who drop through the roof of a house like no other in East Hampton."

"When am I going to get out of here?" Little Edie asks in the Albert and David Maysles documentary *Grey Gardens* (1975).

"She's always talking like that," Big Edie quips.

Little Edie, by then in her late fifties, flirts with the filmmakers; she twirls her baton. Once a greater beauty than Jackie, she now covers her head to hide her lost hair. She's desperate to escape and incapable of leaving.

I have a longtime fascination with stories of girls and women confined to houses. Little girls can't travel far alone—so they explore interiors (think of Lucy Pevensie discovering the portal in the wardrobe). In Shirley Jackson's novel *We Have Always Lived in the Castle*, eighteen-year-old Merricat obsessively protects her agoraphobic older sister and their family home from encroaching outsiders. In *Jane Eyre* and *Rebecca*, young women arrive at isolated manors owned by brooding heroes who are keeping dark secrets from them. One literary ancestor of these novels is the seventeenth-century French fairy tale "Bluebeard," about an aristocrat who forbids his young wife from entering one room in his castle (where he keeps all the corpses of his previous wives)—the story is about how her curiosity catalyzes her to disobey him.

The home, a place of safety and familiarity, can take on a malevolent spirit in gothic fiction. "124 was spiteful," *Beloved* begins. Shelley Duvall told *The Hollywood Reporter* that Stanley Kubrick filmed the scene in *The Shining* of her backing up

the staircase, weakly holding a baseball bat, weeping as Jack mocks and berates her, 127 times over
the course of three weeks.

Duvall, then seventy-one, started crying in front
of *The Hollywood Reporter* interviewer as she re-
watched the scene. "Jack [Nicholson] was so
good—so damn scary. I can only imagine how
many women go through this kind of thing," she
said.

Women read gothic suspense because the terror
is recognizable: What if the person you followed
to the isolated dream house turns out to be the
person most capable of destroying you?

When I think of the contemporary gothic, I
think of the controlling behavior of Brittany
Murphy's husband, Simon Monjack, and her
dramatic physical decline in the final months of
her life. But the villains in these stories aren't
always men. I also think of Shari Franke, growing up on YouTube, weakly smiling for the camera with mono and a 102-degree fever when her
mom, Ruby, hit her first million followers. The
income from their YouTube channel enabled the
Frankes to buy their dream house in idyllic
Springville, Utah, but the fame made Ruby mon-
strous (or the fame drew out the monster that
had been inside her all along). She is now serving
up to thirty years in prison after being convicted
of four counts of aggravated child abuse.

In her introduction to Shirley Jackson's *The
Haunting of Hill House*, the literary critic Laura
Miller writes, "Eleanor may be the target of the

haunting of Hill House, or *she* may be the one doing the haunting."

When I think of the contemporary gothic, I think of the internet: the haunted house we all inhabit. The internet is alive; it feeds on us. It's a decadent manor, filled with rooms we know better than to enter.

Like Little Edie, twirling her baton, losing her hair, we're desperate to escape and incapable of leaving.

Thank you so much for reading *If You're Seeing This, It's Meant for You.*

Leigh Stein
March 31, 2025

| If You're Seeing This, It's Meant for You | |

Did you mean?

- ρ Ennis House
- ρ Dooce
- ρ #accidentalinfluencer
- ρ novels with orphans
- ρ the Thorne Rooms
- ρ rabbits free roam
- ρ what it means if you find feathers
- ρ Deborah Turbeville Comme des Garçons
- ρ hot girl walk
- ρ compression and release
- ρ Eight of Swords meaning
- ρ couples dance challenges
- ρ the Taliesin murders
- ρ #WhiteyyNation
- ρ couples breakup videos
- ρ Brittany Murphy
- ρ viral girl crying
- ρ when does the Lion's Gate Portal open this year
- ρ #channeledmessage
- ρ Francesca Woodman
- ρ ideas of reference
- ρ #thatgirl
- ρ *House on Haunted Hill*
- ρ Helen Lundeberg self-portrait
- ρ Bible verses that denounce astrology

QUESTIONS AND TOPICS
FOR DISCUSSION

1. *If You're Seeing This, It's Meant for You* is a twenty-first-century gothic novel that includes Easter egg references to classics such as *Jane Eyre, Wuthering Heights, The Yellow Wallpaper,* and *Rebecca.* What are some gothic tropes or familiar characters you found? In what ways does Leigh Stein subvert expectations of a gothic novel?

2. "This house will make you do things," Dayna thinks (p. 16). How does the Deckler House exert its influence on the characters in the novel? What are the parallels between the Deckler House and "the platform"? Why do you think some characters feel the influence of the house more strongly than others?

3. What do you think Stein is trying to say about the ways in which the internet affects us? Did she change your mind about anything, or expose dangers that you had never considered before?

4. Dayna is nostalgic for the internet of the early '00s, when she posted self-portraits to her photography blog. The internet where she came of age is very different from the one she confronts, years later, at the hype house. What are your earliest memories of being online? Do you think 2025 is a better or worse time to be a creator, compared to 2005?

5. A 2023 survey by Morning Consult found that 57 percent of Gen Z want to become influencers. Why do you think so many young adults want to make a living by creating content? Do you personally know any successful (or aspiring) content creators?

6. The Deckler House is home to three generations: Gen X, Millennial, and Gen Z. How does the author use satire to explore the different beliefs each generation has about the others? How do these generations come into conflict with one another over the course of the novel?

7. How has your own generation been unfairly stereotyped? What do you think older (or younger) generations misunderstand about your generation?

8. Olivia arrives at the mansion with a special talent for crying. When is she acting and when are the tears real? Or is anything on camera "performance"? When you see someone crying in a video on the internet, does it trigger your empathy, or your skepticism?

9. "Mother pressured me to produce an heir before Craig did," Paula says. "A long time ago, it was already too

late for me. But it isn't too late for him" (p. 178). How is the theme of inheritance expressed in the novel? How do different characters face (or avoid) the legacy they're passing on to the next generation?

10. Like many "momfluencers," Mindy Bliss monetized her daughter Piper's childhood and adolescence. With the 2025 release of the explosive *Devil in the Family* docuseries about Ruby Franke, and Shari Franke's harrowing memoir *The House of My Mother*, more Americans are becoming aware of the dark side of family vlogging. Legislation has been passed in Utah, Illinois, Minnesota, and California to protect child influencers. What do you think of parents who earn income by documenting their family's life on the internet? Have you ever seen a video that crossed a line?

11. Astrology and tarot have become powerful spiritual practices and intuitive guideposts for many Americans who don't identify as religious. Where does Becca's gift for tarot come from? Why do you think so many users on TikTok turn to creators like Becca for reassurance, clarity, and guidance?

12. A parasocial relationship is a one-sided relationship in which a fan believes they have a close, intimate connection with a prominent figure (like a musician, a celebrity, or a content creator). Both Becca and Jake have followers who claim to feel a special connection (Olivia starts out as Becca's fan). What causes these parasocial relationships to develop? How do influencers (or podcasters) build intimacy with their audiences? Are there

any celebrities that you think have dangerously para-social fandoms?

13. "The hand was holding a perfect egg. It pulsed with strange light" (p. 285). How did you interpret the final image of the novel? What's next for Dayna? For the rest of the characters?

© MINDY TUCKER.

LEIGH STEIN makes fun of what the internet is doing to us. She is the author of six books, including the critically acclaimed satirical novel *Self Care*. She has written culture pieces and personal essays for *The New York Times, The Washington Post, The New Yorker, Air Mail, Allure, Elle, BuzzFeed, The Cut, Salon*, and *Slate*.

TikTok | Substack | Instagram: @leighstein

RANDOM HOUSE BOOK CLUB

Because Stories Are Better Shared

Discover

Exciting new books that spark conversation every week.

Connect

With authors on tour—or in your living room. (Request an Author Chat for your book club!)

Discuss

Stories that move you with fellow book lovers on Facebook, on Goodreads, or at in-person meet-ups.

Enhance

Your reading experience with discussion prompts, digital book club kits, and more, available on our website.

Join our online book club community!

 randomhousebookclub.com

 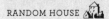